FROM THE PAGES OF SHOSHANIM

Onions Always Make Me Cry

and Other Stories for Teenage Girls

Edited by Sterna Citron and Nechama Dina Smith

The stories in this anthology appeared originally in *Shoshanim Magazine* and are reprinted here with the permission of the authors.

Book design by: Rivkah Lewis

Published by:
Israel Bookshop Publications
501 Prospect Street
Lakewood, NJ 08701

Tel: (732) 901-3009
Fax: (732) 901-4012
www.israelbookshoppublications.com
info@israelbookshoppublications.com

Printed in the United States of America

Distributed in Israel by:
Shanky's
Petach Tikva 16
Jerusalem
972-2-538-6936

Distributed in Australia by:
Gold's Book and Gift Company
3- 13 William Street
Balaclava 3183
613-9527-8775

Distributed in Europe by:
Lehmanns
Unit E Viking Industrial Park
Rolling Mill Road,
Jarrow , Tyne & Wear NE32 3DP
44-191-406-0842

Distributed in South Africa by:
Kollel Bookshop
Ivy Common
107 William Road, Norwood
Johannesburg 2192
27-11-728-1822

....

DEDICATED

TO ALL JEWISH GIRLS

WHO LOVE TO READ

....

ACKNOWLEDGMENTS

When Shoshanim discontinued production of its magazine for teenage girls in August of 2010 (5770), we could not bear the idea of letting Shoshanim disappear completely. Somehow, from the fallen tree of the forest, new growth must sprout; we had to find a way to continue to provide girls with entertaining and uplifting literature. And so, with the help of Israel Bookshop, we have. Here we present the first of a Shoshanim series of stories for girls called Onions Always Make Me Cry and Other Stories for Teenage Girls. B'ezras Hashem, we hope this work will be the first of many.

No book comes to life without the able assistance of several dedicated helpers. Thanks firstly to my husband, Rav Chaim Zev Citron, who is involved in every aspect of Shoshanim and is always ready and willing to let his brain be picked for questions large and small. We are also beholden to Rav Gershon Schusterman, who graciously and meticulously reviews all our material and whose wise counsel we frequently seek.

Thanks are due also to Eli Rothman, our long-time technical consultant; Rachel Malkin, our always helpful editorial consultant; and my mother, Hadassa Carlebach, whose opinion we value. Our writers and illustrators—adults and teenagers—who enthusiastically contributed their talents, have my gratitude, as do the financial contributors who made Shoshanim a reality. And, of course, thanks to the most important people: our ardent readers.

It would be unthinkable not to express my heartfelt thanks to my hard-working co-editor, Nechama Dina Smith (my daughter), who has, since the inception of Shoshanim, never lost her enthusiasm and fire to reach our goal of providing exciting, high-quality literature for Jewish girls.

Lastly, thanks to the editors at Israel Bookshop who went over every word of the manuscript and attended to all the details.

A special note of thanks to Nietzah Benbeniste who came up with the title for this book.

May Hakadosh Baruch Hu bless all these people generously.

Sterna Citron
Elul 5771

THANKS TO THE
SPONSORS OF THE BOOK

Marsha Alperin

Mark Donchin and Ruth Stone

Ruth Gelman

Lois Grayson

Louis Kemp

Henny Klein

Batya Lokey

Alan and Marilyn Rich

Roth Plumbing

The *Chevra Kadisha* of Los Angeles

Moshe and Miriam Fishman

CONTENTS

1

Compared to her older sister Ruth, Baila could never be good enough, not in her parents' eyes or her own.

Onions Always Make Me Cry

BY BETH FIRESTONE

My best friend Estie was always complaining that she didn't get enough attention, but as she had three brothers and four sisters, that was easy to understand. I always said I'd rather have her problem than mine. I'd rather be ignored than doted on. With just myself and my older sister Ruth, my parents seemed to have more than enough time for us. This shouldn't have been something to complain about, but in my case it was. They watched everything I did and knew everything that was going on with me, from every test I took and paper I wrote to what I was wearing, eating, or doing with my free time. I knew they were just trying to do a good job bringing me up and that I should be thankful. The problem was that they were never satisfied.

The year I started high school, the situation got worse. My parents had always expected me to follow in Ruth's footsteps.

Ruth was my very smart, very pretty, ultra-talented-in-many areas and nothing-short-of-amazing sister. That explained my having to enroll in Mrs. Brown's honors English class. I knew I'd have to work twice as hard as my sister to get a decent grade. Even then I'd have to face my mother's raised, disapproving eyebrows when I showed her a B or, even worse, a C.

We were one month into my ninth grade year. I had worked hard the entire week on my first essay for Mrs. Brown, and my mother couldn't wait to see my grade.

"Baila, is that you?" my mother called only moments after I walked through the front door. "Well? Did Mrs. Brown hand your papers back today?" she asked expectantly.

Never underestimate the impact of a red letter on clean white paper, especially if it's not the first two letters of the alphabet. Mrs. Brown had the reputation for being a very hard grader, especially in the beginning of the year. Nevertheless, Ruth had gotten A's from the beginning to the end of the class last year.

My mother looked at the C and raised her eyebrows, nodding disapprovingly. "Did you really apply yourself?" she asked for the millionth time.

I hated that question. I had worked really hard on this paper. I had listened in class and followed the instructions. Was I missing something? I swallowed a lump in my throat. The same lump I had learned to swallow for so many years. The lump that said maybe I just wasn't that smart.

"A C in her class is like a B in any other class," I argued.

"You can do better," she said for the gazillionth time.

How many more times would I have to suffer through those words? Saying nothing more, I headed for the kitchen to grab a snack before going upstairs to tackle hours of homework.

"Why don't you have some rice cakes?" my mother said

when she saw me reaching for the bag of chocolate chip cookies. My mother was always stressing the importance of a slim body. Ruth had the appetite of a bird and was naturally thin. I wasn't heavy, but I wasn't skinny either. My mother was always worried that I would put on weight.

I popped a cookie into my mouth, then grabbed the bag of rice cakes and headed for my room.

"You'll thank me one day," my mother called after me. I probably would, but sometimes when she said that, it just made me want to eat more.

A few nights later, Ruth and I were in the bathroom getting ready for the monthly Rosh Chodesh party. We stood next to each other at the mirror, brushing our hair. My shoulder-length, dark brown hair was straight and thin. I didn't bother curling it anymore because the curls only lasted for ten minutes. Ruth inherited some recessive family gene, and was blessed with thick, straight blond hair, whose ends curled naturally. She had awesome green eyes to match. She wore a dark blue suit that brought out her natural colors. She looked like a model from a Talbot's Petite catalog. I wore the same suit, only in brown, and somehow it didn't hang right on me. As usual, next to Ruth, I felt plain and ordinary. I sighed and threw my brush into the sink.

"What's the matter?" Ruth asked.

"I'm not going to the party," I said, suddenly deciding not to go. I felt like getting into my pajamas and crawling into bed.

"Why not?"

"It's such a fashion show every month. Everyone is always checking out everyone else. I just don't feel like going through that again."

"You're right," Ruth agreed. "But it's still a lot of fun."

"I hate the way I look," I said, messing up my hair, and making a face at myself.

"Not that again, Baila. Come on, you look really cute," Ruth said earnestly.

"I don't want to be cute. I want to be pretty," I said. Feeling my eyes tear up, I ran out of the bathroom and locked myself in my room. A minute later Ruth knocked at the door.

"Baila, Mrs. Fried is honking. Are you sure you don't want to come?" she called through the door.

"Baila, nobody misses the Rosh Chodesh party," my mother added through the closed door.

"How would you know? And who cares anyway? This nobody is going to miss it!" I called back.

"Baila, please open the door and let me in," my mother pleaded.

"Go away. I don't want to talk to you!" I cried, and then buried my face in my pillow.

"Why do you have to be so difficult!" my mother muttered through gritted teeth, giving one last pound on the door before she stormed away.

• • •

The next week in school they announced auditions for the annual song-and-dance school fundraiser. Everyone was very excited, especially the ninth graders. Growing up, we had seen every performance and looked forward to the day we would participate. Now that the opportunity was finally here, I decided not to audition after all. I told Estie as we walked home from school.

"What do you mean you're not auditioning?" she asked in amazement.

"I just don't want to," I answered, picking up the pace and walking slightly ahead of her.

"But you always wanted to be in this show. What happened?"

Estie was my best friend, but I was having a hard time explaining, even to her.

"Come on, Baila, don't clam up on me," she said, pulling on my elbow.

"Face it, Estie. I don't sing very well, and I'll take basketball over dance any day. I'd rather be in the stage crew. Building sets will be fun. Besides, I won't have all those rehearsals, and I won't have to stress out over keeping up with homework." This was the truth, though not the whole truth. The whole truth was that I didn't want to be measured against Ruth. With her fantastic singing voice, she would probably land a leading role just as she had last year.

That night at dinner Ruth talked excitedly about the auditions. I sat, quietly eating.

"You're so quiet tonight, Baila," my father observed. "Aren't you excited about the tryouts?"

"I'm not trying out," I said softly.

"What?" my mother exclaimed.

"I decided I'd rather help with the set designs," I said.

"Set designs?" my mother asked in the high-toned voice she used when she was getting emotional.

"What's wrong with that?" I asked defensively. Designing sets suddenly seemed very important to me.

"That's for all the untalented girls," she said.

"Well, I guess that's me," I said sullenly. "At least I won't have to go through a harrowing week of auditions to find out just how untalented I am."

Neither of my parents said anything. I looked at Ruth. She

looked at me guiltily. I knew it wasn't her fault that she was so talented, but I couldn't help feeling angry at her.

"Set design is very important. A lot of the girls opt for that," Ruth said, coming to my defense. Then she turned to me and said, "You're not untalented, Baila. Maybe if you auditioned, you'd surprise yourself."

"I doubt it," I replied.

"You took ballet and gymnastics. If you'd just apply yourself more—" my mother started to say.

"I do apply myself!" I stood up and yelled. "I wish you would stop saying that!"

"Baila, don't talk back to your mother like that!" my father said, raising his voice above ours. I looked from him to my mother to Ruth. My mother bit her lower lip and angrily poked at her food. Ruth looked down at her lap, like she felt truly bad. My father frowned and rubbed his beard.

"May I please be excused?" I asked.

My father nodded, and I quickly cleared my place and left the kitchen. As I started up the stairs to my room, I stopped when I heard my mother say, "She's become so defensive. I can't talk to her anymore."

"It's because you expect too much of her," Ruth said.

"I don't expect any more of her than I do of you," my mother said.

"Maybe that's the problem," Ruth suggested. "She's not me."

"We always believed if we had high expectations, we'd get good results," my father said.

"It isn't always about the results," Ruth offered.

"Are you saying we should lower our expectations?" my mother asked.

"Don't lower them," Ruth said. "Just change them. Expect

Baila to do the best *she* can do, not the best *I* can do."

As I stood at the bottom of the stairs listening to their conversation, I felt a tightening in my chest and throat. The truth hurt. I tiptoed slowly up the stairs to my room. I lay down on my bed in my favorite position, arms supporting my head, staring at the ceiling. This was where I always did my best thinking. Ruth's words echoed in my head. She had said, "Expect Baila to do the best *she* can do, not the best *I* can do." It dawned on me that I had always thought of *best* as being objective. There could only be one best. All the rest were second, third or fourth place. Maybe Ruth was right. *Best* could be subjective. There was *her best* and *my best*. Why hadn't this occurred to me before? *My best, my best*—the words drifted and floated around my head, lulling me to sleep.

A few nights later, Ruth and I stood next to each other in front of the bathroom mirror, brushing our hair before bed. We weren't our usual talkative selves. After a few minutes, Ruth broke the silence.

"What's wrong with being cute anyway?" she asked, picking up our conversation from a few days ago.

"I don't know," I shrugged.

"You know what your problem is?" Ruth continued.

"What?"

"Instead of looking in the mirror and seeing all of the good things you are, you see everything you're not. You'll never be happy with yourself if you do that."

She was right. That's exactly what I did. I knew it, but I couldn't stop myself. "You're right," I said. "But when everything you're not is standing next to you each night, it's hard to see what you are."

"Just be yourself, Baila. That's good enough," Ruth said with confidence.

"Is it?" I said doubtfully.

Ruth looked at me thoughtfully, then said, "It is, if you're okay with it."

Back in my room, on my bed waiting to fall asleep, I thought this over. Would I ever be okay with myself? I'd have to stop always comparing myself to Ruth, or to anyone else for that matter. It was a hard habit to break, especially when my own parents were always doing it to me. Ruth had told them to change their expectations. Would they? Would I ever be good enough in their eyes?

The next week was a flurry of excitement at school with all the auditions. Estie tried to convince me to change my mind, and I did think about it. But in the end, I stuck with my decision to be on the stage crew. From seeing past shows, I knew how beautiful the sets could be. No matter what my mother thought, I really wanted to be a part of creating them. As expected, Ruth did get one of the main singing and acting roles. People don't change overnight, and I had to admit that I felt a twinge of jealousy. But then I stopped myself. It was my choice, and I was happy with it. That's what mattered. It felt good to know I had the power to change, however slowly.

I wasn't the only one changing. In the weeks that followed, I started noticing small changes in my mother too. I didn't feel like she was always watching my every move. It felt strange, but I wasn't complaining.

A few weeks later, Mrs. Brown assigned our next essay. I'd been thinking a lot about what "my best" really was. Maybe there was some truth to what my mother had always told me. Maybe I could apply myself a little more. Maybe my best could be a little better. I was usually timid when it came to talking to my teachers, especially Mrs. Brown. Nevertheless, I decided to "apply myself" and stayed after class one day to discuss how I could make this next essay better than the last one. This time, I wrote three drafts instead of my usual two.

The next Friday, I waited anxiously as Mrs. Brown handed back our papers. Finally, she walked over to my desk. She held out my paper and gave me a small nod and a smile. I glanced at the paper and saw a big red B and "Good job!" scrawled next to it. My first reaction was disappointment. Would that red pen ever yield an A from her? But moments later a new inner voice, one that was getting stronger every day, said, "Don't see the A that isn't there. See the B that is." I had applied myself and improved. That was good enough for now.

When I got home my mother was in the kitchen cooking dinner. She said hello as I plopped my backpack down. I put three cookies on a plate and poured myself some water without her saying anything about rice cakes.

"How was your day?" I asked, sitting down to eat my snack.

"Good. And yours?"

"Okay. I got back my essay," I offered before she could ask. I was very curious to see how she would react, given what seemed like her new and different attitude.

"How did you do?" my mother asked.

"I got a B," I said cautiously.

"That's an improvement. Good for you," she said.

I felt like jumping out of my chair and hugging my mother, but instead I just smiled at her. She smiled back at me. I took a bite of a cookie and a drink of water. My mother finished chopping an onion and threw it into the pot. She walked over to the kitchen table and sat down across from me. She reached over, took my hand and squeezed it.

"You're a good girl, Baila," she said. Her words caught me off guard. Tears welled up in my eyes, and one rolled down my cheek. My mother reached over and brushed it away.

"It feels so good to hear you say that," I said.

My mother gave my hand another squeeze. The onions started to sizzle, and she got up to stir them. A moment later I saw her make a gesture that looked like she was wiping tears away from her eyes. "Onions always make me cry," she said.

I didn't think it was the onions, but I didn't say so. I took another sip of my water, drinking in the sensation of a strange new feeling—the feeling that I was good enough.

2

Why was the alarm clock ringing at 6:30 on a Sunday morning? And my sister wasn't letting me sleep either. What was going on?

Monday Morning Trouble

BY BRACHA GOYKADOSH

Even before I rolled out of bed in the morning, I had a gloomy sense that things would not work out the way I liked that day.

I was having this strange dream: it was summer, and I was sitting under a sprinkler. When I woke up, my face was all wet. It turned out that I had left my windows open, and it was raining.

But I was okay with that. It's not like it was so terrible. I could go back to sleep, right? It was Sunday, so...

Suddenly my alarm went off. I thought I must have made some kind of mistake. Maybe I had set my alarm last night by accident or something? I pulled out the plug and tried to go back to sleep. I wouldn't dream of getting up at 6:30 a.m. on a Sunday morning.

Then my younger sister came into the room. What in the

world did she want from me at 6:31 a.m. on a Sunday morning? Gosh! Like, sensitivity would be a good thing!

"Elisheva, can I borrow one of your uniform shirts? I can't find any of my own."

Why in the world did she want to wear my uniform shirt on Sunday? Was she out of her mind?

Okay, I'll humor her. "Sure, Bina, why not? Go right ahead!" I answered from underneath my blankets.

"Thanks!"

What a strange girl! Who else would wear a uniform shirt out of school? Sometimes even being related to her is embarrassing!

"By the way, why are you still in bed?" she asked. "The bus will be here in an hour! Don't you need to get dressed?"

"The bus? Bina! What in the world are you talking about?! It's Sunday!"

"Actually, Elisheva," she laughed, "it's Monday. Wake up and smell the iced coffee."

No way, no way, no way! This was not happening to me! I pulled the covers over my head. I needed to sleep. There was no way anyone was going to make me get out of bed.

By the time I opened up my eyes, the house was quiet, threateningly quiet. Uh-oh, where was everyone? Why didn't I hear the usual hustle bustle of my family?

I cautiously got out of bed, washed *negel vasser*, and went downstairs.

On the kitchen table sat a lone paper lunch bag with an "E" scribbled on top, my lunch that Ima had probably hastily prepared before going to work. So it *was* Monday. Oh, boy was I in trouble now!

I glanced at the clock. 8:00. Okay, not so bad. Class didn't begin until nine; I still had an hour. But how would I get to school? It was too far to walk, and I had already missed the bus. I pondered this for a few seconds, and then it came to me—the subway! My mother didn't like when I went on the subway by myself, but I was sure it would be okay just this once. After all, she would never know, and what she didn't know wouldn't hurt her. I rummaged around in the kitchen drawer until I finally found a metro-card. I checked the date. *Baruch* Hashem, it hadn't expired!

I quickly ran upstairs to change into my uniform. If I could hurry I would probably be able to catch the F train. I searched my closet for a shirt. My eyes quickly scanned my wardrobe, but I could not find any of the drab gray and white shirts that I so despised. Bina must have borrowed my last clean shirt! I threw all my drawers open, trying to find at least one decent shirt, as I needed to be out of the house by 8:30, and it was already 8:13! Finally, I found a shirt that was wrinkled and stained and missing a button stuffed into one of my bottom drawers. I had no choice but to wear it. I put a sweatshirt on top of it, hoping nobody would notice the stained shirt. I then pulled on the dull, long, gray pleated skirt. The uniform definitely needed some brightening up, so I put on my pink shoes and a blue and green striped headband.

I ran down the stairs, almost tripping on the way. (Those platforms really don't work well for running!) It was 8:20; I could still make it in time. My stomach started to grumble just then, and I remembered I hadn't eaten breakfast. I grabbed a yogurt from the fridge and a spoon from the cupboard; it was all I had time for.

I ran out onto the street and raced to the subway station. By the time I figured out how to use the metro-card, it was 8:32, and the train had already left. It was just my luck. Now I had to sit and wait another ten minutes for the next one. I knew I would be late.

I sat down on one of the grimy benches. I immediately started going through my mental checklist, a habit I got into last year when I forgot to buy a planner. Math homework, check, I did it on Thursday night. *Navi hachanah*, check, I did it on the bus on Friday. *Chumash* test...?

"Oh, no!" I screeched. A nearby pigeon flew up in fright, a tall businessman stopped in middle of his cell phone conversation. Two dark-skinned men whispering in a foreign language (tourists, I'll bet) pointed at me, and a thin old woman with white hair that was almost blue raised a wispy eyebrow. I heard people laughing and whispering.

"*Tzniyus*, Elisheva, *tzniyus*," a small voice whispered in my head. "And remember that wherever you go you represent the Jewish people."

Oops. I guess my voice was louder than I had meant it to be. But I had forgotten to study for the *Chumash* test that was going to take place in the second period.

It wasn't too late yet! I felt my back, looking for my knapsack. Maybe I could study *Chumash* now. Oh, no, it wasn't there! Neither was my loose-leaf notebook! I didn't have my lunch either. Uh-oh! In my rush I had left everything at home. No wonder I was able to walk so fast, not having all that weight. The only thing I had with me was my yogurt and metro-card. This was not good at all.

I tried to review the material for the test in my head, but I couldn't even remember what *perek* the test was on—*aleph* or *beis*. Or maybe it was both? Was *gimmel* included too? I couldn't remember. Where was I when we learned this stuff?

Then I remembered.

Every day so far I had either been late to class or had cracked one too many jokes, and my teacher, Morah Furst, had not let me back into class. I was supposed to photocopy my friend Batya's notes, but somehow I forgot. Not too smart.

Finally the train arrived, three minutes late. How come, I wondered, the train was late when I needed it to be early, and early when I needed it to be late? I got onto the subway and waited patiently for the 'ding-dong' of the doors closing. I waited and waited. After about five minutes of anxious waiting, I heard the deep voice of the conductor say, "We regret to inform you that there has been a slight delay. Please stay seated and we will get into motion as soon as possible."

The passengers all around me groaned. I groaned too. Now I would be late for sure! Maybe that extra sleep wasn't really worth it! But I really had thought it was Sunday!

Needless to say, the 'slight' delay was not so slight after all. By the time the train started moving again, it was 9:00. I had to be in school in the next forty-five minutes to take my test, which I probably was going to fail anyway. Still, a forty is better than a zero.

The ride to school was pretty uneventful, except for one thing. I was eating my yogurt, and when the train made a short stop, the yogurt spilled. Great! Now my sweatshirt was as dirty as my shirt. It was definitely one of those days that was not going as planned.

I practically flew down the block and a half from the subway station to the school. I was running so fast that my lungs were killing me. I arrived, panting, at Morah Furst's room on the second floor just in time to hear the bell signaling second period.

My friends gave me quizzical looks as I dashed into the classroom.

"Leora, can I borrow a pen?" I asked the girl next to me as the teacher handed out the test papers.

Leora held out her blue pen toward me and took out another pen from her pencil case without even a glimpse of a smile. Whatever. Leora is one of those goody-goody types whose shirt is always tucked in, eyebrows perfect, hair perfect, who studies for tests months in advance, and who follows every rule. Not my type at all. But still some feedback, such as a 'hi' or a 'sure' or something would have been nice.

Morah Furst slapped a test onto my desk with a slight smirk. The extent to which this teacher hated me was just not funny! Ever since the first day of school she hadn't stopped picking on me! Whenever she asked a weird question, she always chose me to answer it. I think she liked seeing me embarrassed.

I turned the paper over and was pleased to see that it was in English in a multiple-choice format. Most teachers in my school give long tests in Hebrew and require you to write whole *megillos* for the answers. At least now I had a chance.

"Okay, *banos*," said Morah Furst, "I think this test is self-explanatory. There will be no questions. Be *matzliach*."

I felt a wave of newly inspired self-confidence.

The first question read:

1. According to the Ramban, why did B'nei Yisrael have to stand in their formation with the degalim when they went out to war?

    A. The *degalim* formed the name of Hashem and were a protection.

    B. B'nei Yisrael had seen the *malachim* do this at Mattan Torah.

    C. A and B.

    D. To scare the enemies.

My newly inspired wave of self-confidence turned out to be very temporary. I had no clue what the question was talking about. I didn't even remember learning the Ramban. I decided to pick D because it sounded good.

The whole test became a game. I picked the letters at random. I even stopped bothering to read the questions. They were incomprehensible to me. I would just think, hey, I didn't pick B in a while, why can't I choose that? I even made up my own code!

Leora was scribbling away next to me. It seemed like she wasn't bothering to read the whole question either. She probably just looked at the first word and knew the answer. Figures.

This made me a teeny bit jealous. Why should it be so easy for her to get a hundred? Why not me? Why couldn't I get a good grade and make myself and my parents proud? I forgot about the fact that Leora probably had studied while I hadn't. But knowing her, she probably would have known all the answers without studying too.

It would be so easy just to peek at Leora's test and see which letters she circled. I would for sure get a hundred. No one would ever find out. It would be the perfect opportunity to prove to Morah Furst that I wasn't a total dunce.

But then I thought, *who am I trying to fool? My teacher? Myself?*

I was having a major conflict. Leora's test was right in front of me. No one but me would ever know.

On the other hand, was it so important to get a high grade that I should give up all my self-respect by cheating? So I'd fail. Big whoop. Twenty years from now I wouldn't even remember this stupid test.

With a sigh, I got up and handed my paper to the teacher. I was the first person to hand in her test, and I think the teacher was trying hard not to laugh. You can't win 'em all, I guess.

I placed Leora's pen back on her desk and walked out of

the classroom. I felt a little proud that I had restrained myself from temptation. I would not have to look at myself in the mirror and think, "That's the face of a cheater."

I sat down in a lone chair at the far end of the hallway, calm for the first time that day. Soon, the recess bell would ring, and my friends, classmates, and teachers would come streaming out of the classrooms, laughing and talking. The morning had started strangely enough, but interestingly, the stain on my sweatshirt didn't appear so obvious. I straightened my shoulders as I walked towards Batya who had just left the classroom. I needed to photocopy the *Chumash* notes.

3

I fantasized about what being a mother's helper would be like—the cool country breeze, the ice cream truck, Dr. Seuss books, cuddly kids, and Shabbos afternoon chats with my aunt and her friends on picnic chairs.

Mother's Helper

BY NECHAMA DINA SMITH

After my sister Tova's wedding, I was busy for a week with *sheva brachos* and going places with my relatives. When the house finally quieted down, I was left with four weeks of summer—too late to be a counselor anywhere. I had to think of something to do before my mother enrolled me in a sewing class.

My aunt Mashy called me from the Catskills. "Sara'le, wouldn't you enjoy being someone's mother's helper in a bungalow colony not far from me and come to me for Shabbos?"

"Yes!" I shouted. "That's great!"

I immediately thought of the cool country breeze and the ice cream truck with sweet, creamy vanilla and chocolate flavors, Dr. Seuss books and cuddly kids, and Shabbos afternoon chats with my aunt and her friends on picnic chairs.

I called up my aunt's friend, Mrs. Lewis. Mrs. Lewis said she had three little boys that needed to be put to bed, read to, taken to the swings and slides, and fed and dressed. She added that one was a baby and that he would accompany her most of the day. For Shabbos her husband would come in from the city and give me a ride to my aunt's. How ideal!

Well, there I was—a mother's helper. Only it wasn't quite what I had imagined.

Mrs. Lewis was about twenty-seven and slim. She was neatly dressed and kept a spotless bungalow. My charges, Moishy, barely five, with chubby red cheeks, and Benny, a two-and-a-half year old with curly hair and a quick smile, befriended me and helped me unpack, hoping to find something of interest among my bags. Baby Berel sucked firmly on his thumb as he watched me.

I helped serve supper that first night, and Mrs. Lewis tidied up while I put Moishy and Benny in a bath. Benny got soap in his eye. He screamed. I tried to shout over him, "Calm down! Let me rinse it out!" and then Moishy poured water over his brother to be helpful. Mrs. Lewis came in, and I felt like I had failed already. She calmly splashed fresh water in Benny's eyes, wiped his face with a towel, and all was quiet.

She smiled as she left the bathroom. "It happens!" she said reassuringly.

I dried the boys and helped them with their pajamas. They ran to bed, each dragging about five books to bed with them. They brought me more and more books. I read and read and read. The boys loved how I read to them, but they were not falling asleep. In fact, they were just as wide awake and energetic as they were before I got started! So I got smart and read very slowly in a monotone. Within minutes, they were snoring.

That was the first day. The next day my jobs consisted of feeding the baby while Mrs. Lewis *davened* with the other two boys, then taking Moishy and Benny to the playground, helping with lunch, cleaning up, and finally turning on the sprinklers for a grand water party. After that, the ice-cream truck arrived, and the five Lewises and I each picked what we wanted, and we sat on the porch in the sun and licked. As usual, I closed my eyes to really enjoy. But this time they quickly opened when the two-and-a-half year old stuck his popsicle into my mouth.

That night, by the time supper was cleaned up and the boys put to bed, my head spun and my bones dragged. I lay down to rest for just one second and woke up in the morning.

The boys attended playgroup twice a week for three hours. During that time I assisted Mrs. Lewis with the laundry and entertained Berel while she cooked and cleaned.

I began to dream of a swim in the pool and of curling up with the books I had brought with me. But I was on my feet or hands and knees the whole day. I had never slept so well! I'd hardly close my eyes at night and it would be morning, with my two little friends pulling me out of bed.

When Mrs. Lewis went to a *shiur* one day that week, I felt myself turn red and shaky with frustration. *I can't watch all three kids*, I declared silently.

Sure enough, Moishy scraped his knee while I was changing Berel's pamper, and Benny started to run off "to find Mommy." I was a wreck.

"Benny," I yelled, "come back here!" I was so thankful to Hashem when he listened. I finished changing Berel while I told Moishy softly, "Hold on one second and I'll get you your favorite Band-Aid."

By the end of the week, I made a few resolutions. One was never to fantasize again. I would always prepare for the worst! Another one was that when *im yirtzeh* Hashem I'd be married, I would *daven* to have girls only!

I was delighted to escape to my aunt's bungalow for Shabbos. Mashy hugged me, and I whispered, "Can I call my mother?"

I called my mother and the tears poured out. "Ma," I cried, "it's not what I expected. I can't handle it! Mrs. Lewis doesn't give me a second's break!"

My mother sighed. "Why don't you explain to her that this is not how she described the job?"

"No," I insisted. "I'm quitting and coming home."

My mother was quiet. "I - uh. You can't. Ta and I—well, since no one was home now, we decided to go to Eretz Yisrael for two weeks."

I could scarcely breathe. "Here's Mashy," I said and brought the phone to her. I ran to the bathroom and couldn't even cry. Stuck three more weeks as a slave!

Shabbos was blissful. I listened to Mashy and her husband tell stories and discuss the *parshah*. I read a book. I took a long nap in the afternoon.

Back at work, I began biting my nails in frustration. One day, as Mrs. Lewis was leaving me again by myself, I spotted a bathing suit inside her tote. I had to watch all three children, and I wanted to cry.

That night, instead of going straight to bed, I came out with a book and bravely sat down at the table. Mrs. Lewis was on the phone. She glanced at me. I began to read. Then she got off the phone.

"I want to talk to you," I said clumsily.

Mrs. Lewis raised her eyebrows.

"I'm not happy." My heart pounded. "You didn't say I'd be working every second. You didn't say I'd have to watch all three kids on my own." I was talking fast so no tears would fall. "You didn't say I'd have to do any cooking. I was expecting to go swimming once in a while, to be able to read a bit."

Mrs. Lewis' face looked white. Shucks, I had sounded so mean. Then I thought of something and added, "The kids would have a better time if I were more rested. I could give them more attention."

Mrs. Lewis' lips were tight. She spoke crisply. "You're right," she said. "You do need breaks. Although you *are* getting paid. Okay, so take breaks. Go swimming twice, three times a week. While we're on the subject of criticism" (now I knew she was insulted) "do you mind to take one minute every morning to make your bed? It would make the room nicer."

I nodded.

From then on, I only watched two kids at a time. When Mrs. Lewis would go to a *shiur*, she took the baby with her. I went swimming when the boys were in playgroup. Mrs. Lewis never asked me to do more than I offered. But she never smiled at me either. She'd talk to me in short, crisp sentences. She wouldn't tell me jokes anymore. She seemed to be working harder and resenting it.

Physically, I loved the new arrangement. Emotionally, I was all alone. There was no one my age in the whole colony, and now even Mrs. Lewis didn't talk to me. I couldn't blame her. If someone had spoken to me the way I had to her, I would probably react the same way.

I tried making conversation. I told her the cute things her children did. "Moishy," I said once, "tell Mommy what you did on the swing today."

"Oh, I pumped my legs up and down...and then I went as high as the sky!" he answered.

I made sure to do my jobs well, but I was careful not to offer to do more. I was scared to get stuck again. After the kids were asleep, I'd read in the bedroom with a nightlight because

I couldn't handle sitting in the kitchen with a stonily silent Mrs. Lewis. Once in a while I contemplated apologizing, but apologizing was never my forté. Besides, wasn't my complaint legitimate? I battled with myself.

One day everything changed.

Mrs. Lewis and I took all three children to the big pool. We were both to watch all of them carefully in the shallow part. She was holding Berel, I kept my hands an inch away from Benny because I was paranoid, and we both eyed Moishy splashing.

Soon, more people came, more kids, and more noise.

Suddenly, I heard a silence in my ears. I looked down at Benny, and he looked happy. Berel was holding tightly to his mother.

Moishy. Where was he?

And then I saw him. He had gone past the rope and was in the deeper part. I saw his arms moving wildly but failing to keep him up. Then he became still and started to sink. Almost peacefully.

I stopped breathing. I lifted Benny to the side of the pool and set him down. I dove in and swam under water toward Moishy, my eyes open and on him. I repeated to myself over and over, "Please no, please no! Oh, my, Hashem, please help, please help, please help."

When I got to him, he was starting to turn upside down. I pulled him up and held him high in the air, screaming "Moishy!" He gave me a glassy look.

No response. I put him on the side, laid him down, and started to check his breathing, hoping someone more professional would take over. Benny came over and crawled on top of him. I was about to push Benny away, but then Moishy opened his eyes and blinked a few times. His face was white.

The whole place was silent. All eyes were on Moishy and me. Moishy's mother came and picked him up. He clung to her. We walked home quietly. I carried Berel, Mrs. Lewis carried Moishy, and Benny walked.

"Will he be okay?" Mrs. Lewis asked me.

"I think so," I answered, "but you should bring him to a doctor."

In my mind, I kept picturing Moishy turning over in the water. I realized how close this little boy had been to *chas v'shalom* losing his life. I realized how fragile life is. And I thought about how I had been protecting my little ego and not saying a simple "I'm sorry" because I was too proud.

The doctor said Moishy was fine, but that he should rest for a while.

We ate a light supper and the children went to sleep, exhausted. Then it was just Mrs. Lewis and me in the kitchen. I wanted to finally get everything off my chest, but I hesitated, having made quite a mess of things last time. I was about to open my mouth when I heard Mrs. Lewis' soft voice.

"Thank you so much, Sara'le," she said.

"Oh, it was nothing. Really."

Now was my chance.

The only way I could apologize was to be casual. "You know," I said, "I'm really sorry I made you feel bad last week. I enjoy working for you, and I shouldn't have sounded like you were treating me badly."

She looked down at the table. "No. Thank you for telling me that. I... guess I'm used to feeling great about myself, and you made me realize I was so imperfect. But thank you for continuing to do an excellent job even when I was sulking."

She came over and gave me a gentle hug. I felt a huge sense of relief.

The last few days as mother's helper were a dream. By that time, I loved the children, and Mrs. Lewis loved me. I did offer to help more than what we had agreed on, but Mrs. Lewis made sure I never took on too much. When we parted, we were all crying.

What a summer!

4

Goldie had never thought of herself as G.O. presidential material, but this was an opportunity not to be missed. She'd be respected, admired, and popular.

Goldie Niederman, Presidential Candidate

BY STERNA CITRON

Sometimes your whole world can change in less than a day. Sometimes all it takes is a few minutes!

It happened like this. Goldie was quietly going over her *Chumash* notes in the lunchroom while simultaneously savoring a pear whose juice threatened to get all over her skirt. Just then, Ruti, the G.O. president, and Sara Michal, the vice president, slipped into the seats next to her.

"So you're having a *Chumash* test, I see," said Ruti. "I had Mrs. Kaufman last year too. I know what it's like. She's tough." She chuckled sympathetically.

Goldie didn't know what to answer. She was never very good at small talk. "Yeah," she grunted, "I guess." But in truth she didn't think Mrs. Kaufman was particularly tough. Still, who was she to argue with Ruti?

"Could we speak to you privately?" Sara Michal asked.

"The student lounge is empty right now."

What could they want from me? Goldie wondered as she followed the girls into the corner of the lounge, out of sight of passersby. *This must be some kind of secret,* she thought uneasily. She might be in the same school as Ruti and Sara Michal, but she was worlds away.

"We hear you're a very good student. You're in all the honors classes," said Ruti in a voice just loud enough to be heard above the hum of the air conditioner.

"You're really a brain," added Sara Michal, smiling. "And you ran the *chessed* committee with Racheli this year and did an excellent job."

Goldie could feel herself melting under the spell of these cool and popular girls.

"You know, G.O. elections are coming up. Sara Michal and I will be graduating, but we're concerned about who is going to take over." Ruti's eyes, like green magnets, fastened onto Goldie's.

"Shoshie Kramer is running for president, as you know," said Sara Michal. She paused significantly.

Yeah, so…? She knew that. What were they were driving at?

"She's a very capable girl and all that," said Ruti. "She'd probably even make an excellent school president. There's only one problem."

"We'll be perfectly frank. She's a bit snobby, and we don't think someone like that should be G.O. president," said Sara Michal bluntly.

"We have to think of what's best for the school. We need somebody who's really a nice girl to run the G.O.," said Ruti.

"And so we feel," said Sara Michal, looking deeply into Goldie's eyes, "that you'd be the best person for the position."

The skin on Goldie's arm tingled. So they wanted her to

run for the presidency. In her wildest dreams, she'd never dreamed of this. She took a deep breath. She had never considered herself to be presidential material, even if she had done a pretty decent job as one of the *chessed* heads. But Ruti and Sara Michal obviously thought otherwise. Maybe they were right. After all, out of the twenty-six girls in her class, they had chosen her.

On the other hand, school was pretty demanding. "G.O. is a lot of work, isn't it?" she asked. "I need time to study." She wasn't the type to just coast along. Anything less than an *aleph* minus would not satisfy her. Twelfth grade would not be quite as hard as the other grades, especially once you got accepted by your seminary. Still…

"The president doesn't do everything herself. She gets other people to do things. That's how smart people work. They delegate," Ruti assured her.

"And we'll tell you exactly what you have to do," promised Sara Michal.

It sounded good. She might not even have to give up her lazy Sunday afternoons with Devorah Leah.

She knew they wanted an answer now, but she needed to get her swirling thoughts in order. She had been an officer once—secretary of her class, but she hadn't done much all year except attend meetings and, oh, yes, take minutes. She hated the minutes part. She wouldn't look at the minutes she had written in shorthand until the night before the next meeting, by which time she could hardly decipher her scribbles. It was not something she would undertake again.

On the other hand, that was last year, in tenth grade, and now she was going into twelfth grade. That was a big difference. She hoped so anyway. And, as they said, she had done a decent job running the *chessed* committee, though most of it was taking orders from Racheli, her co-head.

She wanted to hear what Devorah Leah thought about it, but she was absent today. "I'll sleep on it and let you know tomorrow, okay?" she said to the G.O. officers.

"Of course. We wouldn't want you to rush into anything as important as this without doing some heavy thinking." Ruti patted Goldie on the back as they exited the lounge.

Goldie floated out of the room on air. The whole world looked different. Until now she'd been a nobody, and now here she was, a candidate for G.O. president. She'd be up there at the podium in front of the whole school, giving speeches every day, just like Ruti and Sara Michal did this year.

Not that she enjoyed the prospect of speaking publicly. Her stomach went queasy at the thought. Still, she had been forced to speak a couple of times about the *chessed* activities, and she had survived. She would just do it; that's all there was to it. Look at what was at stake! She'd be admired and respected, known by all the school. The principal and extra-curricular activities director would confer with her. She'd be let out of class to attend important meetings. Everyone would look up to her. The whole thing was unbelievable!

And, Ruti and Sara Michal had been so nice to her. She hadn't realized before what nice girls they were. Not that she'd known them that well. Just the impressions she had from hearing them speak every morning after *davening*. She had always thought that they themselves were on the snobby side, that they thought the world of themselves. Boy, how wrong she had been!

As soon as she got home she called Devorah Leah. "Hey, where were you today, Devorah Leah?"

"I had a bad stomachache this morning, but *baruch* Hashem I'm better. What's up?"

"You're not going to believe this. Ruti and Sara Michal asked me if I'd run for G.O. prez."

There was a long pause. Finally Devorah Leah said, "And what did you tell them?"

"I didn't give them an answer, but I think I'm going to say yes."

Dead silence at the other end.

"Okay, so… what do you want me to say?"

This was weird. Why wasn't Devorah Leah happy for her? She should be jumping up and down for her. Didn't Devorah Leah realize that this was her chance of a lifetime?

"I want you to say what a great opportunity this would be for me," Goldie said. How silly she felt, having to spell out for her friend what she wanted from her.

"Well, if that's what you want to do, go ahead," Devorah Leah replied. "I just never knew you had any interest in being school president."

Devorah Leah sounded so strange, almost like she was angry. Goldie hung up the phone, feeling let down. So what if she had never expressed an interest in being president? She hadn't ever expressed an interest in being a millionaire or a princess either. Did that mean she wouldn't accept the opportunity if it were offered to her? Could it be that Devorah Leah was jealous? Or scared that Goldie would become so popular she wouldn't want to hang out with her old friend anymore?

Goldie hoped her family would be more enthusiastic.

As she mashed the guacamole—her specialty—for supper, she mentioned as nonchalantly as she could, "Ma, I was invited to run for G.O. president."

Her mother was characteristically upbeat. "How wonderful!" she gushed. "I'm sure you'll do very well. *Ein davar omeid befnei haratzon*. If you set your mind to run for president, I'm sure you'll win."

"Thank you for the vote of confidence, Ma," said Goldie.

Her younger sisters, Meira, ten, and Bracha, eleven, always alert to any interesting bits of news, came running from the living room. "Are you going to be high-school president?" Meira asked, her eyes wide with amazement.

"Hurray! Our sister is going to be president! President Nie-derman!" Bracha chanted as she set the dining room table.

Now that was more like it!

"Wait a minute, wait a minute," Goldie hushed them up, chuckling. "I was asked to *run* for president. I wasn't elected yet."

"You'll win for sure! We're gonna help. We're gonna make posters."

She smiled at their enthusiasm. She had forgotten about the posters. Yeah, she'd need a few of them. She could definitely use her sisters' help.

At supper, Meira and Bracha treated her with newfound respect, pouring her juice and bringing her dessert. She kind of enjoyed this kind of treatment.

Her father joined them at the table. "Tatty, did you hear?" Meira shouted excitedly. "Goldie is running for G.O. president."

"Is that so?" he asked in his deliberate, slow tone as he eyed his daughter thoughtfully. "It's a lot of work being president of an organization. I'm not telling you whether to accept or not, but I think you should consider if you are ready to take on so much work. It's not only about prestige."

"Oh, I won't have to work much. The trick is to get others to do the work," she repeated Ruti's wisdom confidently.

"Who says you'll always be able to find others to do the work? Even if you do, people sometimes say they'll do something, and they forget, or they get sick, or their mother needs them. Ultimately, the responsibility will be yours. I'm not trying to discourage you. I just want you to think about what you're getting into."

"Phone for you," her mother called from the kitchen.

It was Ruti.

"I forgot to tell you something important. Sara Michal and I are leaving you our notebook with all our notes of this year's activities and all the committees. Everything will be in there. You'll just follow what it says. Okay? You don't have to worry about a thing."

A notebook with all their notes. All she had to do was follow it. A piece of cake. Why was her father being so pessimistic?

• • •

When she got out of the car the next morning, Ruti and Sara Michal were waiting for her. Goldie felt a rush of exhilaration.

They each grabbed an arm. "So do you accept?" they asked eagerly.

She took a deep breath. "I accept," she answered, trying to sound cool and calm though she was seething with excitement. The gateway had just opened. Everyone would know her; her name would be on everyone's lips, she'd be popular.

By the time *davening* started fifteen minutes later, the word was out. Right and left, students and teachers wished her congratulations and *hatzlachah*. People who had never noticed her before said hi. Girls from all classes came up to her, volunteering to help with her campaign.

So this was what it was like to be popular! It was like being a *kallah*, only you got to be the center of attention all year long.

At lunchtime, as she was cleaning up the crumbs of her sandwich (made by Meira), she heard someone call her name. Someone to congratulate her, no doubt. She got her smile all ready, but then she saw who it was. Shoshie. Her opponent.

Before Goldie could think of what to say, Shoshie spoke. "So you decided to run," she said crisply. "Because it's you, I'm sure it will be a clean campaign, and we won't be slinging dirt and saying *lashon hara* about each other."

"Of course, it'll be a clean campaign," Goldie answered. She felt awkward. She and Shoshie had never been friends, but now it felt like they were enemies. Did it have to be like that? No, she would try and be nice. "I wish you *hatzlachah*," she said.

Shoshie was too much in command of herself to wish her running opponent success. She replied coolly, "May the best girl win."

By the time the principal called her into her office to congratulate her on her nomination, Goldie had forgotten about the bad feeling she was left with after talking to her running opponent. Mrs. Lipshitz stood up, a pleased expression on her face. "I'm delighted that you will be running for G.O. president," she said. Goldie wondered if Mrs. Lipshitz was happy because it was her or because it wasn't Shoshie.

At lunch, some girls got together with her to plan the campaign. They had great ideas which Goldie was happy to go along with. She smiled happily at everybody, and everybody seemed pleased with her. All she had to do was prepare her campaign speech for the next day. Life was good.

She wished Devorah Leah would be a little excited for her. She really wanted to talk to her, share with her everything that was going on, but Devorah Leah was obviously not interested.

That night, while her sisters colored the posters, she worked on her speech, chewing the end of her pencil. What should she say? She didn't know. She got on the phone with Ruti.

"It doesn't really matter what you say," Ruti said. "It's just like a real presidential election. Everyone knows you're just saying these things to get elected. Nobody thinks you're actually going to do the things you say."

Was that how things worked? She had never known.

"Basically," Ruti continued, "you want the girls to see you're a nice person. So just say how you're going to improve the *ruach* in the school. You're going to promote *achdus*. Nice things like that."

Well, Ruti obviously knew more about these things than Goldie did. So she made up a speech with lots of words like *ruach* and *achdus*, adding an idea or two of her own. She tried the speech on her sisters. Meira left in the middle, but Bracha stayed and said she liked it. Goldie hoped it would do.

The whole school gathered together in the auditorium the following day to hear the candidates' campaign speeches. Colorful banners hung all around the room. The ones for Goldie, designed by Meira and Bracha, read, "Go for the Gold; Goldie for President." The others read, "Vote for the best. Vote for Shoshie!" Some of the girls were chanting, "We want Goldie, olay, olay!" while others chanted, "Sho*shie*, Sho*shie*, Sho*shie*." The whole atmosphere was one of happy excitement.

"First we will hear from Goldie Niederman. Please give her your undivided attention!" announced Ruti.

Everyone turned to stare at her. Goldie could feel a red-hot blush slowly extend over her face. She stood up, almost knocking her chair over. "Take it easy," she told herself sternly, grabbing the chair just before it hit the floor, "or you'll make a total fool out of yourself." As she walked toward the stage, some girls broke out into a chant. "We want Goldie, olay, olay!"

Somehow she made it up the stairs and turned to face the audience. As she extricated the microphone from its cradle, a harsh grating sound pierced the silence. Cries of "Ouch! Ooh! Aagh!" filled the auditorium as girls covered their ears. Ruti rushed up to the stage and lowered the sound. The room turned silent. It was time to start. Goldie gazed at all the faces, all two hundred of them, many of them eager and smiling. Goldie yearned to be sitting back among them, safe in her chair. For that matter, she wished she were anywhere besides on stage.

It was now or never. Goldie took a deep breath and plunged into her campaign speech. "If you vote for me, this will be a year to remember," she pledged. (She hoped it would be re-membered for the good.) "I promise to work hard for you to improve the *ruach* in the school." She spoke about the impor-tance of *achdus*, ideas she remembered from a *hashkafah* class. *Achdus* would be her goal, as well as making the coming year the most memorable year the G.O. ever had. She finished off by saying, "I hope everyone will join at least one committee. Our G.O. will be not just for the select few, but everyone will be involved. If we all work together, we'll have a great G.O., and it'll be a really fun year."

As she descended from the stage, she heard applause and cheers. "Go, Goldie, go!" they chanted. So maybe she wasn't so bad?

"And now… Shoshie Kramer." It was Shoshie's turn.

Just looking at Shoshie and how she stood at the podium, head held high, exuding self-assurance, Goldie's heart sank. "If I get elected, I'll work with the administration on behalf of the students to reduce our homework so that no teacher gives more than one half-hour of homework a night and we have no more than three tests a week."

The girls cheered and clapped for so long that Ruti had to take over the mike and say, "Okay, girls, quiet down, please." Goldie could kick herself. Shoshie knew exactly what the girls wanted. They wanted their burden lightened so they could breathe a little, not have to work every minute from the time they came home from school until the wee hours of the night. Now that was a good campaign platform!

Shoshie went on to boast about her past experience. She had been G.O. treasurer the last year and before that, class president. Shoshie sounded capable and competent, whereas she, Goldie, had just sounded… nice.

Everyone's going to vote for Shoshie, Goldie thought. *I'd vote for Shoshie too if I could.*

Ruti and Sara Michal, however, thought differently.

They took her each by one arm and led her to their corner in the student lounge and sat her down at a table. They sat down opposite her.

"You did fine," Sara Michal reassured her. "Shoshie might have been more polished than you, but the girls could tell who the better, nicer person is."

"But what about her pledge to cut down the number of tests and have one half-hour of homework per teacher every night? Who doesn't want that?"

"Oh, like anyone believes that's really going to happen," Ruti answered with a roll of her eyeballs. "Dream on! Don't worry. We have the election wrapped up."

"I sure hope you're right," said Goldie, some of her flagging confidence restored.

"So now we'll go over some of the G.O. activities of the year," Sara Michal said.

"Can't we talk about that after the election?" Goldie asked.

She had been through so much that day! "Or tomorrow, okay?"

"Hey, this is important. You do want to be prez, don't you?" Ruti pursed her lips like a teacher who doesn't know what to do with her naughty student.

But seeing how unhappy Goldie looked, Ruti gave in. "Okay," she said, "we'll wait until tomorrow. By the way, we'll be having a debate the day after tomorrow. The students will be asking the two candidates questions. And then the following day we'll have elections."

"Debate?" Goldie leaped up, panic-stricken. "Tell me you're joking!" Hadn't she been through enough? How much more did she have to go through to get the coveted prize? Besides which, she had to finish studying for tomorrow's *Chumash* test.

"Don't worry," said Ruti, seeing her horrified expression. "It's off the cuff, impromptu. You don't have to prepare for it."

"You don't understand! I'm going to sound like a real idiot next to Shoshie. Why do we have to have a debate?"

"The girls expect it. We have one every year. But Sara Michal and I will give you some good things to say. You'll do fine. Just smile and don't lose your cool."

Goldie felt she had no choice. "Okay," she agreed with an unhappy sigh. Ruti and Sara Michal had a way of getting her to do things she never would normally. She hoped she wouldn't disappoint them and make a fool of herself.

But by the time she got home, she was having doubts about the whole thing again. The glamour part of it was wearing off too. At suppertime, Goldie called out to Meira, who was helping in the kitchen, "Can you please bring me a fork when you come in?" She didn't really have an appetite, but she'd try and eat something.

"I know you're a presidential candidate and everything, but

you'll have to wait a minute," Meira called back.

Boy, her special treatment hadn't even lasted two days.

"*Nu*, so how's the campaign doing?" her father asked her at the table after he said *Hamotzi*.

"I don't know if I like this whole campaign thing," she blurted out, surprising everyone, including herself. "And now they want me to take part in a debate."

Her father sat back in his chair and gave her a quizzical look. "You know the saying, 'If you can't stand the heat, get out of the kitchen'?" He tore off a piece of bread. "Public speaking, discussions, debating, and arguing—that's what you're going to be doing when you're school president. If you don't like it now, what are you going to do next year when you're going to have to do that kind of thing all the time?"

He murmured in a low voice so no one else should hear, "You can still change your mind and withdraw. But if you do that, you should do it immediately. Once you're elected, you're stuck."

Change her mind? Ruti and Sara Michal would be furious. Everyone would be disgusted with her, including the principal—and they had a right to be! She should have realized all this before! There was no way she could withdraw now.

Anyway, she comforted herself, it would be fun if she won. She, Goldie Niederman, president of the G.O, would be in the spotlight every day. What more could a teenager want?

• • •

But then, that night, came the dream. To be more exact, it was a nightmare. She was walking, and with each step her legs felt heavier and heavier as if pulled down by a great weight. Her steps grew slower and slower until, try as she might, she couldn't take another step. It was like her feet were stuck in cement. She was helpless, unable to move.

Goldie woke up with a start, her heart thumping so hard that it hurt. What did the strange dream mean? Unable to move. Stuck. Yes, stuck. If she went on with this, she'd be stuck, stuck in a position she was clueless about and, to be honest, that she had no real interest in.

In the morning, she left the house ten minutes early and hurried around the block and across the street to Devorah Leah's house. "Can we walk to school together?" Goldie asked when Devorah Leah appeared at the top of her stairs, hoisting her purple-colored backpack over her shoulder.

"Yeah, sure," she answered. Her tone was not exactly warm, but at least it wasn't cold.

She took a deep breath. "Why were you upset when I got nominated for president?"

They crossed the street. Devorah Leah looked thoughtful. "Well, if you really want to know, I never thought of you as a school president. It's so not you. And I couldn't figure out— and I *still* can't—why you suddenly wanted to do it."

So not her. Devorah Leah was right. And deep down she had known it all along, but she had been so charmed by Ruti and Sara Michal's attentiveness. And so tempted by the lure of being popular. She sighed. She wished she could push the clock back to three days before. Life had been so uncomplicated then.

She had to get out of this mess. She momentarily entertained the thought of running away, leaving town, disappearing. Then she wouldn't have to deal with anyone. But no, that was a wild idea. She couldn't do it.

That morning she *davened* with more *kavanah* than usual. "Hashem," she whispered at the end of *Shemoneh Esrei*, "I know what I have to do. Please give me the strength to do it."

After *davening*, she approached Ruti. "Can I talk to you for a minute please?" Her voice shook despite herself.

"Sure," Ruti said, searching Goldie's face for a clue.

They went into their usual corner of the student lounge. "What's up?" asked Ruti, at her most pleasant. "I hope you're not worried about the debate. Sara Michal wrote some really great things for you to say."

"No, it's not that. It's something else." Goldie realized this meant the end of her short-lived but exciting relationship with Ruti and Sara Michal, the end of her brief era of popularity and admiration. She'd be *persona non grata*, mocked by everyone, except maybe Devorah Leah.

"You're not chickening out on us, are you?" Ruti asked guardedly.

Chickening out. Oooh, it sounded awful.

"I can't run. I'm really sorry to pull out at this late stage," she said, her eyes glued to a crease on her skirt.

"What came over you, Goldie?" Ruti asked, astonished. She put her arm around Goldie affectionately. "Listen, I know it's hard. You've never done anything like this before. But Sara Michal and I are here for you. We'll help you. And we have confidence in you that you'll do a good job."

Her charm was really hard to resist. Goldie had to steel herself. "I'm just not cut out for it. I'm not presidential material. I'm sorry," Goldie said.

Ruti's smile vanished. Her fury came swiftly, like lava pouring forth from an exploding volcano. "Now you realize you're not cut out for it? Ruti's voice had a sharp, jagged edge to it. Gone was her charm, replaced by undisguised wrath.

Sara Michal added, "After everything we did for you! We could have picked anyone, but we picked you. You didn't even have to do much! We did most of your campaigning for you! And now you're letting us down like this!" Her voice dripped with scorn.

Mercifully, the bell rang at that moment. Ruti and Sara Michal flounced out of the room in disgust. The meeting—and their relationship—was over.

Totally weak and drained, Goldie dragged herself to class, not daring to meet anyone's eyes. The teacher had already started. As she squeezed behind Devorah Leah's chair to get to her place, Goldie muttered in her ear, "I dropped out of the race. I just told them."

Devorah Leah looked up at her. A smile spread over her face. Her thumb went up in a sign of approval.

It was good to know she had Devorah Leah's support. The other girls would probably be contemptuous of her for changing her mind at this late point. It would not be pleasant for a few days, but eventually they'd forget about it, *b'ezras* Hashem. Then life would go back to the same as before. She wouldn't be the center of attention, she wouldn't be popular, but that was okay. She'd definitely rather have it this way.

5

A Taste of Perfection

BY BRACHA GOYKADOSH

I'm so jealous of Shifra! She is perfect. There is no other adjective to describe her. She has perfectly long, silky, golden-brown hair. Her eyes are a perfect shade of delicate china-blue. Her nose is perfect—not too big and not too small. She is also the perfect height—5'6"—not too tall and not too short.

I don't think Shifra ever got anything less than a ninety-five on a test. Once I asked her how long she studied for a chemistry test. She casually shrugged and said, "Oh, maybe half-an-hour or forty-five minutes." And that was the chemistry final. Not just a little quiz or something. Chemistry is the hardest subject. All those ions and protons floating around. And she just studied forty-five minutes! And so, guess what she got on the final! A seventy-seven? An eighty-two? No way! Miss Perfect got a ninety-five-and-a-half! You should have heard her sobbing in the bathroom when we got the finals back. "I wanted a hundred!" she said, big tears streaming down her perfect, oval face. "I should have known the answer to that dumb question!" she sobbed. "I'm so stupid! Everyone knows that the answer was noble gases!"

What was she was talking about? I studied six hours for that final, and I got an eighty-four, a really good mark for me. I was really happy about it. But now I felt stupid. Shifra studied for maybe forty-five minutes and got a ninety-five-and-a-half, and she's complaining! I mean, like, come on!

Shifra plays the piano and has even won a few awards. Shifra swims like a pro. (What am I saying? She *is* a pro!) Shifra has a stunning voice. She was choir head last year when we were freshies. It is virtually unknown for freshmen to be head of anything, especially choir. So it was a really big thing. This year Shifra is head of dance.

Shifra has two older brothers. Both of them are in yeshivah in Israel. She has three younger sisters. She has no older siblings at home to boss her around!

I, Ruchy Leff, on the other hand, have three older sisters, two younger sisters, and two younger brothers. Okay, so Shaindy's in seminary and can't boss me around anymore, but Leah and Ricky do their fair share of telling me what to do. And Goldie and Gitty, my younger sisters, are just so annoying! Shloimy and Moishy, the twins, are spoiled; they're only five, but they are so bratty!

• • •

Aaaaaaahhhhhhhh! Morning! I'm so cold! I shiver and pull my comforter closer. Strange, it's not my usual gray comforter with pink flowers. This one is really gorgeous. It's made out of this soft, satiny material, and it looks like new. Maybe Ima bought it for me and wanted to surprise me? Perhaps I was just so tired last night that I didn't realize? I don't know why I am so tired. Usually, I just jump out of bed. Today I feel exhausted.

"Shiffi! Wake up!" says a woman with a Brooklyn accent. First of all, my name is not Shiffi, it's Ruchy. Second of all, my mother does not have a Brooklyn accent. My mother has lived in good old Chicago, Illinois, all of her life. "It's almost 8:00, Shiffi! Get out of bed! I mean *now*, Shifra!"

I resist the temptation to crawl back under the covers. I throw the comforter off and jump out of bed. That makes me feel dizzy. It makes me so dizzy that I can't even recognize my room.

Where am I? The room I'm in is done in shades of green and blue. My own room is pink! What's going on here! Where are my beautiful antique dresser and bureau and lovely desk? Where are my books? My seashell collection? My gold and silver mirror that I won at a Chinese auction? My *Shoshanim* magazines?

Instead, there is a modern, white Formica desk and dresser. In fact, the whole bedroom set is made of stunning, ice-white Formica. It gives the room a clean, modern look. There is a brand-new Apple computer (flat-screened!) on the desk. On the wall is a beautiful portrait of Shifra Greene! What is a painting of Shifra Greene AKA Miss Perfect doing here!? Is this her room?

I look into the shiny white Formica mirror. I used to have fluffy (and frizzy) dark hair and big green eyes. I had a little bit of acne on my forehead. My nose was long and thin. I now have silky sleek, golden-brown hair and delicate china-blue eyes. My skin is clean and pimple-free. My nose is just right— not too big, not too small. I look exactly like Shifra Greene!

"Oh, there you are, Shiffi!" said the woman with the Brooklyn accent rushing into my—no, Shifra's—room. "Why aren't you dressed yet?" She looks at me. I look at myself. For the first time I realize I am wearing blue pajamas with stars on the pants. I saw these pajamas in a boutique on Central Avenue, but my mother said they were too expensive (fifty bucks!), so I couldn't get them.

"Shifra! Space in!" said the lady who I now presumed to be Shifra's mother. "I need your help! Yael is having a temper tantrum downstairs, and Blanca can't calm her down, and I have to run to the office, and Daddy is still at shul, and he probably won't come home afterwards because he has to go to his office because he has an appointment with a client, so I need you to take Yael and Rena to school because Esty's at a friend's house, and I can't because I have to run, and Blanca has to scrub the floor because Yael spilled her cereal which is why she's crying, and oh, gosh, it's 8:15 already, and I have to go, and you know Yael's pre-school starts half-an-hour earlier than the high school, so you really have to get moving because it starts at 8:30. Thanks so much for your help, darling. Bye, honey, I love you!" With that, Mrs. Greene blew me (in Shifra's body) an air kiss and ran out of the room.

I stood there, amazed. Could she really say so much in one breath and in less than a minute? That was amazing! Wow!

Then suddenly my responsibility dawned on me! I had to get both kids and myself ready for school! I ran around the house like a madwoman. I called Rena and Yael. Blanca thought I was nuts when I asked her to show me where Yael's clothes were. It was 8:45 when we finally left the house. Yael was late for pre-school. Rena, who I figured was in second grade (she told me that Gitty Leff, my sister, is in her class) would probably also be late. If I didn't get to school in the next fifteen minutes, I would for sure be late. Suddenly, it dawned on me that Shifra had come late to school the past few days.

Yael had another tantrum, and I was stuck in Morah Blimie's nursery class for another twenty minutes until she finally calmed down. By then I had totally missed *davening* in the auditorium. I was about ten minutes late for *Ivrit*. I got a note from the secretary, Frumie, who gave me a stern look and said, "Hmmm… third time this week! This is going to have a bad effect. If you're late one more time, I'm afraid I'll have to inform the principal and your parents." I quickly ran out of the office. The secretary was really scaring me! She was usually nice to the real me, but it was obvious that she disliked Shifra.

When I got to *Ivrit* class, Mrs. Ben-Zion, my teacher, gave me a stern look. As I handed her my late note, she said that since I had already been late six times in the past two weeks my GPA went down three points. I sighed.

I sat down in Shifra's seat next to her best friend, Judy. Judy didn't even look up at me. Suddenly, I felt a pang of longing for my friends, Chava, Chanie, Feigy, and Tzirel. I wished I could sit with them.

Out of the blue, I had a weird idea. If I was Shifra, then who was me? I looked at myself (my old self, in the old Ruchy Leff body). I, or rather Ruchy, was furiously taking notes. Is that what I really looked like from another person's view? My frizzy, fuzzy dark hair that I always thought looked so limp, for some reason suddenly looked shiny and full of body. And my pimples didn't show that much! My nose looked so much better than I thought! And I seemed so smart! I just kept taking notes and looking at the teacher! If I didn't know the truth, I would almost think that I was, well… perfect!

All of a sudden Mrs. Ben-Zion called on me! Arrgh! "Shifra," she said, "do you know the answer to this question?"

"Err…ummm?" I said nervously. "Do you think maybe that you could repeat the question?" I felt so stupid!

"If there is a *shva b'rosh milah*, is it a *shva na* or a *shva nach*?"

"Oh, sure, a *shva na*!" All of a sudden, I felt as if a fountain of knowledge had been poured on me! I felt so smart! The bell rang, signaling that class was over.

The next class was *Navi*. I quickly rushed to my locker and took out a *Navi*. Oh no! I had gone to my old locker! My Ruchy Leff locker, not my Shifra Greene locker! Abruptly, I remembered that I did not know Shifra's locker combination, or which locker was hers! That was really frustrating! Now how would I get a *Navi*? The bell would ring any minute now! I had to hurry! All of a sudden I saw Shifra's friend, Michali.

Michali has a different schedule. She has *Navi* last period, not second period.

"Michali," I asked breathlessly, "may I borrow your *Navi*?"

"Sure," said Michali, giving me a weird look. "Just be sure to give it back to me before fourth period."

I quickly rushed to *Navi* class, and thank G-d I was on time! That's because Mrs. Jacobowitz, the *Navi* teacher, has a habit of coming late to class.

"Hi, Shifra!" said Mimi, Shifra's friend.

"Oh, hi, Mimi," I answered nonchalantly.

Mimi then proceeded to describe in great detail the whole new wardrobe that she had gotten last night from Garden City Shopping Plaza. In ten minutes, I knew exactly what she had gotten, from which store, at what price, and why Mimi thought it was a good bargain. "And then," continued Mimi, oblivious to my immense boredom, "I got this really cute, dark denim skirt with such a cute suede camel belt. I got it from Ann Taylor Loft for only twenty dollars! Isn't that a good price? Then I got a charming pair of shoes from Banana Republic. They're just gorgeous! They're made of this dark blue really nice soft leather made from lambs, and they have a little suede strip, sort of like a buckle, but not really. I just, like, love them! They were only forty-three dollars, which I think is a really good price! And then, I got this lavender cotton jacket from Kenneth Cole. It's sort of like plaid and has these green lines running through purple boxes. It was thirty-two dollars, and I didn't really like it, but my mother said I should get it because it brings out the green in my eyes, and I have a purple skirt that matches it. And then…"

Mimi totally did not realize that I was dying of boredom. I'm not kidding, I really was. Clothes do not interest me in the least! I was really overjoyed when Mrs. Jacobowitz walked in. The teacher launched into a fascinating discussion about how Elisha and Eliyahu were similar. I knew the answers to all the questions. After I answered the sixth question, Mrs. Jacobowitz told me to give other girls a chance.

Finally, it was recess. There was no way I was going to hang out with Shifra's friends anymore! They were just too boring! I went to my friend Tzirel who was talking to Chava. "Hey!" I said. They both gave me really strange looks. "So, what's up?" I said, making a real effort to try to talk to them. "Do you guys like computer games?" I knew they did, and once they got started they couldn't stop!

"How did you know?" Chava asked curiously.

Tzirel just stared at me like I had fallen from planet Mars.

"Oh, I love computer games!" I said in an amiable voice. "I just got a new game. It's called Mall Tycoon! It's a total blast! You make this mall…"

"Oh, Ruchy got that, too!" said Chava. Tzirel was still staring at me like I had lost it.

"Really!" I said, acting like I was surprised, which of course I wasn't. "Where is Ruchy?" I asked.

"You want to speak to Ruchy?" asked Chava. Her voice

made it sound like I was crazy.

"Yeah. Why?" I answered.

"Oh, I dunno."

"So where is she?"

"I told you I don't know!"

"Oh."

I suddenly needed to speak to Ruchy! She was me! If I was in Shifra's body, then maybe Shifra was in mine.

Then a weird thought entered my head. Maybe for some people it wasn't so weird, but for me this was really weird. I thought that I should go and fix my hair. Why is that weird? you ask. Well, the thing is, I never fix my hair in school. None of my friends do either. The lighting in the bathroom is so bad, and I would need a brush, and also I cannot make my hair without gel or mousse. I never even think about making my hair in school!

So I went to make my hair. After all, I couldn't let everyone think Shifra Greene was having a bad hair day just 'cuz I wasn't in the mood of making her hair!

In the bathroom were all of Shifra's friends. Shouldn't I have known?! "Oh, Shiffi!" squealed one of Shifra's really good friends, Leah'le. "I haven't seen you all day! Where've you been? So what's doing?"

"I'm great. What's up with you?" I answered her.

"'What's up with you'?! What is going on, Shifra?" she twittered. "You sound just like one of those *nebby* girls!" Then Leah'le proceeded to make her hair in a messy bun, as opposed to her usual neat clip. She slumped down and put this really gruff wanna-be look on her face. "So, hi, sup? Yeah, sup?" Leah'le broke out in gales of giggles. All of her friends (well, technically my friends, too) burst out laughing.

You see, the thing is that perfect people like Shifra and her friends do not, under any circumstance, ever say, "What's up?" or anything of that sort. They think it sounds loser-ish. They all speak in these fake Brooklyn accents and say stuff like, "So, what's doing?" or, "I like such a skirt or shirt," or whatever.

Then one of Shifra's (my?) other friends, whose name is Kayla, asked me what happened to my hair. She said it looked awful and that I totally needed to get it permed. When I heard that, I got really mad at her and told her that what I did with my hair was my business and it really shouldn't make the least bit of a difference to her. Then I ran out of that place as fast as I could. I didn't even want to know what they were thinking.

Okay, so now I was standing in the hall, all by myself, looking like the biggest loser *ever*! So what should I do? I couldn't go to my real friends, my Ruchy Leff friends, because they would think I'm totally nuts. And I couldn't go to Shifra Greene's friends because they already thought I'm mad. Help!!!

• • •

"Drrrriiiiinnng," went my alarm clock. I was jolted awake from a restless sleep.

"Ruch...honey...wake up dear!" said a woman with an accent from good 'ole Chicago, Illinois! It must be...

"Ma!" I screeched happily. "It's you! It was just a dream! I'm not really Shifra! I'm me! How wonderful it is to be me again! I was so jealous the whole time, and now I see that I have nothing to be jealous of because I have my own talents and gifts!"

"Uh... Ruchy, I don't know what you're talking about, but why don't you start to get ready for school? It's almost 8:30, sweetie."

"Okay, Ma." I jumped out of bed as my mother left my

room. I was back in my own beautiful pink room with the stuff that I loved. I felt alive and energetic once again.

Thank goodness, it was all a dream. What if it really was true? What if I really was Shifra? Hey, wait a second. Before I wished that I was Shifra. I thought that she was just perfect and that her life was totally perfect. But now in my dream I got a little taste of her life, and believe me, it sure wasn't perfect. I mean, come on. The way her mother dumped all the responsibility on her, and the way her friends treated her. And what her friends talked about! Yuck!

I realized my life was just the way I wanted it to be. I had lots of good friends with whom I enjoyed spending time, and my mother would never put so much responsibility on me. (She would drop it on Ricky or Leah or Shaindy instead! Ha!)

And also, so what if I wasn't good at all the things Shifra was good at? Even though I was never choir head, it doesn't mean I don't have an okay voice. And just because I'm not dance head, it doesn't mean I can't dance. And besides, I don't even like dancing, now that I think about it objectively. I enjoy using the computer and I like crocheting. I also like to paint, and I am head of scenery this year. I don't want to brag or anything, but I'm a pretty good chef. And even though I'm not that smart, I'm not stupid either. While chemistry and math are not my best subjects, I do pretty well in creative writing, biology, and Spanish.

So I don't have Shifra's life, which I thought was perfect but really isn't. But I do have my life, which, now that I think about it, is, well, pretty near perfect!

6 Chana Leah lived in an elegant mansion on a wide boulevard. Her husband was a philanthropist. Suri couldn't believe it was the same Chana Leah who was so poor and shabbily dressed in high school! And here, Suri and her husband were struggling. Was it fair that life ended up this way?

Strange Tricks

BY STERNA CITRON

That twangy voice! It didn't matter that she hadn't heard it since graduating Torah Academy of Youngville ten years ago; she'd recognize it anywhere.

"I can't believe it," Suri Blattner exclaimed. "It's Chana Leah! I haven't seen you in ages!"

Suri dropped her packages on the sidewalk of Manning Avenue into a pile of snow, and shifted her squirming baby to her left arm. Right in front of Moshe's Kosher Essin, the two former schoolmates hugged.

Suri gazed at Chana Leah. She looked the same. Her eyes were still large, black, and haunting, her forehead wide and intelligent, and her chin determinedly pointy. Only now she looked more mature, more serious. Which wasn't surprising. They were both twenty-eight now.

"It's so great to run into you! Let's see, it's been how many years?" Suri asked. She snuck a peek at her friend's gray tweed coat with its stylish cape. It was a far cry from the dingy brown peacoat that Chana Leah had worn day in and day out in high school. Suddenly, Suri became self-conscious about her own down-filled jacket which was overdue to go to the cleaners.

"The last time I saw you was at graduation ten years ago," Chana Leah exclaimed. They both stood for a moment, lost in memories good and bad. They hadn't been close friends, but it had been a small class, so everyone knew each other well.

"What are you doing here? Do you live here in town?" Suri asked.

"Yes, I do. I live on South Maple Street. I moved here four months ago. Maybe you'll come over? Do you have a few minutes?"

Suri checked her watch. "Sure, I have about an hour until I have to pick up my son." Maple Street. The rich section of town. Wow, life does play some strange tricks.

"Great, I'll see you at my place in a few minutes," Chana Leah said as she scribbled the address for her.

Suri strapped her daughter into the safety seat of her nine-year-old Camry and got behind the wheel. In her rear-view mirror she could see Chana Leah open the door of a sleek Infinity, the color of vanilla pudding. Even Suri, ignorant as she was about cars, could tell it was a luxurious car.

As Suri headed down Third Avenue to Maple Street, she had a crazy idea to stop at her house and put on her Anne Klein coat which she wore usually on Shabbos. But then she realized how ridiculous that was. Who was she trying to impress, after all? Just a few years ago, Chana Leah had been a poor girl who wore her hair in a long black braid and fastened her skirt hems with safety pins.

Suri pulled into Chana Leah's broad driveway. So this was

where her former classmate lived—in a two-floor brick mansion with rows of French dormer windows staring down at her. A gigantic elm tree spread its leafless branches over most of the front lawn. The wide brick walkway had been carefully cleared from the snow. (Suri's place, on the other hand, hadn't been shoveled at all; you had to walk in the footsteps of the last person who had tramped through.) Suri ascended the front steps with Mimi pressed against her side and pressed the bell. Little Mimi listened in awe as the chimes echoed and re-echoed throughout the house.

"Isn't that nice, Mimi?" Suri cooed, but her voice sounded hollow. How was it possible that all this was Chana Leah's? She tried to compose herself so she wouldn't look as incredulous as she felt.

Her friend opened the door. "Please come in," she said. Behind Chana Leah there stretched out a vast marble-floored vestibule with a gleaming chandelier that hung down from the second floor. Suri's eyes opened wide. Of the few homes she had been in on this side of town, none matched this one. From somewhere deep in the recesses of the mansion the sound of vacuuming could be heard. The housekeeper. Full-time, no doubt, Suri deduced from the immaculate, hushed sweep of a carpet that covered the living and dining room floor.

"Can I get you something?" Chana Leah asked graciously after she had taken Suri's and Mimi's jackets and hung them up. "A hot drink to warm you up? What can I get for the baby?"

"Thanks, we're fine. Don't worry about us. Just sit."

Chana Leah sat down on a handsome velvet burgundy couch that was easily twelve feet long, while Mimi, sensing there were new worlds to explore, crawled away, babbling happily. Suri's eyes roamed around the high-ceilinged, elegant living room. On one wall was a hand-carved china cabinet with gleaming silver Judaica. Spots of light were aimed at each piece of silver. Paintings of florals and landscapes that could have been in a museum hung on the walls. Cream-colored silk drapes with sheers of silk chiffon adorned the tall French doors.

How did a young woman design a room like this? Oh, yes, a decorator. Of course!

Suri tried to assume an interested but not overawed look. It wasn't easy. Her mind reeled. This wasn't a house; it was a palace. And Chana Leah, who in school had been an outsider, who was regarded as a bit eccentric, was its fortunate owner.

"I know what you're thinking. I've come up in the world. Yes, Hashem has been good to me," Chana Leah said. Was Suri imagining it, or did she see just a hint of a smirk behind Chana Leah's smile, as if to say, "You never thought much of me. What are you thinking now?" *It reminded her of that certain look that the old Chana Leah used to have back in high school. Was it pride? Or standoffishness? But now, of course, it was a different story. Chana Leah had plenty to be superior about. She wasn't just rich. She was fabulously wealthy.*

"So tell me about yourself," said her hostess. Her voice was warm, encouraging, and actually not superior at all.

Suri tried to gather her thoughts. She'd much rather hear about Chana Leah. How had this all come about? "Well, I have three kids, *b'li ayin hara*, a six-year-old boy, and two girls, one who is four and this little one, Mimi, who is turning one soon. My husband's a really good guy, *baruch* Hashem. He taught for a few years after *kollel*, but he felt teaching wasn't for him. Now he and his brother own a car wash, and every night he goes to the *kollel* to learn."

"Yeah, go on," Chana Leah said, nodding.

"We bought our own home last year. We're very happy, *baruch* Hashem. It's a very nice home." At least, until now she had thought of her home as very nice. She wasn't so sure now. "And," Suri finished, "I'm pretty busy between the children and the house, and I give piano lessons two evenings a week and Sundays."

"I remember how you played the piano when we put on that performance for Chanukah in eleventh grade. You were really good," Chana Leah said admiringly.

"Thanks," Suri said. It was a nice feeling to share those memories with someone else who went through it. Nobody here knew her from her girlhood days. "And what about you?"

"Me? I don't have much to tell," Chana Leah answered in a vague tone. That was just how she was in school, Suri remembered. Evasive. She never spoke about herself or her family. If they had a project, she never revealed what her topic was until the day of the presentation. Her classmates had tried here and there to break down that barrier of secrecy without any success.

"As you can see, my husband and I are doing very well, thank G-d. Our son Yoni is eight years old…" her voice trailed off into silence.

Only one son. Suri's heart filled with compassion for her friend.

Then Chana Leah brightened up. "Yoni's coming home soon. In one hour. Can you stay?"

"I wish I could. Maybe some other time. I'd love to meet your son. What about your husband?"

"Gershon?" Chana Leah paused. "He's—he's involved in lots of things. He's extremely busy. He's on different boards and committees. I can't even keep up with him half the time. But he's doing good things, so that makes me happy."

Suri wasn't sure what it all meant. Boards, committees. Was it like the boards of schools and *yeshivos* and things like that? Yes, that must be it. They were involved in *tzedakah* organizations, probably in a big way, which was why Chana Leah was being so vague. She didn't like to boast.

"Come," Chana Leah jumped up, "I'll show you a picture."

Scooping up Mimi, Suri followed her hostess into another large room which appeared to be yet another living room, only a little more casual than the first. Here the couch and matching loveseat were made of yellow leather, and on the ebony coffee table was a careful arrangement of hand-blown glass shapes, all differently colored, and a pile of oversized photography books. Above the fireplace was a huge, gilt-framed painted portrait of the three of them, Chana Leah seated on a Louis XIV armchair, wearing a brocade gown, her son standing at her knees, and at her side an aristocratic, proud-looking man with a small black beard flecked with gray. Suri realized with a start that Chana Leah's husband was older than she was, at least ten or maybe twelve years older. Quite a contrast from her boyish-looking husband.

There were lots of photographs on the wall, mostly of Chana Leah's husband smiling and shaking hands with different people. One of them she recognized as the principal of Yesodei Haemes. She also noticed a lot of plaques on the wall with the Weinfelds' names inscribed on them.

They returned by way of a kitchen gleaming with stainless steel cabinets and counters. A woman in a white uniform stood in front of a large antique stove, stirring a pot from which a warm tantalizing aroma came forth. "Remember, Amanda, easy on the chili pepper, please," Chana Leah cautioned her. She opened up a cabinet and took out a fruit leather which she handed to Mimi.

"Tah-too," said Mimi promptly. It sounded exactly like thank you. Chana Leah pinched her on the cheek. "Cuuuute!" she said. A pang went through Suri. She hoped and prayed Chana Leah would have more babies, *b'ezras* Hashem. One child in nine years of marriage!

Suri couldn't help staring at the woman in the white uniform. "You have a cook?" she asked, astonished. She wished she didn't sound so naïve and excitable, but she couldn't help it. *Nobody* she knew had a cook.

Chana Leah laughed good-humoredly at her friend's ingenuousness. "Yes, I do. I'm pretty lucky. Amanda makes the best Indian food too. One day you'll taste her tandoori chicken."

Chana Leah made it sound like she expected there to be other times when they got together. *But could they really be friends?* Suri wondered. What did they have in common, this old classmate and her? This old classmate who drove an Infinity, lived on South Maple, and had a cook working for her, making food that she had never even heard of.

And then the other problem. Chana Leah would expect to be invited over to her place. She cringed at the thought. Her house was, well, kind of informal, homey maybe. She had some second-hand furniture, a slightly frayed Persian rug and some original paintings that her mother-in-law, an artist, had let her choose from her collection. But, she thought with a pang, the house needed a lot of fixing. She could not let Chana Leah see it the way it was.

"Come, Mimi… we have to go home," said Suri, pushing her daughter's arms into her jacket sleeves.

As Chana Leah let her guests out into the waning afternoon, Suri saw two men with black hats and beards approaching the house, clutching attaché cases. "Gershon Veinfeld *voynt du?*" one of them asked Suri. They were obviously collecting for some yeshivah or organization.

"Yeh," she answered. Her Yiddish wasn't great, but that much she understood.

From her car Suri caught a glimpse of Chana Leah as she greeted her visitors, *meshulachim* from Eretz Yisrael obviously. She started the ignition and waited to put the heater on. She was surprised to see how attentively and respectfully Chana Leah was listening to them. Most people, herself included, made short shrift of *meshulachim*, handing them a few dollars and hoping to be rid of them quickly. Chana Leah was being so... so nice. Then Chana Leah disappeared inside, probably to write them a check, while the two men waited at the door. Interesting... Had Chana Leah always been like this? Now that she thought about it, she had to admit that yes, Chana Leah had always treated everyone respectfully.

She drove to school to pick up her son, and then home, impatient to call her mother and tell her whom she had met— and most of all, how she had come up in the world. She wondered what her mother would have to say.

Her arm wrapped tightly around Mimi, she carefully climbed her snow-packed stairs, holding on tightly to the banister with her free hand. Her eyes caught the flecks on the wall where the paint had peeled off. Ugh. It was really awful.

She set Mimi down in her highchair and sat down to spoon-feed her sweet potatoes, while her son went to play with his building blocks. Her eyes swept over the parquet floor, graying with age and dotted with stains. There was no way she could invite Chana Leah to her home.

With her free hand, she dialed her mother. "Ma, you won't believe who I saw today."

"I give up."

"Chana Leah. She moved here. She's married to a guy

named Gershon Weinfeld and has one son who's eight years old. And Ma, she's rich. I mean, really rich. Can you believe it?"

"You're kidding! Who would imagine? Well, I'm happy for her. She didn't have an easy childhood. Her father came from Romania, and he never learned the language, so it was hard for him to get a decent job."

"Yes, she used to wear the same shabby coat every day—all day, even in class." It suddenly occurred to Suri why she had done that. Chana Leah didn't want anyone to see her shirt, which was probably either not ironed or missing a button. She had never realized why... until now. Maybe if she had thought about it then, she would have had more sympathy for her. "But anyway, Ma, she invited me to her house, or rather mansion. My whole house can practically fit into her living room. And she has a maid and a cook. Ma, a cook!"

"Okay, so she's wealthy! So she has a cook. *Baruch* Hashem! *Auf ala Yiddishe kinder gezokt!* (It should happen to all Jewish children.) I hope you don't begrudge her?"

Suri flinched. It was hard to admit, but maybe her mother was right. Maybe a little part of her (or a big part of her) did begrudge her friend.

Suri went to cook supper. It would be baked fish with green beans and potatoes (thank you, but no tandoori chicken for her). Something bothered her. If Chana Leah, who had been somewhat of a misfit in school, who had been kind of, well, strange, if she could now be the wife of a tycoon, then why didn't she—Suri—deserve better? After all, she had been president of the G.O. She had graduated salutatorian of the class. So why didn't she deserve just as much as Chana Leah? It wasn't fair.

The rest of the evening she couldn't stop analyzing her

home, comparing it to her friend's. Nothing measured up to her friend's house and furniture. Her second-hand furniture, which had that old, well-made feel, suddenly looked shabby. Her mother-in-law's paintings which livened up the walls and which she used to admire seemed mediocre. The rice-paper shades on the windows were ragged around the edges. Anyway, they were supposed to be there only until they could afford miniblinds or curtains. But somehow now, it looked like they should be replaced urgently. And then, of course, there was the old wooden floor which she had always thought of as having a rich patina, but now she saw all the gray spots, the stains.

Ugh, the place looked really awful. How could she be expected to live like this? What would Chana Leah think when she saw it? She must talk to her husband—immediately. Lazer was a reasonable man. He would understand. He would find a way. She wasn't exactly sure how, especially since they had had to borrow money to get the car wash business started and they hadn't even begun to pay back their debts. But Lazer was smart. He could come up with a solution.

That night, after the children were asleep, as she and her husband sat at the kitchen table munching some freshly made popcorn, Suri told Lazer about her unexpected meeting with her former classmate and her visit with her.

"What did you say their name was? Weinfeld?" he sounded excited. "I heard that Gershon Weinfeld had moved here with his family. Gershon Weinfeld is a big philanthropist. He's pretty famous. My *rosh yeshivah* says he's a '*gaon*' in *tzedakah*-giving. I had no idea his wife was a good friend of yours."

"I can't really say we were good friends. We were in the same class. She was kind of an outsider, socially. None of us really knew her well, as she kept herself apart and she was kind of poor. But you should see where she lives now. She lives in this magnificent mansion. It's like a fairy tale; the rooms are so grand and the house is so tastefully furnished."

"Hmm, I hope you're not getting any ideas of moving to South Maple Street?" he asked teasingly.

She laughed, but it wasn't a real happy laugh. "No, no, I realize Hashem distributes riches to whomever He sees fit. But I just want to know, how long do we have to live… like this?"

Lazer almost choked on his popcorn. "What do you mean 'live like this?' Like *what*?"

"Like this," she said, sweeping her arm towards the rest of the house. "Look at it: the windows, the floor…"

"Is something wrong with them?"

"Is something wrong with them?" Her voice rose a notch. "The rice shades—can't you see—they're all askew, their tassels are gone, and the edges are ragged. They were only supposed to be there until I got normal curtains."

"Oh. I never noticed."

Suri kept her eyes focused on the bowl of popcorn, which was still full. She knew that if she looked at her husband's face, she'd feel sorry for him, and she wouldn't be able to go on. But she had to go on! This was too important!

"And the floor. It's full of stains! It's embarrassing the way it looks!"

"The floor? Something's wrong with that too? Listen," he said, "I thought you were happy with this house. Most of our friends our age don't even own their own place! We were really fortunate to be able to buy it."

Suri said nothing.

Lazer went on. "I don't understand what happened to you. You were perfectly happy until today. Just because you met someone who's wealthy you suddenly have to own the perfect house. What do you expect me to do? Rob a bank so you could remodel? You know we can't borrow money. We just borrowed to start my business."

Her husband didn't understand her. Suri stared off into space.

Lazer got up and pushed back his chair, his shoulders sagging dispiritedly. "What do you want me to do?" he asked. "Take on a second job so we can have the house of your dreams? Fine, I'll do that! I'll stop learning in *kollel* at night and on Sundays, and I'll work for Menashe, fixing computers. Is that what you'd like?"

Her husband should give up his learning so she could have nice drapes and a refinished floor? "No," she whispered hoarsely. But surely there had to be some solution. If there was a will, there was a way, wasn't there?

Suri heard her husband walk up the stairs, his steps slow and heavy. She had really hurt him. She had made him feel that he had disappointed her, that he could not live up to her expectations. How could she have done that to him?

Suri sat unmoving. The clock struck twelve. Finally, she forced herself to get up, empty the untouched popcorn into the garbage, and go upstairs. She lay awake for a long time, staring into the darkness, until she eventually fell into an uneasy sleep.

The next morning Lazer left without saying goodbye. Despite the unusually warm sunshine and beautiful, blue sky outside, Suri's heart was heavy. They had fought—over what? Nothing, not even a beautiful house, was worth ruining their relationship! She wished she had never said anything. A beautiful house would be nice, but not at this price.

If only she could turn back the clock to before their conversation! She and her husband had always loved and respected each other. All she wanted was to get things back to how they were before.

She forced herself to make breakfast for the children and get them ready for school and playgroup, but she felt miserable. Just after Donnie and Esty were picked up, her phone rang. "I'm outside your house," said a twangy voice. "Can I come in for a few minutes?"

Suri was too stunned to answer.

"Hello?" asked Chana Leah. "Are you there?"

Forget about the worn-out shades and stained floors, thought Suri in dismay. She hadn't even cleaned up the house. It was a mess!

"Okay," she gulped, "but I'm not dressed. And the house is a wreck."

"Don't worry, I'm not coming to inspect. Just to say hello," Chana Leah answered gaily and hung up.

Chana Leah, looking flawless in a neatly combed *sheitel* and perfectly applied plum lipstick, was genuinely happy to see her.

"I'm really sorry about the way the house looks," Suri apologized, lifting her hand up to her own disheveled *tichel*.

"You don't need to apologize. It has a wonderful, warm, homey feeling. And these paintings are lovely." She walked up close to examine them. "Who did them?"

"My mother-in-law."

"Wow! She's good!"

Chana Leah wandered around the living and dining room, picking up this knickknack and that photo. "And here's your children's collection." She stopped before the arts and crafts of the children which Suri had arranged on a shelf. A wistful look seemed to pass over her face. Suri got a sudden glimpse into Chana Leah's life—the vast mansion occupied by her and her husband and one only child.

Chana Leah spied Suri's wedding album on top of the bookcase. "May I?" she asked.

"Sure! Here, let's sit down. Sorry about the mess." Suri quickly shoved the toys and books on the couch to one side to make room for them to sit.

"Really, don't worry about it! I like a house that feels lived in!"

That was a new way of looking at things. Suri had never thought of a room littered with playthings as an asset.

The two women sat down and pored over the album.

"Oh, wow, here's Mrs. Daitch, our *Chumash* teacher. She's gorgeous, isn't she? Oh, and look, here's Sima from our class. How's she doing? Have you kept up with her?"

They reminisced about the times they had at Torah Academy while Mimi busied herself with the toy cell phone she had gotten for Chanukah.

"Oh," Suri jumped up. "I forgot my manners. How about a cup of coffee? Tea? Juice?"

"Actually," said Chana Leah, "it's such a gorgeous day outside. It's warmer than yesterday, and the snow is melting. How about if we put Mimi in the stroller and go for a walk?"

"Okay, let's do that. I'll just make a quick phone call first."

Suri ran upstairs. She grabbed the phone and quickly dialed. "Lazer," she whispered.

"What?" His voice was guarded.

"You'll never believe who's here."

"Who?"

"Chana Leah!"

"You're kidding. Did she faint when she saw our house?"

Suri laughed. "No, but *I* nearly did when I heard she was coming over."

Now it was Lazer's turn to laugh.

"Guess what?" she asked.

"What?" He was sounding a little less glum.

"She likes the house!"

"Really? Discolored floor and all?" He paused. "Suri, you think you can be okay with the rice-paper shades for now? It's just a matter of time. *Iy"H* the business will pick up next year, and then we'll be able to fix up the house, one thing at a time, slowly. Do you think you can live with that?"

Her heart lifted. He was sounding like the old Lazer. What a good, kind, thoughtful man he was! He wanted her to be happy. "I could definitely live with it," she said, swallowing back a lump which had unexpectedly risen in her throat.

7

My choice, Rebbetzin Gordon, may come as a surprise to you. Yocheved Bloom is definitely not your typical *Eishes Chayil* Award winner.

The Eishes Chayil Award

BY NECHAMA DINA SMITH

Dear Rebbetzin Gordon,

You asked us to choose the perfect girl from our ninth grade for the *Eishes Chayil* (Woman of Valor) Award. You'll count up the number of votes for each candidate, and the lucky winner will receive a set of Bais Yaakov Production videos.

Well, my choice may come as a surprise to you. Typical *Eishes Chayil* winners are soft-spoken, never utter a word of *lashon hara*, and accomplish many *chessed* hours a week. Yocheved Bloom is definitely not one of those perfect girls. (She's my friend, so I know her pretty well.) She's smart, matter-of-fact, has a couple of good friends, and comes from a big family. She's very involved with her friends and family. She does exactly one *chessed* hour a week at the old-age home.

But, Rebbetzin Gordon, I think that sometimes a person can do something so special that all the heavens are filled with the dancing and singing of angels. I don't mean to be poetic or anything. But something like that happened with Yocheved which I'm sure caused rejoicing in the heavens. Let me tell you about it.

Three weeks ago, Bais Yaakov held its annual Mother-Daughter Tea. In actuality, not only mothers and daughters attend this event. Grandmothers, sisters, aunts, neighbors, friends, and even strangers—all kinds of people—come too, anxious not to miss out on the fun. As one of the volunteers, I was there in the afternoon in the spacious rented hall with the sparkling chandeliers, helping to set the tables. (I was not asked to assist with the seating. If I had, things might have been different.) Anyway, when I finished my job, I rushed home and got dressed. By the time my mother and I arrived, many of the seats were already taken.

I picked up our place cards. My mother and I had been assigned to Table #11. It took a while until we reached our table because my mother was busy talking to everyone. She stopped to admire the green and yellow color-coordinated tablecloths and seat covers and the matching centerpieces—tall, white candles with green vines twined around them. By the time we got to our table, with me practically pulling my mother along, all the seats at our table were filled, except for two.

Next to one of the empty seats sat a middle-aged woman in a dress that looked suspiciously like a housecoat, and a stained one at that. It was Rita. We knew Rita because she comes to all Bais Yaakov events; in fact she attends just about every *simchah* in town.

Now, I understand that Rita, being a bit "slow," simply

does not know many social norms, including the importance of showering regularly. Still, even though I understand this, I knew I could not and would not be able to sit next to her and stand the smell. No money in the world would induce me to do it.

I stood there, waiting impatiently as my mother chatted to one of her PTA friends. I was waiting for her to finish so I could explain to her very quietly what the situation was. Suddenly, I noticed Yocheved in a beige linen suit and matching headband walking up to my table with her mother, Mrs. Bloom.

"Hi," she said.

"Yocheved? Are you supposed to sit here, too?"

"Yeah!" she answered. "Are there not enough seats?"

I turned my face so Rita couldn't see. "I cannot sit here," I mouthed to Yocheved. "This lady smells!"

I was almost crying. But I couldn't be so mean as to let Rita see that I was upset at the prospect of being her neighbor. She would be terribly hurt.

Then a flash of inspiration hit me. I said aloud, "Oh, we should sit together! Since there aren't enough seats at this table for all of us, how about if we look for an empty table?"

Meanwhile, my mother and Mrs. Bloom had noticed each other and had started a conversation. They only vaguely heard me. The people at the table, thankfully, were all busy chatting. All except Rita. She just stared straight ahead, occasionally scratching her unkempt light-brown hair. I had a feeling she was aware of what was going on. On the other side of Rita sat an old woman, whose sense of smell was obviously not too keen, as she looked like she was doing fine.

I scanned the other tables in the hall. "Look, Ma," I pointed to Table #9. "I see some empty places there. It's kind of late already, so maybe those people aren't coming!"

I looked imploringly at Yocheved. "Should we go?"

"Oh, I'll just sit here. You go ahead." Matter-of-fact as usual, Yocheved pulled out the chair next to Rita and sat down. As her mother sat down next to her, I gently pulled my mother to the other table. I breathed a happy sigh of relief. I felt good that Rita didn't have to feel shamed, because if I had sat there, I'd have held my nose or buried it in a napkin the whole time, and that would really have embarrassed her.

I couldn't help but be in awe of my friend. She was so natural. She sat down without any hesitation, just as if she was an old buddy of that woman.

The program ran smoothly. I enjoyed some of my friends' recitals on the piano, the comedy skit from the twelfth grade, and even the speeches from the mothers and teachers.

I kept looking over from where I was sitting to see how Yocheved was faring. I couldn't believe what I saw. In between the speeches and performances, she talked to Rita. Yocheved was going out of her way to make Rita feel comfortable! When now and then Rita would tilt her head closer to Yocheved to tell her some secret or something, I watched, holding my breath, waiting to see how my friend would take it. But Yocheved didn't bat an eyelash. (Afterwards, when I asked her if perhaps she hadn't smelled anything, she shrugged and told me that she just breathed deeply into her spicy Chinese chicken and her mother's perfume.)

All evening long, Yocheved was just as friendly as could be. When the Mother-Daughter Tea was over, Rita said goodbye, and then before my astonished eyes, she gave Yocheved a hug!

There were tears lurking in my eyes when I saw that. Yocheved had made a *nebbach* kind of person feel good. She had treated her with respect and attentiveness. She had made her feel important. There was no question about it. Up in *Shamayim*, Hashem, with all the angels in Heaven, were exulting at that moment. And I was proud to be the friend of such a great girl.

That's why I'm nominating Yocheved Bloom for the *Eishes Chayil* Award.

Sincerely,
Batya Rosen

8

She suspected that something was wrong with what she was planning to do, but she couldn't quite put her finger on it.

The Chinese Auction

BY YONINA HALL

Rivki glided out of the schoolyard feeling ten feet tall. Just before the bell rang, her ninth-grade math teacher had handed out the midterm exams, each one folded over so no one could see the score. As the teacher dropped the test on Rivki's desk, she shared a private smile with her top student. Rivki peeked at the paper. Then the bell pealed, followed by a whoosh of excitement as girls jumped out of their seats, grabbed their briefcases, and headed for the door. Rivki let herself be buoyed along with the flow, her feet barely touching the ground.

She heard someone huffing and puffing right behind her. Before she had a chance to turn around, she heard her best friend's voice at her shoulder.

"What'd you get?" Ayala demanded.

Smilingly, Rivki withdrew the paper that hadn't left her hands and showed it to her friend.

"A hundred! I knew it!" Ayala said admiringly. "You're a whiz at math!"

"I probably inherited it from my father," Rivki said modestly. Mr. Weinstock worked at a big accounting firm downtown. "And how did you do? Did my tutoring help?"

"It sure did," Ayala replied. "I got a seventy-eight, my best mark so far this year. Let's make another date for a week before the next test, okay?"

"Sure," Rivki replied. "But I think we're going to be seeing each other a lot more before then. Didn't you ask me to help with the Chinese auction for Bikur Cholim this year?"

"How could I forget?" Ayala smiled. "My mother said she's going to have us working every day as soon as the first ticket orders come in. I've been helping her since it started, but now the auction is getting so big that she needs more than one pair of hands to finish."

"I've never done a Chinese auction before, but it sounds like fun," Rivki said as they turned onto their street. "Lots of prizes and lots of winners, right?"

"Well, there's only one winner per prize, but everyone who participates is going to get a lot of *s'char*," Ayala replied.

Rivki had no idea how prophetic her friend's words would be.

• • •

When Rivki knocked at Ayala's door the following Tuesday afternoon, a grateful Mrs. Pfeiffer greeted her warmly. "Come in, come in!" she said. "Can I get you something to drink? Here, I've made a whole worktable for you and Ayala in the dining room. Let me take your coat. Ayala's coming down in a minute. Please make yourself at home!"

As Mrs. Pfeiffer bustled about in the kitchen, Rivki turned toward the dining room. The table looked like a storm had hit it. Colored boxes, white papers, and multicolored slips covered most of the table. Two chairs faced each other across the mess.

Peering closer, Rivki tried to make some sense out of the disorder. A row of colored boxes ran down the middle of the table. The slips—which were actually blank ticket stubs—were stacked in piles all around. White forms lay in other stacks, covered with grids of numbers and checkmarks. In front of each chair lay a few pens and a calculator. The whole setup reminded Rivki of her father's office in the middle of a major accounting project.

Mrs. Pfeiffer entered the dining room with Ayala in tow. She showed the girls where to sit and explained to them what they had to do.

The job seemed pretty straightforward. The prizes were numbered according to category. Electronics were the 1000's, housewares were the 2000's, clothing was the 3000's, etc. Each raffle ticket cost five dollars; for every twenty-five dollars, however, the bidder received a free ticket. Rivki and Ayala had to check each order form, write the name and phone number of the bidder on one side of the raffle ticket and the number of the prize on the other side, and finally toss the tickets, checks, and order forms into the appropriate boxes.

"This whole operation really should be computerized, but we just don't have the staff for it," Mrs. Pfeiffer apologized. "Four of us started this auction three years ago, and it's grown way beyond our expectations. Maybe next year we'll find someone who can put the information onto computerized labels, but this year, our womanpower will have to do." She chuckled at her choice of words.

Mrs. Pfeiffer showed the girls the prize catalog that had been mailed to thousands of homes. Rivki's eyes widened when she saw prizes like a refrigerator, a camera, a ten-speed bike, jewelry, and clothing.

"The grand prize is a new living room set," Mrs. Pfeiffer said proudly. "Our prize committee really outdid themselves this year. Last year we raised twenty thousand dollars for Bikur Cholim, and this year we hope to raise a lot more!"

Rivki was impressed by all the figures. Her mathematical mind began calculating the number of catalogs and how much each bidder might contribute.

"Come on, let's get started!" Ayala cried, grabbing an order form. "Here's our first customer—Mrs. Malka Edelman, with a twenty-five dollar donation. That means she can bid on six prizes. One-two-three-four-five-six… all in order!"

Soon Ayala and Rivki were busy poring over the order forms, tapping away on their calculators, and scribbling names and phone numbers onto raffle tickets. It was the beginning of what would be days and weeks of ticket processing before the official prize drawing one month hence.

An hour and a half later, Ayala stretched her arms over her head and groaned. "So many numbers! I can see them with my eyes closed. Let's call it quits for today, okay?"

Rivki looked up and grinned. "Personally, I think this is fascinating," she said. "I see certain prizes are being checked off on almost every form. Those must be for the big prizes like the camera and the refrigerator. Other prizes aren't being checked off at all. Can I take a look at that catalog again?"

Ayala passed the booklet with a shrug. "Help yourself. I couldn't remember what anyone checked off if you paid me."

But her friend wasn't listening. Rivki was gazing at an elegant leather desk set with a scientific calculator. She made sure to commit the prize number to memory.

• • •

Day after day, the girls sat down to newly received order forms and scratched out names and numbers onto hundreds of raffle tickets. While Ayala often felt that her head was
swimming with figures and had to take frequent breaks, Rivki
was enjoying herself immensely.

As she picked up yet another order form and saw the grand
prize box checked off, she glanced down at the box for prize
#6026—the desk set—and saw that it was empty. Strange. It
was a really nice desk set, with a calculator that had scientific
functions like her father's did.

"See anything you like?" Ayala asked one day.

"Yeah," Rivki said. "The leather desk set."

"What does it look like?" Ayala asked.

Rivki reached for a catalog and opened it to the Books and
Stationery section. "There, see? Pretty neat, huh?"

"It certainly looks like something you could use," Ayala
smiled. "Personally, I could go for the sapphire necklace or the
pearl ring."

"Are you going to bid on them?" Rivki asked.

"Nah," Ayala said with a little laugh. "What chance do I
have against all this competition?"

The girls turned back to their work, but Rivki kept thinking about the desk set. No one else has bid on it yet, she marveled. What if no one bids on it at all?

At dinner that night, Rivki's mother asked her how the
Chinese auction was coming along. Rivki vividly described
how she and Ayala were plowing their way through never-
ending piles of order forms.

"It's so interesting to see what people bid for," she added. "Most people put their bids in on several different prizes. But some put in two or three bids on the same prize."

"Doesn't that show a lack of *bitachon*?" interrupted her older sister Penina, who was in twelfth grade. "I mean, it only takes one ticket to win the prize."

"True," Mrs. Weinstock answered thoughtfully. "You know, an auction can teach us something about life. There are so many interesting things we could acquire, but Hashem gives each of us exactly what we need."

"If I'm supposed to get the jewelry, no one can take that away from me," Penina echoed. "And if my friend is supposed to get the camera, nothing I can do will take it away from her."

"That's right," her mother said. "It's good to give *tzedakah* and support the auction, but we have to trust Hashem. He knows what's best for us to win."

That desk set is the only thing I want to win in the whole catalog, Rivki thought. I wonder if Hashem wants me to win it.

• • •

Three weeks later, the piles of blank ticket stubs had dwindled significantly. Every afternoon at four o'clock, Rivki and Ayala sat down to process more forms. Mrs. Pfeiffer was beside herself with excitement.

"The response is unbelievable!" she exclaimed, rubbing her hands together. "We're well over last year's returns, and more ticket orders are still coming in every day!"

"When is this going to end?" Ayala wailed as she scribbled the same name and phone number onto forty-eight different raffle tickets.

"Next week is the deadline for receiving ticket orders," her mother reassured her. "After that, we'll spend a few days sorting out all the tickets and putting them into raffle boxes. We'll have the prize drawing here on Thursday afternoon. You girls are invited to watch, of course. We couldn't have done it without you!"

Rivki smiled and began to process the forms in her pile. Her nerves were tingling with excitement. She had looked at hundreds of order forms for nearly a month. No one had checked off prize #6026. Every so often, when Ayala had to leave the room for a minute, Rivki had leaned over and skimmed through Ayala's order forms as well. She couldn't believe it! No one was bidding on the desk set at all!

I could just put in my bid right now and walk away with it, her heart told her. Maybe it's like my sister said. Hashem wants me to have it so much that He's dropping it right into my lap!

She decided to wait a little longer to be absolutely certain. If she saw no bids on prize #6026 by the deadline date, Rivki decided, she would enter her bid right before the bidding closed. That way she would be sure to win.

• • •

That evening Rivki sat quietly at the dinner table, her mind and heart sending conflicting messages back and forth. Something was wrong with what she was planning to do, but she couldn't quite put her finger on it.

On the one hand, since no one was bidding on the desk set, what's the auction committee going to do with it anyway? Her heart demanded. Surely it was better to have someone win it than to have to store it away for next year's auction. And I have as much right to bid as anyone else! Mrs. Pfeiffer never said I couldn't bid on something just because I'm working for the auction committee.

Yes, but you know a lot more than the bidders do, her mind retorted. You have inside information. You know that no one else bid on it and that you'll win it for sure.

So no one will care if I win it because no one else wants it! her heart crowed.

The rest of her family had no idea of the silent debate Rivki was having. Penina had everyone's attention as she told the family about the part-time job she'd just landed for Pesach vacation at the Kosher Mart.

"The grocery needs extra cashiers because they'll be open more hours for the pre-Pesach rush," Penina explained.

"Are you going to take money and make change?" asked five-year-old Bentzy curiously.

"Sure!" Penina laughed with a toss of her black curls. "And guess what—I'm going to be bonded!"

"Bonded?" repeated nine-year-old Shevi. "What's that?"

"That means they're guaranteeing that I won't steal any money," Penina explained. "Of course, I would never think of stealing, but in the business world, storeowners have to be sure. The bonding agency checks out your record and ensures that you're honest."

"What happens if you steal something?" asked a wide-eyed Bentzy.

"How could you say such a thing?" Shevi reprimanded him.

"It's a fair question," Penina replied thoughtfully. "Then you're not considered trustworthy enough to handle money, and you're not bonded anymore."

The conversation filtered slowly through Rivki's consciousness. She wondered if what she was planning to do would be considered honest or not. If she had to apply to a bonding agency, would she be considered trustworthy?

• • •

On the afternoon of the deadline, Mrs. Pfeiffer encouraged Ayala and Rivki to finish up as many order forms as they could so that the drawing could begin.

Weary of the never-ending march of numbers, Ayala cried out, "Hurray! The end's in sight!" Then she turned to Rivki and whispered to her, "We should do something to reward ourselves when this is over. How does a banana split sound?"

"Heavenly," murmured Rivki, engrossed in her work.

But Rivki's mind was not on banana splits. As she continued processing one order form after another, the box for prize #6026 was still coming up empty.

It would be so easy to bid on that desk set right now, she said to herself. No one would know, not even Ayala, not even the auction committee. If you had bid on it at the very beginning, you could have won it fair and square. But now that you know there's no competition, it wouldn't be right at all. It would be like cheating on a math test. Even if no one ever found out, you'd know that you hadn't earned that "100" fair and square.

As Rivki finished processing the last order form in her stack, a sense of elation washed over her. Somehow, her yearning to win the desk set was losing some of its appeal. In its place had arisen something more powerful, a feeling of purposefulness that was guiding her toward doing the right thing rather than just giving in to the impulses of her heart. She felt invigorated.

She put down her pen. Someone was standing at her shoulder. She looked up into Mrs. Pfeiffer's smiling face.

"Good work, girls!" Ayala's mother beamed. "We could never have done it without you! And all our prize winners are indebted to you, too, for handling their bids so efficiently. You deserve prizes of your own!" Saying that, Ayala's mother handed each of the girls a small box, neatly gift-wrapped in pink and gray paper. "This is just a small token of our appreciation for your hard work," she said, smiling affectionately.

Rivki's heart leaped. The box was too small to hold a desk set, but not too small for a calculator.

But no, that was impossible. There was no way Mrs. Pfeiffer could know how much she had longed for that prize.

Ayala quickly tore open the wrapping of her box and admired the pearl ring nestled inside, similar to the one in the catalog. "Wow, this is beautiful! Thank you, Ima!" she exclaimed, jumping up to hug her mother.

Rivki forced herself to unwrap her box slowly. It was too light to be a calculator. Oh, well.

"Thank you so much for the lovely gold bracelet," she said cheerfully as she gave Ayala's mother a peck on the cheek. She wasn't one for much jewelry, but the bracelet was so small and dainty that she might actually wear it. Anyway, it really didn't matter, she reminded herself. She had made her decision, and it had been the right one. Only Hashem would ever know how hard it had been to overcome her *yetzer*. That was enough *s'char* for her. She didn't need anything else.

9

She didn't express her feelings easily to others, but when she wanted to do something nice, she certainly didn't expect this kind of reaction.

The Red Steps

BY YONINA HALL

"You're kidding!" shouted Esti, jumping up out of her seat in the lunchroom and waving her hands theatrically. "You're leaving?"

"Who? What?" Bayla's head spun around in curiosity and excitement.

"Hey, Esti," called Chani, "what's the scoop?"

Bayla waited, along with everyone else in her tenth-grade class, to hear Esti's answer. She obviously had a juicy piece of news to tell them.

"Temi's moving to Chicago!" Esti exclaimed breathlessly. "She just told me the news and said I could tell anyone I wanted!"

"Really? When?" the other girls cried, rushing over to Esti's and Temi's table. Temi was sitting quietly beside Esti.

Temi roused herself to meet her audience. "It's true," she admitted, her voice scarcely more than a whisper. "My father's going to replace the principal of a girls' school who has to leave in middle of the year, so we're moving next month."

"Do you know where you're going to live?" asked Chani.

"Do you know which school you're going to?" echoed Yocheved.

Temi looked a bit overwhelmed. "I… I don't know yet," she stammered.

Bayla felt sorry for Temi and tried to think of a way to smooth over her obvious unease. "Maybe you'd like a goodbye party?" she suggested brightly.

Temi shot her a withering glance. "Thanks, but no thanks. Goodbye parties are fun for those who are staying, not for those who are leaving," she sneered.

Bayla reeled as though she'd been struck. "I… I'm sorry," she mumbled, backing off. Thankfully, no one else seemed to notice the exchange, as more girls moved in to pepper Temi with questions.

Bayla slunk back to her chair and wrapped up the remains of her sandwich with trembling hands. *What was so wrong with what I said?* she thought, feeling a wave of hot tears sting her cheeks. *I was just trying to make her feel better. Is that so terrible?*

The rest of the day was a total waste. Unable to concentrate much on anything, Bayla gratefully welcomed the sound of the last bell. Chani was waiting for her by the door for their walk home.

Bayla was so quiet that Chani started chattering about the first thing that came to mind. "Isn't it exciting about Temi?" she babbled. "Imagine—fifteen years old and ready to explore the world! New places, new faces, a whole new life!"

"It must be pretty hard for her," Bayla replied thoughtfully. "She's been with us ever since first grade. I'm sure she expected to graduate with us in two years."

Chani smiled fondly at her best friend. While Bayla loved staying home with her family, Chani looked for adventure around every corner. The two were as different as night and day. Maybe that was the reason they liked each other so much.

"You're such a mommy," Chani teased.

Bayla didn't mind being teased. If truth be told, Chani's words warmed her like a fire on a snowy winter night. From her friend's lips, she knew it was a compliment. She decided to share with her something she hadn't told anyone.

"Do you have a few minutes to see something?" she asked as they turned the last corner to her house.

"Sure, what?"

"Come out back," Bayla said mysteriously, pushing open her backyard gate.

The house where Bayla lived with her mother and stepfather didn't have an official backyard surrounded by a fence. Instead, the rural property blended into an open field, beyond which lay a small woodland. Kids from the neighborhood headed for the woods every Erev Shavuos to collect greenery to decorate their homes and every Erev Sukkos to gather s'chach. Chani remembered running around in the woods with her brothers and sisters when they were little.

"What are we doing back here?" she asked curiously.

"Shhh—this way," Bayla said, stepping carefully across the field and over to a big tree with a deep niche at its base. "Is she here? Yes!"

Chani came around behind her and looked where Bayla was pointing. A furry white rabbit, looking a bit worse for the wear, was snuggled in the niche and was nibbling from a pile of carrot and cucumber peels.

"Oooh, she's so cute!" she exclaimed. "Where'd you get her?"

"She's not mine," Bayla corrected her. "There are lots of rabbits in these woods. You see those marks on her hind legs? I think a dog attacked her. I found her limping around when I went out here for a walk one Sunday afternoon. I made her this soft bed out of down from an old pillow. Every day I bring her vegetable peels, oats, and seeds."

"Very nice," Chani said approvingly.

"But it's a secret," Bayla warned her. "You're the only person in the world who knows about this, except me."

"I can keep a secret," Chani promised. "What will you do if she has babies?"

Bayla giggled. "Then you can call me 'Bubby!'"

• • •

The aroma of whole-wheat pancakes and scrambled eggs wafted up to Bayla's room as she dressed for school the next morning. She hurried into the kitchen to set the breakfast table as her mother flipped another batch of pancakes off the griddle.

"Smells delicious, Sima," said Bayla's stepfather from his seat at the table. "This and a cup of coffee… Gan Eden!"

"It's in your honor, Yaakov," Sima Bergman replied. "Don't you remember buying me real Canadian maple syrup on your last trip to Toronto?"

"Oh, so that's what it was for," Mr. Bergman joked.

"Here, try some of it with the pancakes," said Sima, placing the pitcher of maple syrup on the table.

"Pinny! Bruchi! Breakfast!" Mrs. Bergman called. Bayla's eight-year-old stepbrother and six-year-old stepsister raced each other into the kitchen and slipped into their chairs under their mother's watchful gaze.

"Where's Nachum?" Bayla asked, waiting for her brother.

"He stayed overnight at a friend's house to study for a test," Mrs. Bergman said. "Soon he won't be eating breakfast with us at all when he starts *yeshivah ketanah*. Can you believe it, Yaakov? He was only seven when we got married…"

"… and now his bar mitzvah is around the corner," Mr. Bergman finished for her. "Which reminds me: Didn't you say we're going to pick out bar mitzvah invitations this afternoon?"

"Oh, I'm so glad you reminded me! Bayla, would you like to come along? We're going to pick out invitations at Aunt Leah's and Uncle Shmuel's print shop."

"I'd love to!" Bayla replied happily. Aunt Leah, her late father's older sister, had always held a warm place in her heart for her only niece. Bayla remembered how her aunt had let her play with her costume jewelry and porcelain knickknacks whenever she and Nachum came to visit with their parents. After her mother remarried and they moved to a bigger house out of town, she and her aunt didn't see each other very much. Every chance to visit was a special treat.

"Then we'll leave right after you get home from school," Mrs. Bergman decided. "I've already arranged for a babysitter for Pinny and Bruchi."

• • •

The new day looked a little brighter, Bayla reflected as she hitched her schoolbag up on her shoulder and trotted to school. The good breakfast had washed away the bitterness of Temi's remark and replaced it with renewed sympathy for her classmate's plight.

As Bayla crossed the main street, a window display in the

corner stationery store caught her eye. A huge envelope was inscribed with the words, "Remember family and friends. Write home."

A new idea flashed through Bayla's mind and in seconds her heart approved. She slipped into the small store and asked the girl behind the counter, "Do you sell address books?"

The salesgirl placed a few samples on the counter and Bayla chose one with a cover of pretty yellow pansies.

"Could you gift-wrap this, please?" she asked. "And do you have a note card that I could put inside?"

Bayla paid for her purchases and hurried out of the store. During the break after homeroom, she composed a short poem:

> *Dear Temi,*
> *Wherever you go,*
> *Whatever you do,*
> *All your friends will remember you.*
> *Keep in touch!*
> *Your friend,*
> *Bayla*

She tucked the note inside the package and placed it on Temi's desk. She waited for recess to end, anticipating Temi's response.

It wasn't long in coming. At first, when she saw the gift-wrapped package on her desk, Temi declared, "What? A present for me?"

When she opened the package, a furrow appeared between Temi's eyebrows. After reading the note, she turned to Bayla in a huff. "Why do you have to remind me I'm leaving?" she almost shouted. "It's easy for you to be nice—you get to stay! How could you be so insensitive?" Angrily, she flung the address book aside and threw herself into her seat, her shoulders twitching.

Bayla was speechless. She didn't express her feelings easily to others, but when she wanted to do something nice, she certainly didn't expect this kind of reaction. *Am I weird or something?* She moaned silently. *Is it a crime to care? Sometimes I care so much that it hurts if I don't do something. Am I wrong to keep on trying?*

The room grew hot and stifling as the class dragged on. As soon as the bell rang, Bayla grabbed her food satchel and fled.

While the other girls headed for the lunchroom, Bayla went outside the building and sat down on a low stone wall. She didn't like to eat alone, but a cold, hard wall had sprung up around her, and she needed to retreat behind its protective guard. She unwrapped her sandwich and went to wash her hands. When she came back to say a *brachah* and take a bite out of her sandwich, she heard the sound of sobbing.

It was a little girl, half-hidden by the bushes growing next to the low wall. Bayla's soft heart went out to the youngster. She coughed to make her presence known and then walked around the bushes until she came face to face with the tearful child.

"What's the matter?" she asked gently, sitting down beside her.

"Ruchi doesn't want to eat lunch with me," the little girl sniffled.

"Is Ruchi your best friend?" Bayla asked knowingly.

"Uh-huh. But she says she's not my friend anymore."

"What happened?"

"She didn't do her homework and she wanted to copy mine. I wouldn't let her. It's cheating!"

Bayla nodded sympathetically.

"Ruchi never does her homework anymore. She says it's too hard for her."

"It sounds like Ruchi's having a hard time," Bayla said.

The little girl's blue eyes opened wide. "She is," she agreed. "She says her mommy's sick and can't help her with her homework, and she doesn't have any big sisters who can help her. She can't do it herself."

"Maybe you could help her," Bayla suggested quietly. "Instead of letting her copy your homework, do it together with her."

"But isn't that cheating?" the girl asked.

"No, it's called studying," Bayla replied with a grin.

The little girl's face brightened as she pondered this new idea. Then she stood up, wiped her cheeks, smiled at Bayla, and skipped back to class.

I wish I understood myself as well as I do little girls, Bayla thought ruefully as she went back to her sandwich. *I've never met anyone else like me.* Feeling not just a little sorry for herself, Bayla *bentched*, packed up her satchel and hurried back to class.

The morning's unpleasant incident hadn't yet worn off in Bayla's mind when she joined her parents in the afternoon. But she eagerly climbed into the back seat of their car for the ride to the print shop.

Located on a busy boulevard in the heart of the city, the store had definitely seen better days. As they pulled up to the modest, white stucco building, Bayla couldn't help but notice the paint peeling off the walls and the faded sign tacked over the doorway.

Aunt Leah's welcome, though, was as fresh as ever. To Bayla's delight, her aunt fussed over her, commenting on how tall she'd grown and how ladylike she had become. She produced drinks and a box of cookies and invited Bayla to sit with her on the faded chairs in the showroom while Uncle Shmuel and the Bergmans went into the back room to look at invitation catalogs and print styles.

Time passed unheeded as Bayla chatted with her aunt. There was so much to talk about. Bayla found herself relaxing in the warmth of her aunt's undivided attention. After they'd finished their drinks and cookies, they stepped outside to get some air. The traffic on the busy street sped by, oblivious to the older woman and the young girl standing on the sidewalk.

"*Baruch* Hashem, we still have customers," Aunt Leah confided to Bayla. "Many of them had their own bar mitzvah invitations printed here when they were children. They like the idea of supporting a family business, and they appreciate the personal attention we give them. But most of our business has gone to the high-tech, computerized print shops downtown. Their computer operators never learned how to set type by hand, but it's the only way Uncle Shmuel knows how to do it. One day, we'll have to close our shop for good."

Bayla felt sorry for her aunt though she was surprised to see that her aunt didn't seem too upset about it.

"Breathed in enough exhaust fumes?" Aunt Leah teased. "I'll bet you're not used to this kind of air, living out in the country. Come, let's go inside and see what your parents have picked."

As they turned to go back inside, Aunt Leah suddenly stopped and reached for Bayla's arm. Her other hand pointed to the two small, chipped steps they were about to ascend.

"Hundreds of people have climbed up those steps, but no one really noticed them," she said in a faraway voice. "Only your father did. He said to me, 'Leah, someone could trip on those steps, they're so tiny and close together. I have an idea.

I'll paint them red.'"

Bayla stared at the crumbling steps. She could see that they had once been red, but time and weather had faded the cement to a mottled pink.

"That was your father, always thinking about others," Aunt Leah said. "Even though he's not here, his caring goes on. And you know what? He was right. People *did* trip on those white steps now and again, but not one person ever tripped after he painted them red."

Bayla's heart filled with pride at her father's sensitivity. Who would ever look down at two lowly steps and worry about the people who trod over them?

Then it occurred to her that that was the trait she had inherited from her father. For as long as she could remember, she had always thought of ways to help others, especially with quiet, inconspicuous gestures. The red steps spoke to her: There's nothing wrong with you, Bayla. The same way your father cared, you care, too.

"Thank you for telling me this," she whispered gratefully.

"Your father was a special person... and so is his daughter," Aunt Leah replied, squeezing her arm.

Together, they climbed up the red steps.

• • •

Bayla peeked through the homeroom door and quickly looked around before entering the room. She felt different today, more self-assured, but she still hoped she wouldn't run into Temi before class started. She darted over to her desk and set to work, organizing her books and papers for the first lesson.

Chani sat down across the aisle. "Ready for the *Navi* test?"

she asked jovially.

"Ready as I'll ever be," Bayla groaned. The two shared a laugh.

Bayla glanced at the clock. Two minutes until the bell. Their teacher was nowhere in sight. Then she felt someone standing beside her shoulder. She turned and almost jumped in surprise. It was Temi. Temi lowered her eyes self-consciously. "I just want to apologize for the way I've acted towards you lately," she murmured in such a small voice that Bayla strained to hear her. "It's not like me to fly off the handle like that. I... I guess it's just the stress of having to pull up roots and switch to a new school and leave in the middle of the year..."

Her voice trailed away. Bayla summoned the courage to look up into Temi's face and saw a far different person than she'd known for the past ten years. The prospect of leaving her home, her school, and her friends had turned Temi's normally rosy complexion pale, and a worried look had appeared around her eyes and mouth. With newfound confidence, Bayla decided she had heard enough. She let her heart reach out once again.

"It's okay. I understand. I forgive you," she said reassuringly. "And if there's anything I can do to help you, please let me know."

Temi looked stunned. She had been sure that no amount of apologizing would make up for her disagreeable behavior. "Um, thanks," she answered, visibly relieved. "And, um, thanks for the address book. Would... would you be the first to sign it?"

Bayla gazed at the address book with its cover of pretty yellow pansies that Temi held out to her like a prize.

10

The news that Miriam gets that her family has to move to another country does not fill her with excitement at all. All she feels is dread.

The Big Move

BY BRACHA GOYKADOSH

I'll start my story from the beginning of the end. The end of the world, the night my parents announced that they were moving to England, and I was going to be dragged with them to the city of the Buckingham Palace and Big Ben.

It all started as a regular day. Of course, in most occurrences like this, the day starts out horribly; usually there's a thunderstorm happening, but this day I had no indication, no reason, to suspect anything dreadful would occur.

So anyway, as I was saying, it was a regular, boring day. I went to school, I came home, and I did my homework. I admit that I wouldn't have minded some excitement, but never this!

As soon as my father came home from work, my parents sprang the big news on me. My younger brothers Dovid and Aaron and my sister Naava were already sleeping (it was 9:30), and my older sister was in seminary in Yerushalayim, so it was just my parents and me.

"Miriam," my father began, "your mother and I have some exciting news to tell you." At that second I knew the news was not going to be something that I would find very exciting at all. After all, the last time my parents told me they had exciting news was when I was stuck at my Aunt Cheryl's house in some little hick town in California while they went on a trip to Israel. It was in the summer, and Aunt Cheryl didn't even have air conditioning.

"Yes, Abba?" I asked, like a good, obedient daughter.

"Well," said my mother in a whisper—she has this thing that she doesn't like to talk loudly after the kids go to sleep because she's afraid they'll wake up—"your father has been offered a magnificent job opportunity in England. He'll be getting triple his current salary and—"

"But it's too bad you couldn't take it, right, Abba?" I quickly interrupted. "Like, you would never make us move halfway across the world just because—"

"I accepted the job, Miriam."

"What!" I shrieked.

"Miriam, not so loud, you'll wake up the kids!" said my mother, still whispering.

"Oh my! You're kidding, right? How could you do this to me? Ima, how could you let Abba do such a thing? My life is over!"

"Miriam," said my mother, a little more loudly than before, "you are really overreacting. You know, my whole family lives in Manchester—my parents and siblings. I grew up there! Let me tell you, it's a wonderful place. I really have missed it all these years living in the States."

I guess I forgot to mention that my mother is British. She grew up in Great Britain. (Wow, what egos! What makes the

British think they're "Great" anyway?) She moved here when she got married to my father.

Anyway, the point is, wasn't the grand old U.S. of A. my home?!! Didn't they realize that I would miss it?! But I knew that, however I felt, it did not justify my being rude. So I just quietly asked to be excused and went to bed.

The next few weeks were a whirlwind of activity. There were boxes everywhere in the house. We were moving in three days. You can guess how I felt!

The day before we left, my friends threw me a goodbye party. Parties are supposed to be festive, but I basically cried the whole time. I was being shipped halfway across the world against my will, and there was nothing I could do about it.

The day before the big move, I was reading a magazine in the kitchen. I couldn't help overhearing my younger siblings chattering in the room next door. They were all talking in fake British accents. They were so cute! I couldn't help but join them!

"Really? I think so too!" said Naava in an accent that sounded more Irish than British to me, if I wasn't mistaken.

"I wonder what we'll have for breaky on the airplane," said Dovid.

"Breaky?" asked Aaron. "What's breaky?"

"Breakfast!"

"Oh…"

Before I knew it, I was totally involved in their conversation, speaking with a British accent too. Then I realized what I was doing. No way, I was not happy I was moving to England, and I would derive no pleasure from that fact either! I quickly retreated to my room, which now only consisted of a bed frame and mattress since everything else had already been shipped.

The dreaded day arrived. The day when the world ended, the day I moved to England. The first few days after we came weren't so bad. I didn't have to go to school because I was "recovering" from jet lag. Tons of relatives kept pouring in with tons of food. And speaking of pouring, so was the weather. It did not stop raining from the moment I got off the plane. And when it wasn't pouring, there was a slight yucky drizzle. Eww, totally and completely eww. I need sunshine to live.

But then I started school. Starting school is always hard, especially if you are the new girl. And especially if you come in the middle of the year. And especially if you come from a place where you are told that you speak English, and then you come to England and realize that the English you speak and the English spoken there are two totally different languages. I didn't even realize that some of the girls were speaking English at first, their accents were so strong. I thought they were speaking French or something. And, of course, they all thought that I was the one with the accent when it really was them.

And the school was really weird. My grade had its own separate building with an auditorium, gym, cafeteria, lab, and even five or six classrooms. But it was only for our grade—all twenty-five of us! Strange, I know. Don't ask me why!

All in all, things were not going well.

But then one day everything changed. We were learning chemistry, and as usual I was totally spaced out because I wasn't even trying to understand what the teacher was saying because her accent was so weird, maybe she's Cockney or something. So I was doodling this really cool picture of a giraffe, and just then the fire bell rang.

So I was just, like, okay, they're having a fire drill, but I guess they don't have fire drills in England, or at least not in this school because all the girls were totally panicking!

"What's going on?" I asked.

"There's a fire!" they yelled.

So guess who got to be heroine of the day? Me! I made all the girls line up and walk quietly out of the building. They all stared at me with newfound respect.

Anyway, it turns out the fire wasn't really anything serious, *Baruch* Hashem. One of the janitors unthinkingly threw out a lit cigarette into the bathroom garbage can. He got fired, so whatever.

From then on, things began to look up. A girl in my class, whom I hadn't spoken to before, came and introduced herself to me.

"Hey," she said in an American accent. (My heart did cartwheels!) "I'm Orah."

"You're American!" I almost jumped up for joy. Finally a fellow American!

"Oh, yeah, my family moved here last year. I just wanted to let you know how impressed I was with how you handled things during the fire."

"Uh, thanks," I said.

Then Orah asked me about my old school, and it turned out she knew some of my friends from camp! It looked like I had a new friend.

After that, things began to look up. I guess the sun shines sometimes in England too!

11

She had this strange feeling that Mrs. Lewin was watching her every move. Well, it was Mrs. Lewin's house, after all. She was probably making sure Devori did everything just right.

The Secret Chessed

BY YONINA HALL

"Devori, I don't know what I'd do without you," said Mrs. Lewin gratefully, as she and her sixteen-year-old helper stood side by side at the kitchen sink. "Ever since you came to help me, my house is in order, the clothes are clean, and the meals are so tasty. You are a gem!"

Devori Miller blushed, although she knew she deserved the compliment. She'd never worked so hard in her life since her mother had suggested that she volunteer a few hours a week to help their neighbor. She was constantly bending over, reaching up, sorting, washing and tidying, only to return to a messy house two days later. *Why can't things stay the same while I'm gone?* she thought irritably, tossing her auburn ponytail back over her shoulder. Still, with praise such as this, maybe it was all worth it.

Devori turned off the water and reached for the towel to dry the dishes.

"Oh, don't do that now," Mrs. Lewin protested. "I hear the dryer buzzing. Could you take out the clothes and fold them before you leave?"

Do this, don't do that... Devori wasn't used to being ordered around, but she said nothing. Mrs. Lewin was a really nice person despite her bossiness. As the eldest girl in her family, Devori was given a lot of leeway to decide when she wanted to fulfill her chores at home. More often than not, the tall, athletic teenager could be found at the swimming pool or the softball court in her free time. In fact, that's probably where she'd be right now, if not for this *chessed* project.

She went to unload the dryer. Scooping out the warm, clean clothes was actually one of Devori's favorite tasks. She loved to press her cheek against the fresh-smelling laundry without having to worry that it would dry out her skin, the way working around the oven did. She also relished the chance to do something away from her neighbor's prying eyes. She had the strange feeling that Mrs. Lewin was watching her as she moved around the house... But how could that be? She was probably just making sure that Devori did everything the way she wanted. It was her house, after all.

A few times, as Devori folded the laundry in the bedroom, she overheard snatches of whispered telephone conversations. One time someone had even knocked at the front door and murmured something in a low voice that Devori couldn't make out. When Devori emerged from the bedroom, she saw Mrs. Lewin hastily stuff something into her pocket, totally flustered. "Oh, there you are! Finished already?" Mrs. Lewin babbled. Devori felt embarrassed without knowing why.

Something funny is going on here, but I can't put my finger on it, Devori concluded. *I'm going to keep my eyes and ears open to find out what's really going on.*

She left the laundry sorted in neat piles and went to fetch her purse. "Thank you so much! Have a good Shabbos!"

Mrs. Lewin called after her. "See you again Sunday afternoon!"

• • •

When Devori arrived the next week, she began her routine automatically. She prided herself on how quickly she had memorized the entire layout of Mrs. Lewin's house and where everything belonged.

First on her list of "things to do," as Mrs. Lewin called it, was to pick up all the stray items scattered about and deposit them on the dining room table. Then she picked up each item one by one, sorted it according to where it belonged in the house and carried armfuls of the stuff to their designated places.

She mentally patted herself on the back for putting the house back into order so quickly today. Humming a little tune, she headed for the kitchen to peel and chop vegetables for dinner.

Mrs. Lewin was sitting at the kitchen table, steadying an onion on the chopping board. Her other hand clutched a knife in midair. She sat frozen in that position, like a statue. Her face, normally so pleasant, was gripped by an expression of such utter hopelessness that Devori cried out, "Is everything all right, Mrs. Lewin?"

Mrs. Lewin started. "Oh, yes, dear. Here, take the chopping board. You can continue with the vegetables now."

Puzzled, Devori slid the chopping board over to her side of the table and rolled the vegetable trolley beside her. As she started peeling potatoes with a practiced hand, she looked over to the sink, where Mrs. Lewin was now standing. The water was streaming out of the faucet, but Mrs. Lewin stood paralyzed, her hand suspending a dish under the gushing torrent.

"Mrs. Lewin!" Devori called.

The dish slipped out of Mrs. Lewin's hand and smashed into the sink, jolting her out of her reverie. "What? Oh, dear! Quick, bring the squeegee and dustpan!"

Devori hurried to help. Or, more accurately, it was Devori who turned off the water and scooped all the shards of glass out of the sink while Mrs. Lewin stood by, wringing her hands. When Devori had finished, she noticed that Mrs. Lewin had returned to the kitchen table and was sitting immobile again, her blue eyes fixed on a distant object without really seeing it.

Devori sat down opposite her. "Mrs. Lewin?" she whispered. "Is everything all right?"

Two tears welled up in the woman's eyes.

"Mrs. Lewin, please tell me what's wrong," Devori begged. "Maybe I can help?"

Mrs. Lewin turned to her as the droplets seeped out of her eyes and two more rose to take their place. "Oh, my dear, I don't know... I don't know..."

"Know what?" Devori persisted.

"What I'm going to do about Yom Tov!" Mrs. Lewin confessed, breaking down into a fit of sobbing. "My husband has been ill for more than four months, and I just lost another job. Between taking care of my husband, looking for another job, and worrying about our future, I can't keep my mind on anything lately, not even keeping the house clean. And I used to be such an excellent housekeeper, too. What am I going to do?"

Devori sucked in her breath. No wonder Mrs. Lewin was eyeing her strangely, she realized with a start. It must be hard to have someone else cleaning up a house that you once were able to care for yourself—even if the help is free.

Mrs. Lewin kept sobbing. Through the tears and sniffles,

Devori could hear her saying, "All the money that dear man gave us has run out. Yom Tov is two weeks away and I have barely any food left in the pantry!"

Devori couldn't believe her ears. Barely any food? How could that be? She looked around the tidy kitchen. The refrigerator, the stove, the countertops—all looked clean and neat. The house didn't *look* poor. What was that about a man and money?

"No one knows, no one knows," Mrs. Lewin muttered. "We have friends coming to us for the *seudos*, as always, and Michael and Danny both want to bring home some classmates from yeshivah. I need flour to bake challah and meat to make a *seudah*. What will I do? What will I do?"

Devori's head was spinning. Didn't the Lewins have relatives they could turn to? Why didn't the neighborhood *chessed* committee know about this?

Mrs. Lewin suddenly realized she had revealed her secret to a mere sixteen-year-old girl. "Now, Devori," she said, wagging her finger at her wide-eyed listener, "I don't want anyone to know anything about this. Even your mother! It's a secret, you understand? Why, if your mother were to find out, she'd never look at me the same way again!"

Devori nodded weakly.

"Hashem will help, Hashem will help," Mrs. Lewin muttered, brushing away some imaginary crumbs. "Come, finish peeling the vegetables and fill up the soup pot. That will be enough for today."

• • •

Devori walked home slowly, her mind awhirl. Could it be that Mrs. Lewin was really as poor as she said she was? Why hadn't anyone else in the neighborhood realized it?

Like an apparition, a warning finger shook before her eyes. "No one knows, no one knows," Mrs. Lewin's voice rang in her ears. "It's a secret, you understand?"

Devori's head swelled with the trust Mrs. Lewin had placed in her. *Secret or not, I'm sure I can do something about it*, she resolved. *I bet she confided in me because she knew I could figure out a way to help. Let's see… I have plenty of birthday money. I could give her some of that!*

Devori imagined the grateful look on Mrs. Lewin's face as she proffered the life-saving envelope. For a moment she considered another scenario, of Mrs. Lewin refusing to take the money, but she quickly pushed that image out of her mind.

She has to take it—it's the only way she can make Yom Tov, Devori decided. *It will be our little secret. Of course I won't make a big fuss over it. I'll just hand her the envelope when I'm finished working. She'll be so grateful to me. I'm going to save her whole Yom Tov!*

Energized by her decision, Devori dashed into her house and bolted up to her bedroom. She pulled her coin purse out of its hiding place and poured its contents onto her bed. A puzzled look crossed her face. She had expected there to be a lot more. Then she remembered that she had already used most of the money to pay for an overnight trip with her classmates last *Chol Hamoed.*

Seventeen dollars and forty-five cents, she thought dispiritedly after counting up the bills and coins strewn across her bed. *How far can that go?* The rosy picture of her magnanimous gesture fizzled out like a sputtering candle.

A new idea popped up the next day at school when everyone was called to Minchah early to say Tehillim for a student who had been injured in a car accident. As the girls filed into the auditorium, Devori noticed Aliza Grossman setting up some *tzedakah* boxes on a table next to the exit. A few were for recognized Torah institutions, while others were for poor families in the neighborhood.

• • •

The next day, when the girls were called into another Tehillim session for the girl who was still in critical condition, Devori brought in her own *tzedakah* box. She slipped it in beside the others on the table before going to find a seat.

After Minchah, Devori trailed the throng of girls making their way out, hoping that her *tzedakah* box had filled up with coins. As she neared the exit, she saw Aliza hurrying over to the table and with a loud cry exclaim, "Who put this *tzedakah* box here?"

"What's the problem? I did," Devori said.

"You have to get special approval from Rebbetzin Roth to put a box here," Aliza said imperiously. "No one can put a box here without her permission! Only *I* have permission!"

Devori watched in shock as Aliza turned over her *tzedakah* box and shook out the few coins it contained.

"Either you're going to tell Rebbetzin Roth what you're collecting for, or I will," she said in the tone of someone chastising a small child.

Devori knew she was cornered. She wasn't about to betray Mrs. Lewin's trust in front of all the girls who had stayed behind to watch what was going on. Weakly, she motioned to Aliza to take the *tzedakah* money from her box and use it for her approved charities, and silently she left the hall.

"Is anything the matter, Devori?" Mrs. Lewin asked, as her usually efficient helper went about her tasks rather lethargically.

"Everything's fine," Devori replied, pursing her lips. "I'm going to sort the laundry now."

In the privacy of the laundry room, Devori gave her thoughts free rein. She had just peeked into Mrs. Lewin's pantry and seen fewer cans standing on the shelves than there had been a few days before. *I'm sure she's just pretending to be cheerful for my sake,* she told herself. *But how long can she fool herself? If she doesn't get some kind of help soon, her whole life might fall apart. I must think of another way to get her some money!*

Desperately she tried to come up with more possibilities. She could line up extra baby-sitting jobs and give all of her earnings to Mrs. Lewin... But no, it would take months before she had any amount of money to speak of. She could go door-to-door collecting in a neighborhood where no one knew her... No, it didn't seem right for a sixteen-year-old to go out collecting alone in a strange neighborhood. She would ask a friend to come along. No, that wouldn't work either; the friend might ask too many questions.

Maybe she could make a yard sale? Her parents had so much stuff in the basement; surely they'd be willing to part with a few things. But then, of course, her parents would ask her why she was suddenly so interested in selling things. This sworn-to-secrecy business was getting problematic.

There's not much I can do on my own, Devori thought ruefully. I must convince Mrs. Lewin to let me tell just one other person. It just won't work any other way!

The doorbell rang. "Could you answer that, Devori?" Mrs. Lewin called from another room. Devori jumped up and ran to open the door.

It was a man collecting for his son's *chasunah*. Knowing Mrs. Lewin's financial situation, Devori didn't dare bother

her. She was sure that there wasn't an extra penny in the house. Feeling awful, she murmured an apology to the man and gently closed the door.

"Who was that?" asked Mrs. Lewin, coming into the hall-way.

"Oh, just someone collecting *tzedakah*," Devori replied.

"Did you give him anything?" The look on Mrs. Lewin's face was so serious that Devori regretted not giving the man some of her own money.

"Uh, I didn't have my purse handy," Devori stammered.

"You should never pass up a chance to give *tzedakah*," Mrs. Lewin chided her. "You might think, how much can one person give anyway? And even if you had a lot of money to give, you wouldn't be able to give all of it, as you wouldn't have anything left for yourself. But when everyone gives together, it adds up and can really make a difference." She looked off into the distance. "That's what the man said to me. He said he wanted everyone to have a *chelek* in the mitzvah."

"What man?" Devori blurted out.

"Mrs. Lewin looked like she was about to cry again. "My husband's co-worker. He realized what was happening when things started to get bad for us. He went around collecting from all the people at the factory—anonymously, of course—and raised enough to tide us over until now."

So that's what the whispered conversations and strange telephone calls were all about. Devori's heart went out to Mrs. Lewin, who had started to weep.

"Don't cry, Mrs. Lewin!" she pleaded. "I can help, really I can! You just have to let me tell someone so I can start collecting money for you!"

Mrs. Lewin's eyes flew open in shock. "You mustn't tell anyone!" she almost shouted. "I'd be ashamed to face them!

We still have children to marry off—we have a name in this community!" She quickly wiped her eyes and straightened her *sheitel*. "Hashem will help, you'll see. Just please don't tell anyone!"

Devori felt like she'd run into a brick wall. Here she knew so much but couldn't do anything about it. Late into the night she tossed and turned in her bed, trying to think up other ways to raise money for Mrs. Lewin. But all her ideas came to a dead end when she realized that someone else would have to know why she was doing such a wonderful *chessed*. Even something as simple as getting a note from a *rav* meant telling the *rav* whom she was collecting for.

It's not fair! she cried in frustration. *Here I am, ready to help, but Mrs. Lewin isn't giving me the chance!* Finally, spent with emotion, she fell into a dreamless sleep.

• • •

Someone was ringing the doorbell. With a start, Devori looked at her alarm clock. It was 10:00! Why hadn't someone awakened her? As she washed her hands, threw on her robe, and hurried downstairs, she realized that her mother probably had tried to wake her, but she had been too tired from her sleepless night to even hear her.

No one was downstairs. Devori peeked through the eyehole of the front door and saw a young woman standing with a plastic shopping basket at her feet. When Devori opened the door, the young woman said simply, "Yad Sima."

"Where's the little girl who usually comes?" Devori asked.

"Oh, that's my sister. She's helping me this afternoon, so I offered to do her rounds for her this morning," the young woman explained.

Devori nodded and went to get something from the pantry. She was familiar with the procedure. Every neighborhood had a *chessed* coordinator who sent girls around to collect basic foodstuffs for needy families. The donations were sorted out at the *chessed* coordinator's house and put into baskets for delivery to the families. The whole system worked smoothly—and anonymously.

Devori came back to the door and looked into the young woman's basket. A bottle of oil, a bag of oatmeal, and a few cans of vegetables were already inside. As she extended her package of wafers, she suddenly heard Mrs. Lewin's voice in her mind: "You might think, how much can one person give anyway? But when everyone gives together, it adds up and can really make a difference."

Thoughtfully, Devori placed her package in with the other staples. Then she turned to the young woman and asked her, "Do you know who your sister's coordinator is?"

"Mrs. Edelstein on Campbell Street," the young woman replied. "I'll be taking this basket over to her soon."

"*Tizki l'mitzvos!*" Devori said, suddenly feeling better than she'd had in a long time.

That afternoon she knocked on Mrs. Edelstein's door. The woman received her so warmly and listened to her request so attentively, that Devori immediately knew that she had found the right address for her problem. Without mentioning any names, Devori explained that one of their neighbors was going through a very hard time and had no food in the house to make Yom Tov.

Mrs. Edelstein understood at once. "My girls are used to going door-to-door to collect food for poor families," she assured Devori. "No one will know who this collection is for. I'll just send them out on their usual rounds at the end of the week, and we'll collect four or five baskets of food. Then you can come to my house to pick up the baskets to deliver to your friend."

"I don't think I could carry them all by myself," Devori worried aloud.

"That won't be a problem," Mrs. Edelstein assured her. "My daughter will help you carry them as far as you'd like. She could even carry them over to the exact address, but she won't notice a thing. She's very good at this kind of *chessed*," she added with a wink.

Devori laughed in relief. "Thank you, Mrs. Edelstein. You don't know how much *chessed* you're doing—for me as well as for my neighbor!"

• • •

On Erev Shabbos, Devori stood outside Mrs. Lewin's door and waited for her heart to stop pounding. Her gaze swept over the five brightly-colored shopping baskets bulging with enough bottles, cans and packages to fill several pantries. For a fleeting moment she wished she had collected all this food single-handedly. Now, that would have been something to be proud of!

She reached up and rang the bell.

"Devori! What are you doing here today?" Mrs. Lewin greeted her with surprise.

"I, uh, have something to show you," Devori answered, purposely avoiding the word *give*. She motioned toward the baskets. "These are for you. For Yom Tov."

Mrs. Lewin's hand flew to her heart as tears welled up in her eyes. "For me? But—from where? How?"

"Don't worry, Mrs. Lewin, no one knows," Devori assured her quickly. "Except for Hashem."

A slow smile lit up the woman's face. "You don't have to tell me where these came from. Just—thank you. Devori, you're a lifesaver!"

Devori pushed aside the compliment as if she was swatting away a pesky fly. "It wasn't me," she said truthfully, "though for a long time, I wished it would be. I couldn't do it alone. But I found I could be part of something much bigger. Remember what you said about everyone having a *chelek* in *tzedakah*? You really can do so much more that way than if you try to do it all by yourself."

Mrs. Lewin, her face beaming, still hadn't moved from the doorway.

"Come!" Devori laughed. "Let me get these into the kitchen for you!"

A surge of energy flowed through her muscles as she lugged each basket into Mrs. Lewin's house. Then she sat down at the kitchen table, watching as Mrs. Lewin pulled out one item after another from the baskets, exclaiming with delight that it was just the brand she always used.

This anonymous chessed *business is such a good idea, maybe I could start one at school,* Devori mused. *I could organize tutors, run a* gemach *for school supplies, set up a note-taking service for girls who are out sick... the possibilities are endless. I could call it "Tomer Devorah"—that has a nice ring to it. Whoops!* She caught herself in time. *Maybe I better rethink this. Perhaps "Ahavas Chessed" would be a better name.*

"I'll put the stuff away in the pantry, Mrs. Lewin," Devori said with a smile.

12

Shira was Ephraim's sister. She knew what was best for him. Ephraim needed a girl who was beautiful, or at least extremely pretty.

The Shidduch

BY NECHAMA DINA SMITH

"Shira, can I come in?" Leah pleaded.

Do you have to? thought Shira. She wasn't in the mood to get up, and the yearbooks spread out on her bed would give away what she was doing.

"Shira, can you open up? Pretty please?"

Hmm, on the other hand, maybe Leah could help, Shira thought, relaxing her hunched shoulders. "Coming," she called out and released the locked door to let her younger sister in.

"Guess what?" Leah began excitedly.

Shira raised her eyebrows. "What?" she asked guardedly. Leah needed no prompting. "Ta told me that he and Mommy are looking for a *shidduch* for Ephraim! Did you know?"

"Yeah, Mommy told me." Shira sat on her bed and Leah leaned over.

"They must really need our input if Ma even told you," Leah commented as they looked over the books.

"*Our* input?" Shira smiled. "You're only thirteen!"

Leah frowned.

"Well," Shira softened. "Look for the best, most glamorous girls and we'll make a list for them to look into."

"G-glamorous?" Leah stumbled on the word.

"Ephraim is a good boy. A very good boy. He's the best in his whole yeshivah. So besides all the good qualities that we have to look for, he also deserves a very beautiful girl."

The girls pored over every page of every book, noting one, question-marking another, circling yet another, until finally they came up with a list of the ten top girls who had graduated Bais Sarah two or three years ago.

"Here you are, Ma," Shira announced triumphantly as she handed over the list. "These are the best of the whole Bais Sarah."

Mrs. Siegel set down the iron on the ironing board and looked at the paper. "Did you also consider any teachers in the school?"

"Teachers? No." Shira thought for a minute. "Miss Rubin is mean and nasty. Forget her, please. Miss Levy—she's my math teacher, she's not that frum. And Miss Cooper must be thirty. Everyone else is married."

"And from the other grades?"

Who was her mother thinking of?

"Not Miss Reich, Ma, right?" Shira asked, alarmed.

"Well, actually a *shadchan* mentioned her name and said she's an excellent girl. What do you think?"

"Mommy, she's...she's..." but Shira couldn't finish. She couldn't find the right word. If she didn't act mature, her mother wouldn't continue to confide in her.

"Do you know her at all?" Mrs. Siegel asked.

"No," her daughter admitted quietly.

Shira went to the kitchen where she could chew on an oatmeal cookie as she thought. The problem with Tziporah Reich was simply that...she wasn't pretty. Nor thin. How could her mother consider her? Tziporah had not even entered Shira's head. Ephraim was a real *lamdan*, a treasure of a *bachur*. He himself claimed that looks were not that important to him, but, thought Shira, *I'm his sister! And I care! And I want what's best for him! I know he needs someone beautiful! At least extremely pretty. Or at least someone who knows how to dress, who has a sense of style. Is that asking too much?*

Shira and her mother didn't talk about *shidduchim* anymore that week. It dawned on Shira that she might not be all that useful in helping her parents find a *shidduch* for her brother. It seemed like her parents were doing all their research and work on their own. But Shira and Leah kept alert, checking with each other to see whether either of them knew if anything was happening.

Sometimes her father would mention news that their mother wouldn't. So, before he dropped her off at school, Shira asked, "Ta, what's going on with Ephraim?"

Rabbi Siegel stroked his beard and whispered, though no one besides him and Leah was in the car, "He's going out."

"Oh." Her heart began to pound. "With whom?"

"Well, there were a few girls we were looking into, a couple even from your suggestions. And—*hashgachah pratis*—one of them happened to go to New York for a wedding, so we quickly did all the back and forths, and Ephraim went out with her!"

Shira waited, still as stone.

"Her name is Tziporah Reich."

Shira nodded mutely.

"*Daven* for him. It might get serious," said her father. He pulled up to the drop-off point, and Shira opened the door and jumped out.

Shira was stunned. "What's wrong?" her friend Yaeli asked, sliding next to her on the bench in the *davening* hall.

"Nothing," Shira said glumly.

"You're white," her friend observed.

"I'm a little worried about the *historia* test."

"Me, too," Yaeli said, and squeezed Shira's hand as they both began to *daven*.

When they reached *Shemoneh Esrei*, Shira remembered what she was doing and decided she'd concentrate. She wouldn't care what people thought of her. Only the really holy girls covered their faces with their *siddurim* by *shema koleinu*. She and her friends would never do that. But today she did, pressing the siddur with its cool pages over her face.

"Hashem," she whispered and then stopped. What was she really asking for? "Hashem," she continued, "please, please give Ephraim the best possible *kallah* that he deserves, and please make it clear and obvious to me that she is the best." She uncovered her face and finished *davening*.

It was Thursday afternoon. Shira and Leah came home from school. Leah went to her room to do work, and Shira helped her mother knead the challah dough. Side by side, they silently turned and pushed, sprinkled and pressed, turned again and pummeled masses of dough.

"Shira," her mother's voice was gentle, but energetic, panting a little from her exertion with the dough. "I think they're going to get engaged."

"Who?" Shira realized that Ta must have told Ma that he'd spoken to her.

"Ephraim and Tziporah."

Her heart sank to her stomach. She turned her shoulder so her mother wouldn't see the tears that flowed like a sudden downpour from her eyes. She kneaded vigorously.

Her mother continued confidently, "She's talented, brilliant, kind, a *baalas chessed*, a dedicated teacher, comes from a good family... and most importantly…"

"What?" Shira couldn't hide her sniffle.

"Ephraim is crazy about her!"

They both chuckled, Shira surprising herself.

Making challah was a good time to talk to Hashem and ask Him for one's needs. Again she asked Hashem in a whisper, "Please make me see how this is good..."

The next week flew by. Shira was glad that schoolwork demanded her utmost concentration. She didn't have much time to worry. Fortunately.

A week later the two were engaged. The l'chaim was scheduled for Tuesday night.

Ephraim arrived from New York. The *kallah* arrived. The shul was filled with happy chatter and light music. Shira helped an older woman fill her plate with salad. She turned around to gaze at the *kallah*. Tziporah sparkled. And Ephraim looked like he'd won the lottery. His smile didn't leave his face the whole night.

Shira looked at her future sister-in-law, heard the kind way she spoke to everyone, sensed the warmth of the hugs she gave her many students who came to wish her mazel tov, admired her modest yet stylish dress, and decided, with tears in her eyes, that Hashem had given her what she wanted: a beautiful sister-in-law.

13

I glance at my watch. I've been here for exactly one minute. Fifty-nine more minutes to go.

The Empty Chair

BY NOMI DAYAN

I pushed open the thick door and sucked in my lower lip as a sickly odor hit my nose. Oy, I told myself. Why am I starting this? I know I won't be able to keep it up. I'm just going to go in, do my thing, and I'm out.

I shifted the weight of my black case to my other hand that was not yet sweaty. I felt so uncomfortable and out of place! I should have picked babysitting. I knew I should have. Or tutoring. I could have done that. What compelled me to check off "Nursing Home" to fulfill my *chessed* hours at school? I'm just going to have to tell them I changed my mind.

I stood there, my eyes following the tired line of the elderly people in wheelchairs. Some turned to look at me, as if expecting something. I swallowed and tried to smile. I attempted to lift my feet, but they seemed to have planted themselves into the shiny linoleum floor. I glanced at my watch. I was there for exactly one minute. Fifty-nine more minutes to go. I felt tense and uneasy. What was worse was that I didn't know what to do.

"Will you play for me?"

I turned around. She sat in a wheelchair with her hands neatly resting in her lap. Her dress sported a childlike floral print with soft splashes of blossoms. Her hair was drawn back in a tight bun, and I could see the fluorescent lights reflected in her gray eyes.

Had she been there when I came in? I hadn't seen her. How did she know I was carrying a musical instrument in my case? Anything could be in there...

I found myself hauling up a chair and clicking my case open. It took a few minutes for me to put my clarinet together, but she watched patiently. I moistened the reed, aligned the parts correctly... and suddenly I didn't know what to play. Relax, I told myself. You've been playing for years. Play anything!

I played a simple Shlomo Carlebach tune. She listened and watched. I probably made more mistakes than played the right notes. But she enjoyed it so much that tears welled up in her eyes.

When I was done, she said softly, "That was beautiful. You play wonderfully."

"Thank you," I answered.

She kept beaming at me.

"Can you play?" I asked, even though it seemed like a silly question.

"I used to play when I was a girl," she told me. "I loved to play."

I wanted to ask why she doesn't play anymore but didn't want to seem nosy.

She saw the question in my face. "I have bad arthritis in my fingers, and I cannot play much anymore. I wish I could play."

She moved her fingers gingerly. "But you can play."

I came back the next week, again with my clarinet. She was there, waiting, in the same spot as before. I could tell she was waiting for me from the empty chair next to her, ready.

I sat down easily. This time she was wearing a soft wave print of poppies. Her hair was styled neatly with a lavender pin. I knew she did all of these in anticipation for my visit. I hadn't told her I would be back. I guessed she was just hoping.

I played better this time. My clarinet really sang. I let myself unbend and loosen, allowing my fingers to slide where they knew they belong.

"You play from the heart," she said. "And your heart smiles."

I did not come the next week because of a family *simchah*. There just wasn't time. As I pushed open the thick door again, I wistfully realized that she waited for me every time. But I couldn't always come. How do I tell her?

She saw me and was delighted. But there was no chair. Our eyes met.

"I didn't put out a chair because I don't want you to feel beholden to come," she told me. "I don't want you to feel uncomfortable if you cannot come, or feel that you have to be here."

I was glad she said that but was almost ashamed. How could I skip visiting her like that? I put the mouthpiece to my lips slowly.

Before I left that time, she touched my hand. I've never felt such old hands before. She always kept them nestled in her lap.

We never talked much. I was never much of a social person, and I never know what to say. I would come, sit down, and play. Shortly after that, I'd leave. She would just smile and listen the whole time.

"I was like you once," she told me on one visit. "I did the same thing, and I hated it. I would visit the old people only because I had to. I was very young and plump, and they would squeeze me all over and pinch my cheeks, probably because they missed their little girls. I resented them because I reasoned it was because of them that I missed some sunny afternoons when I could be reading or playing the clarinet. And I hated being pinched. I told myself that when I got old, I would never make anyone do such a thing. And now...look at me, making you come and play! And you! You still do it. Instead of feeling bad about coming, you feel bad about not coming."

The next two weeks I could not come. I had told her beforehand because I did not want her to wait for me. But during those two weeks I realized something. I missed her.

14

Sima thought she hadn't heard right. Since when did her family have anything to do with *gemachs*? Donate to them maybe, but use them?

A Change in Plans

BY YOCHEVED LEAH PERKAL

"Sima, we're waiting for you!" Chaya called.

Sima headed slowly toward her classmates who were lingering outside the schoolyard. For once, she wouldn't have minded being left behind.

The small group of eleventh graders made its way down the street.

"I can't believe we're having another history report!" Brochi said.

Chaya nodded. "Yeah, this is the fourth one this year."

"Oh, let's change the subject," Sara Leah declared. "Look!" she pointed to the display window of the elegant clothing boutique they were passing. "Rubin's put out their latest designs."

The girls slowed their pace.

"I love that green two-piece," someone commented.

"It is nice," Sara Leah agreed, "but I could never afford it. Not even when they go on sale. But what about you, Sima?

Don't you shop here pretty often? And now with your sister's wedding coming up, you're probably buying lots of stuff."

Sima tried not to show her consternation.

No one seemed to notice the effort it cost her except Chaya. Smoothing back the blond curls that always seemed to escape her ponytail, Chaya said to her friend in a low tone, "I don't think she meant anything."

Sima didn't answer. She had never minded the occasional comments about her family's financial means. She had even taken a certain pride in them. But Chaya didn't know—and how could she when Sima couldn't bring herself to tell her— that Sara Leah's remark had hit an unusually sore spot.

Most of the girls parted at the corner; Sima and Chaya continued on for another two blocks as usual.

"Did you decide on the color for the gowns yet?" Chaya asked as they crossed the street.

Sima shook her head, the fine brown hairs of her neatly-made ponytail bouncing against her neck.

"What's with the cream and apricot you were thinking about?"

Sima shrugged.

"Those colors will look gorgeous with your dark hair and light skin."

Still Sima said nothing.

"So what's the problem?" Chaya persisted. "Your sister wants another color?"

"Um...I don't know," Sima mumbled. *I don't care,* she wanted to yell. But really, she did.

"Want to come over and start on the history report?"

Sima's "no" sounded abrupt even to her own ears. "I mean, no, not today. I have things to take care of," she corrected herself.

The surprised expression on Chaya's face turned to one of understanding. "Yeah, I know you're busy. Weddings are much more exciting than a report, that's for sure."

Sima was silent. The appointment she had that afternoon wasn't exciting at all. How could she tell Chaya that she was on her way to meet her mother and sister at a *gemach* for sister-of-the-bride gowns?

The conversation with her parents last night was so fresh and raw, it was painful to remember. Financial setbacks, they had told her. A simpler wedding. That didn't sound so bad until she heard the details. They would be changing the hall. Baila's *chasunah* would be at Bais Miriam. Sima just couldn't envision it. What would her friends say? What would everyone say? They were expecting a grand wedding like her brother's had been.

But there was more. Sima hadn't expected the news to affect things like the matching gowns they had been planning for her and her younger siblings, including a matching dress with a bubble skirt for her six-month-old niece. But then her mother had said matter-of-factly, "If you want a nice gown, we should make an appointment at the *gemach* right away."

At first Sima had thought she hadn't heard right. Since when did the Feldmans have anything to do with *gemachs*? Donate to them maybe, but *use* them?

"Many of your friends' families get their gowns at the *gemach*. They often find beautiful things there."

"But we wanted matching and everything, and the colors..." Sima's voice had trailed away. What she had wanted to say was, "But I'm not my friends. And they know that. They're expecting some fantastic creations. What will they think?"

"I know," her mother had said in a softer tone. "But that's

not a reason to splurge."

"It's not that we're about to starve," her father had finished. "It's just that business isn't doing well now. So it would be wisest not to spend too much."

When she was sure that Chaya was out of sight, Sima retraced her steps and headed down a different street. She proceeded briskly for ten minutes until she found herself in front of a large apartment building. She glanced up at the address and then checked it against the paper in her hand. 5689. Yes, this was the right address.

Sima stepped out of the elevator and looked around. The apartment doors being clearly marked, she had no trouble finding 3D. She drew a deep breath and raised her hand to knock, hoping she wouldn't meet anyone she knew inside.

"Can I help you?" An elderly woman in a short, dark *sheitel*, wearing a neat white blouse and black skirt was smiling at her.

"Um...I'm here for the...for the *gemach*..."

"You mean you've come to help? That's wonderful! Come inside!"

Sima stumbled into the apartment. The elderly woman apparently thought Sima had come to help with the *gemach*, but soon, too soon, she would have to explain that she hadn't come to help; she had come to be helped.

But the woman, who introduced herself as Mrs. Ricky New, didn't show her into a room with rows of hanging gowns. Instead she led her into a small but airy living room and invited her to sit down on the immaculate, maroon velvet couch.

"I really appreciate your coming, and so fast, too. I only spoke to Esther yesterday."

Sima stared. "Esther?"

Mrs. New nodded. "Maybe she didn't tell you, but Esther is my niece."

"I – I don't understand," Sima stammered.

Mrs. New pushed her glasses back firmly on her nose. "Didn't Esther explain anything to you before she sent you here?"

"E-Esther?"

"Didn't my niece Esther Green send you here?"

"Esther Green?!" *Who was she anyway?* "My mother sent me here. I mean, she told me to meet her here."

"Meet you here?"

Sima nodded. "To try on gowns."

"Gowns?" Mrs. New paused. "Oh, you must mean the gown *gemach*. But you're in the wrong building. You see, 5689 has two entrances. I live in A and you need building B."

Why hadn't anyone told her that? Sima frowned and extracted herself from the velvety softness of the couch. "I'm sorry for bothering you."

"No, don't be sorry. *I'm* sorry. It would have been nice…"

Sima rushed out of Mrs. New's apartment, glad to escape the confusing conversation. It was late and her mother was probably wondering where she was.

Now that she was looking for it, Sima found entrance B quite easily. When she reached apartment 3D, she knew she was in the right place. Under the "Family Weiner" nameplate was another sign that stated clearly "Wedding Gowns."

As soon as she rang the bell, the door was flung open. "Where were you?" her mother demanded. "I was starting to worry."

"I got lost. No one told me that 5689 had two entrances." She said nothing about the mix-up with Mrs. New. It was too complicated.

Her mother led her into a large room filled with clothing racks. In the corner, Sima could see her sister Baila, the *kallah*, sifting through a rack. As soon as she saw Sima, she came hurrying toward her with a gauzy peach gown. "Isn't this stunning? It's just like the one we were planning, the same color and everything."

Sima inspected the dress. Just like the cream and apricot she had been planning? Not really. It didn't even come close.

A woman in a wavy blond *sheitel* came toward them, smiling. Sima presumed she was Mrs. Weiner.

"Yes, this does look like it should fit," Mrs. Weiner said.

"But we also need two more for my younger sisters," Baila explained. "Do you have this in sizes twelve and eight?"

The woman shook her head. "I only have one more size in this style—a bigger one."

Baila sighed as she returned the gown to its rack.

Seeing her mother head for another rack, Sima frowned. Did her mother really expect to find something here? Didn't she know they would never find anything really gorgeous in a *gemach*?

Then her mother held up a gown in soft pink. "Sima," she called, "I think this will look great on you."

"I only have one of that," Mrs. Weiner pointed out.

"I want her to try it on anyway," said Sima's mother.

Grudgingly, Sima took the gown into the fitting room and tried it on. When she examined herself in the mirror, she had to admit that it really was beautiful. It had smooth satiny material, the belt fit her waist perfectly, and there was delicate edging on the collar and cuffs. It almost looked like a custom-made creation. Maybe no one would guess that it wasn't.

"Oh, it looks exquisite on you!" Mrs. Weiner exclaimed.

Sima's mother nodded, smiling. "Yes, it looks like it was

made for her."

Baila came rushing over. "It's absolutely gorgeous," she gushed.

"But there's only one," her mother told her.

Baila's large, blue eyes clouded. "I really wanted everyone to match for my wedding."

The blond woman looked around the room. "Let me think…Oh, I know!" She walked over to the far corner of the room and came back with a navy gown. "I have this in a size six, and I probably have it in all the sizes you need. I might even have knickers and a vest for little boys in navy, too."

"Really?" Baila jumped at the suggestion. "We need something for a four-year-old boy."

Sima looked at her mother's and sister's smiling faces. Then she turned sharply and headed back to the fitting room. The navy wasn't ugly, but it couldn't compare to the pink. And as Chaya had pointed out, she always looked better in lighter colors.

After Sima handed the pink gown back to Mrs. Weiner, she went over to her mother who was inspecting a little boy's outfit. "I'm going outside," she said. "It's too stuffy in here." Her mother looked at her thoughtfully for a moment and nodded.

Sima took the elevator down to the lobby. As she pushed the large glass door open, she felt a refreshing breeze tickle the back of her neck. She breathed deeply. It really had been stuffy up there.

Sharp infant wails broke into her thoughts. She looked around. Not far from her, under a shady tree, was a twin carriage. A boy and a lady in a short, dark *sheitel* were sitting on the bench. The woman held a baby in her arms.

Mrs. New and Sima saw each other at the same time. "It's

you, isn't it?" Mrs. New said cheerfully. "Did you find what you were looking for?"

Sima stiffened. She wasn't in the mood of answering questions.

But Mrs. New didn't ask any more. Instead she shifted the infant on her shoulder and rocked the carriage with her foot to calm the second wailing baby inside.

"Are these your grandchildren?" Sima asked politely.

Mrs. New shook her head. "Meet some of my neighbors." She pointed to the young boy fidgeting with the pages of a reader open on his lap. "This is Avraham Mayevsky," she explained. "He and his family moved here from Russia a few months ago, and I'm helping him with his reading."

The baby inside the carriage started screaming again. "And these are the Goldstein twins. They're two months old and *baruch Hashem* very sweet, but they are a bit colicky. Their mother doesn't get much sleep. I took them for a while so she can have a nap, but I can't get him to stop crying."

"Goldstein?" Sima asked as she automatically took over rocking the carriage. The baby stopped crying immediately. "Oh, I know Rivky Goldstein. But why doesn't someone in her family help? She has two sisters in high school and a younger one in seventh grade."

Mrs. New shrugged. "I don't know. Maybe they can't come for some reason. But even if they could, it's not my business. The fact is that Mrs. Goldstein needs help." She sighed. "But I'm only one person, and as you can see, it's not easy for me. And there are more people in the building who need help too. That's why I asked my niece Esther Green to find me some volunteers. When you knocked on my door earlier, I was sure Esther had sent you. I was disappointed when I realized it had been a mistake."

Sima felt uncomfortable. It wasn't her fault she had knocked on the wrong door. Then she heard herself say, "Um…if you want… I mean, maybe, if my mother lets, I can help a bit."

"You could?" Mrs. New beamed. "That would be wonderful!"

Sima found herself smiling back. There was something irresistible about Mrs. New's smile.

"Sima?"

Sima turned around and waved at her mother and sister who were looking for her. When they came closer, her mother exclaimed, "Oh, hello, Mrs. New!"

Sima looked at her mother, surprised.

"We met once in shul," her mother explained.

"So this is your daughter?" Mrs. New said. "How nice! Sima was just offering to help out with some of the neighbors in my apartment building. She was going to ask you for permission."

After Sima's mother agreed to let Sima come back the next day, the three Feldmans headed home.

"I don't know her that well, but she seems like an unusual lady," Sima's mother said as they crossed the street. "When I first met her, she told me that she moved into that building a few months after her husband passed away. She didn't want to live alone in her big, old house, but she didn't want to move in with her children either, even though they had invited her to come live with them. So she decided to rent an apartment, thinking it wouldn't be so lonely with so many neighbors."

As they climbed up the steps to the house, Sima's mother said, "So what do you girls say about the gowns? I really like the pale pink on Sima."

"But there was only one…" Baila's disappointed voice trailed away.

Sima felt her irritation rising. She had also wanted everyone to match, but the navy was so… dark. And here she'd finally found something in a *gemach* that she wouldn't mind wearing. "It's easy for you to say, Baila," she muttered. "*You* don't have to make such decisions. *You* still get to wear your original custom-made gown."

Baila paled. She opened her mouth to say something but thought better of it. She turned away and hurried into the house.

Her mother gave Sima a sharp look. "That wasn't nice. It's true that Tatty and I decided to go with the gown we originally planned for Baila, but remember, it *is* her wedding. This means that as hard as these changes are for you, they're much harder for Baila. It would be nice of you to be a little more considerate."

Sima pressed her lips together. Not knowing what she might say to her mother if she opened her mouth, she went up to her room and threw herself onto her bed.

Just then her phone rang.

"Hello," she said sullenly into the receiver.

"What's wrong?" Chaya asked, concerned.

"Nothing."

"You're sure? You don't sound too great."

Afraid that she was going to burst into tears, Sima said curtly, "I'm fine."

There was a pause, after which Chaya asked, "Do you want to work on the report tomorrow?"

"What's the big rush with the report?" Sima snapped. "We have two weeks until it's due."

"I know," Chaya said quietly. "It's just that…I mean, I thought it would be good to get it out of the way. And it would be fun to do it together."

The phone was sticky with her perspiration. Sima switched the receiver to her other ear. For the first time since she could remember, she wasn't in the mood of Chaya's company. It would be very difficult not to talk about the wedding when it had dominated so much of their conversation until now. And she just couldn't face telling Chaya what was really going on with her family. Then she remembered Mrs. New. "I have other plans for tomorrow, anyway," she said, glad for the excuse.

"More wedding errands?"

"Um, no. Actually not. Um…it has to do with a project I'm doing."

"A what?"

It was pretty strange talking so vaguely to her best friend. "A project," she repeated, unable to think of any better way to describe it.

"Oh." There was a tinge of coolness in Chaya's voice. "Okay, bye."

"Thanks for calling," Sima murmured. But Chaya had already hung up.

The next afternoon Sima came home from school to find her mother and Baila choosing *bentchers* for the wedding.

"*Bentchers*?" Sima asked. "So we're doing *bentchers* and *siddurim* like last time?"

For a moment no one said anything. Then Baila said, "No, Sima. Just *bentchers*."

Sima trod heavily out of the kitchen. *Bentchers*? Just plain *bentchers* like everyone else? The *siddurim* at Ari's wedding had been so attractive. And the challah covers they had given out to the guests at the *sheva brachos* had been really popular. She realized there wouldn't be challah covers this time either.

The clock in the hallway struck five. It was almost time to

leave to go to Mrs. New. It would be good to get away, even for a short while.

"I'm so glad you came back," Mrs. New greeted her. "Follow me to the kitchen for a drink."

After pouring Sima a glass of cold orange juice, Mrs. New took out a white bakery box from the fridge. "I wish I could say it's homemade," she said, winking at Sima, "but it isn't. I don't like baking much. And this cake from Weiss' Bakery is quite good." She opened the box.

Sima couldn't help licking her lips. Checkerboard cake. Her favorite.

"So whom would you like to help?" Mrs. New asked. "There's Mrs. Brody, who could use someone to read to her because she's losing her vision. You might enjoy that. Then there's Mrs. Wald, who's really lonely but won't admit it. And then there are the twins you met yesterday. And there's Avraham, who needs lots of tutoring so he can catch up with his class."

Sima swallowed her last bite. "Whatever you think is most important."

"Well, one of the tougher jobs is one I haven't even mentioned yet. It's a family where the mother needs help with a houseful of children. Do you think you could handle that?"

"Okay," Sima said. She wasn't sure what she was getting herself into, but she was drawn to the lady opposite her, and she couldn't help wanting to please her.

"Wonderful! I'll tell Mrs. Landbaum about you right away."

"Landbaum? Oh, I think I know who you mean. They're a poor family, right? And I think the father got into trouble. Someone even said he's in jail. Is it true?"

Mrs. New sighed. "It doesn't really matter. The point is that Mrs. Landbaum needs help. Would you like to tackle the job?"

Sima nodded.

"Then if you're ready, I'll take you down to her place right now."

Sima followed Mrs. New down a flight of stairs to a sparsely furnished apartment. Mrs. New introduced Sima to Mrs. Landbaum and left. There was an awkward moment at first, but when Mrs. Landbaum broke into a shy smile, Sima saw how young she looked despite the worried lines on her forehead. Sima smiled back and looked around the dining room. It looked more like a playroom. A messy one.

"This is Rivky," Mrs. Landbaum said, pointing to a little girl cutting papers into tiny squares. "She's almost four. And the two-year-old watching her is Binyamin." At the sound of their names, Binyamin and Rivky looked up and gazed curiously at the newcomer.

"That's Dina over there, doing her homework," Mrs. Landbaum continued. Sima recognized the slight fourth grader in the faded uniform blouse from school. "And those are Menachem and Yisrael." Mrs. Landbaum sighed as she looked in the direction of a pair of bickering boys sitting on the large window sill. The older one had a spread of brown freckles across his nose while the younger one's face was adorned with thick glasses. "They really need to get out a bit, but I have to clean up the kitchen and prepare supper."

"Would you like me to take them to the park for an hour?" Sima offered.

Mrs. Landbaum brightened. "That would be an excellent idea."

The Landbaum children were eager to go. As Sima led them into the playground area, Yisrael went racing for the swings. He ran so fast that he tripped over his feet, and his glasses went flying.

Sima picked them up hurriedly and noticed that one handle was dangling from the hinge. "Oh, no! Look at your glasses!"

None of the children seemed particularly perturbed.

"They've been that way for a long time," Menachem explained. "I have some tape in my pocket. I'll fix them."

With his glasses on his nose once more, Yisrael sat down on the last empty swing.

"I also want to go on a swing," Rivky said plaintively.

"You'll be next after Yisrael," Sima promised.

"No! I want to go now!" Rivky threw herself on the ground and started kicking her feet.

"Stop that!" Dina reprimanded her sharply. "You're ruining your shoes."

"I don't care," Rivky sobbed. "They're torn anyway. I want new ones. Everyone in my class has new shoes."

"Well, it won't help if you ruin them," said her sister. "Mommy said she can't buy us new shoes yet. So you'll just have to wear them anyway, and if you do that they'll look worse than before."

Sima breathed a sigh of relief when another swing became available, and Rivky got up from the ground and ran to it.

The hour passed quickly. Soon it was time to take the kids home. Before Sima left the Landbaum's apartment, she arranged with the young mother to come back in two days.

"Do you think I can stay a little longer next time?" Sima asked her mother when she got home. "Mrs. Landbaum looks so tired. Maybe I can help her serve supper or put the kids to bed or something."

"Yes, you can," her mother agreed. "I'm glad you're helping her." She paused. "Now, I know you're not happy about the gowns, but we really must decide. What do you think we should do?"

Visions of taped-up glasses and torn shoes swirled around in Sima's mind. "Whatever you want," she said distractedly.

"Really? Whatever I want?"

"I mean, whatever Baila wants. Whatever she decides. It doesn't matter to me," Sima said resolutely.

Her mother looked at her curiously. "Thank you. That's very thoughtful of you," she said quietly.

The next time Sima went to the Landbaums, she dropped in to see Mrs. New first.

"Mrs. Landbaum said she really appreciated how you came in and knew just what to do," Mrs. New complimented her.

Sima smiled at the compliment. "I'm on my way there now. I just came to say hello."

"Could you please do me a favor on the way? I need to return a dozen eggs to Mrs. Wald upstairs."

"Sure, no problem."

Mrs. Wald opened the door, a frown imprinted on her features. "Yes?"

Sima swallowed. So this was the lady Mrs. New said was lonely. Well, she was glad she wasn't going to be the one visiting her. "Um, Mrs. New asked me to return these to you."

"Mrs. New? Oh, that's right." The frown on Mrs. Wald's face became slightly less pronounced. "If you'll come in for just a minute, there's something I need to return to her as well."

Sima stepped hesitantly inside. To her surprise, the hallway and open living room weren't cold and uninviting as she imagined they would be. The walls were decorated with paintings and drawings. And then Sima noticed that all were signed with the same signature, D. Wald.

"Did you make these?" she burst out as Mrs. Wald returned with a book in her hand.

Mrs. Wald's lips stretched into a thin smile. "Yes."

"Oh, I love them. I'm not an art expert or anything, but I could stand here for ages, just looking."

Although Mrs. Wald didn't respond, she looked pleased.

As the door closed behind her, Sima had a sudden thought. Chaya! Her best friend loved art. Chaya had taken basic drawing lessons, but here was a real artist. Chaya could visit Mrs. Wald, and maybe even take lessons from her or something. That way Mrs. Wald would probably not mind that someone was coming to keep her company.

When she heard Sima's idea, Mrs. New said, "That's a great idea! Speak to your friend and let me know if she wants to do it."

Sima slowly shut the door of Mrs. New's apartment behind her. In her excitement, she had forgotten that talking to her friend wouldn't be that simple. She and Chaya hadn't spoken since their strained phone call three days ago. She'd have to explain everything from the beginning, including what was going on at home and how she had met Mrs. New.

On the other hand, she missed Chaya. She welcomed the thought of talking to her again. Sima straightened her shoulders. Somehow, discussing her family's financial situation didn't seem like the end of the world anymore.

When Sima arrived at school the next morning, she had only one thought in her mind. She needed to find Chaya and talk to her—at last. She just hoped Chaya wasn't too upset with her.

As she neared her classroom, she heard animated voices. Her classmates seemed to be discussing something. Hearing her name, she stopped short and listened.

"Yes, I'm sure. My brother told me...Mr. Feldman... money problems..."

"My uncle's brother-in-law...caterer of Majestic Manor. He said they canceled..."

"What? You must be kidding! That's terrible!"

"What's so terrible? Let them be like everyone else for a change. If a plain hall is good enough for the rest of us, why isn't it good enough for them?"

"Shh... Sima will be here any minute."

As she entered the room, her eyes met Chaya's. Chaya looked worried.

Sima slipped into her seat. She had been dreading what everyone would say, and now she had heard it with her own ears. The stab was there, but it wasn't as painful as she had feared, though she had no idea why.

When the bell rang at the end of the period, Chaya came up to her. As if nothing had ever happened between them, she drew Sima by the arm out of the classroom and into the hallway. "You heard what the girls said about you this morning, didn't you?"

Sima nodded.

Chaya took a deep breath. "Well, please don't think that I would just talk about you. I was sitting there, and then someone started talking, and the other girls joined in. People just love spreading rumors."

"It's not a rumor," Sima said softly.

"It's not?"

"No, it's not."

There was a momentary silence. Then Chaya said, "So that's why you didn't want to talk to me about the *chasunah*. I'm sorry I was such a nudge."

"It's okay. How could you have known?"

Again there was silence. But this time it was comfortable and familiar.

Then Chaya said hesitantly, "The girls…they don't mean anything. They're just talking. You know, that's how people are."

Sima nodded. Yes, she did know. She knew people would talk. She knew some would relish the news of her family's financial setbacks. But there were also people like Mrs. New who concentrated on helping people without going into the whys and the wherefores of their problems.

She stopped in mid-stride and looked at her friend. "There's this lady you have to meet." Then, remembering Mrs. Wald and her paintings, she corrected herself. "Actually, two ladies."

"Yes? Who?"

"Remember that project I said I was busy with? You know, the one I didn't tell you about? Well, listen…"

15

Chava's mother didn't share Chava's enthusiasm about the school camping trip. In fact, there was nothing Chava could say to induce her mother to let her go.

A Forest Is a Dangerous Place

BY YEHUDIS LITVAK

Sitting on the living room sofa, Chava gazed at the isosceles triangle she had just drawn in her math notebook. It seemed like the right answer. But Chava's mind was far from her geometry homework. To her the triangle looked like a tent. She imagined sitting in the tent with her friends Gitty and Devora, surrounded by a dark forest, with only the countless stars for illumination. The dead silence of the mountain air was broken by a short, shrill sound. Startled, Chava jumped up only to realize it was just the front door opening. She smiled, getting back to reality. "Hi, Ma," she said, as her mother walked into the living room.

"Hi, Chava!" her mother smiled back, hanging up her coat. "How's your day going?"

"It's going great! We're having a camping trip at the end of the school year! I'm so excited!"

"A camping trip?" Chava's mother asked nervously. "That's something new. Your school never had camping trips before."

"Yes, this is the first one!" exclaimed Chava, not sure why her mother wasn't willing to share her excitement. "We used to have hiking trips, but this year the principal decided to organize a three-day camping trip to the same forest. It'll be so much fun!"

"A three-day trip? Wow, that's a long time. You've never been away from home by yourself for that long. Aren't you afraid to go?"

"Ma, I'm fourteen!" Chava said vehemently. "I'm old enough to spend three days away from home! Besides, I won't be by myself. I'll be with the whole school."

"But a forest is a dangerous place. There are steep mountains and cliffs. And wild animals. And poisonous berries. I'm afraid to let you go, Chava."

"But everybody else is going! I really want to go," pleaded Chava.

"They've never done it before, so they don't realize how dangerous it is. I don't care what everybody else is doing. You're not going!" pronounced Chava's mother resolutely.

"Yes, I am going! I'm old enough to make my own decisions!" Chava shouted. "Nobody else has to ask their mothers. All the girls decided that they're going. And I can also decide to go if I want to!"

"Don't speak to your mother like that!"

"Stop treating me like a baby! I'm an adult! And I can choose what I want to do!" screamed Chava with tears in her eyes. She ran to her room, slammed the door, and sat on her bed, tears streaming down her cheeks. She was full of anger over being treated like a baby, but on top of the anger there was guilt and embarrassment. Chava realized that she had hurt her mother and felt terrible for screaming at her. But her mother was being so unreasonable! How could she not let her go on the camping trip? All her friends were going. Was she supposed to stay home, just because her mother was not willing to treat her like an adult?!

Suddenly Chava made up her mind. She would go on the trip. She just wouldn't tell her mother.

The next morning on the way to school, Gitty and Devora discussed the camping trip. They were both planning to go. Apparently, their mothers had no problem with it. Chava sighed and asked, "Is it safe to go camping?"

"What do you mean?" asked Gitty in surprise.

"Of course, it is!" exclaimed Devora.

"Did you ever have any accidents when you went camping?" asked Chava.

"What kind of accidents?" Gitty wanted to know.

"Well, like falling off a steep mountain, or being attacked by a wild animal, or eating poisonous berries?"

"Chava, what's wrong with you?" asked Gitty. "Did you have a bad dream or something?"

"Don't worry, Chava," said Devora. "We go every year, and we never had any serious accidents. It's perfectly safe."

"Never mind," said Chava. "I don't know what I'm really asking. It's okay."

"You probably never went camping," said Gitty.

Chava nodded. Of course, growing up without a father, she could not have expected to have gone on camping trips. Her mother, who after twelve years still hadn't gotten over her husband's death, was prone to depression. She worked hard during the week and spent most of her free time in bed, reading self-help books. On a good day, she would take Chava shopping. A camping trip was out of the question.

"Don't worry, Chava," said Gitty. "We'll tell you all about camping. We'll help you prepare. You probably don't have a sleeping bag. We'll help you pick one out."

"Yeah, we can go to the store together," said Devora.

"Thanks!" said Chava. "That's so exciting—buying a sleeping bag! Are they expensive?"

"Not really. You can get a pretty good one for less than thirty dollars," replied Gitty.

"That much I have. I don't even have to ask my mother for the money," said Chava.

"There's a great store on Fourth Street," said Gitty. "It's very close—we can walk there."

"Let's go today!" exclaimed Chava.

"Okay," nodded Gitty.

"Sounds like a plan!" added Devora.

Mrs. Cohen, the school principal, walked into the classroom right after lunch. "I have a short announcement to make." She turned to the math teacher, Mrs. Stern, who nodded her assent. Mrs. Cohen continued, "Girls, we need to get your parents' permission for the camping trip. I'm going to pass out a form that your parents must sign. Please bring it back as soon as possible. I know you are all grownups," she smiled, "but I need the signatures. Nobody will be allowed to go without a signed permission form. Okay?"

Mrs. Cohen passed out the forms and left the class. Mrs. Stern wrote an equation on the blackboard. But Chava couldn't concentrate. She was staring at the permission slip. Her mother would never sign it. It would be so humiliating—everybody going camping and she staying home because she didn't have a signed form. And everybody would find out that her mother was still treating her like a baby. Everybody would think that she was immature. Chava blushed, imagining the embarrassment that awaited her. *What should I do?* she thought. *I can't even ask Mrs. Cohen to speak to my mother because then she'll find out what my mother thinks of me. I'll be too ashamed to even tell Mrs. Cohen that I don't have a signature.*

What should she do? She had no choice. She would have to fake her mother's signature. Of course, in a normal case, that's an extremely dishonest thing to do. But her mother was being so difficult! Everybody else said the camping trip was safe. What was her mother so worried about? Her mother was just being irrational. The permission form was not for irrational mothers. She would sign it herself and not have to go through all that embarrassment, and then she'd go with everyone else and have fun.

Chava was relieved. But deep down she felt pangs of guilt at deceiving her mother.

After school, Chava went home and started on her homework. She and her friends had agreed to meet at Gitty's house at five o'clock to go shopping for the sleeping bag. Chava glanced at her watch. It was a quarter to five. She closed her book. Suddenly the front door opened.

"Hi, Ma! You're early today," she said nervously.

"Hi! I had a dentist's appointment, so that's why I came home early. How was your day?" her mother asked.

"It was good," Chava said, trying to stay calm. "Ma, I'm going to buy something for school. I'll be back soon."

"Which store are you going to?" Chava's mother asked.

"Oh… um… just a regular store. I'm going with Gitty and Devora. Why? Do you need anything?" asked Chava.

"I don't need anything. I just want to know where you're going. Can you please tell me?"

"No, I can't tell you! Why do I always have to tell you

where I'm going? I'm old enough to go where I want!" Chava exploded.

"I'm your mother, and I have a right to know where you're going to be," said Chava's mother firmly.

"Other girls my age don't have to tell their mothers where they are every second of their lives!"

"Maybe other mothers are too busy with their younger children, so they can't know where the older children are all the time. But I only have you, so I can make sure that I know where you are."

"Ma, you're being unreasonable! Why do you need to know where I am every minute? Why can't you trust me, like other mothers trust their daughters?"

"You know what, Chava? I'll drive you to the store. We can pick up Gitty and Devora on the way."

Chava got furious imagining the scene. Her mother was going to go with her and watch her every move. And Gitty and Devora would see that her mother didn't let her go anywhere without her knowledge! How embarrassing that would be!

"Ma, I'm going whether you like it or not!" Chava yelled defiantly.

"Chava!" her mother screamed, taken aback.

"I'll see you later." Chava picked up her purse and slammed the door behind her before her mother could say anything else. She walked quickly towards Gitty's house.

It took Chava several minutes to regain her composure. When she was a block away from Gitty's house, she thought of the horrified expression on her mother's face as she left the house. Chava was torn. Should she go back and apologize and forget about shopping with her friends? But what would she tell Gitty and Devora? She couldn't tell them the truth—she was too ashamed. Chava sighed. *Might as well go to the store,* she thought. *I already hurt my mother anyway.*

On the way to the store, Chava pretended that everything was okay. She listened to Devora describing a camping experience she once had with her family. It sounded like so much fun! She couldn't wait to go!

The girls spent a whole hour at the store picking out a perfect sleeping bag. Gitty critically inspected each one, pointing out that one of them wasn't very warm and another one wasn't big enough. Chava liked the light blue one, but she decided that it was too expensive. Finally, they all agreed that the purple one with a thermal lining was the best Chava could afford.

As they stood on line at the checkout register, it dawned on Chava that she would have to hide the sleeping bag from her mother. She could put it in the closet. But how could she sneak such a big package into the house? Then Chava realized that even without the sleeping bag, she wasn't sure how she was going to get back into the house. What would she say? What a mess she was in!

"Here you go," the cashier interrupted her thoughts as she handed Chava the sleeping bag. "Have fun camping!"

The girls thanked her and left the store.

"Chava, what's wrong? Why do you have that expression on your face?" asked Devora.

"Don't you like the sleeping bag?" asked Gitty.

"I really like it. Thanks!" replied Chava, trying to smile.

"So what's wrong?" insisted Devora.

"I have to hide the sleeping bag from my mother," Chava blurted out.

"Why?" Devora asked, surprised.

"She doesn't let you spend this much money?" asked Gitty.

"No," said Chava sadly. "It's my money. I earned it."

"So what's the problem?" asked Gitty.

There was no way out. "My mother doesn't want me to go on the trip," Chava admitted.

"What does she want you to do instead? Work?" asked Gitty, apparently trying to make some sense out of Chava's words.

"No, it's not because she wants me to do something else. She thinks camping is dangerous. She's afraid for my safety," Chava blushed, as if she was acknowledging a terrible sin.

"Really? She should talk to my mother. Maybe she'll convince her that it's safe," said Devora with sympathy.

"Your mother probably thinks that way because she never went camping herself," said Gitty thoughtfully. "Devora's right. She should speak to someone who's done it before."

Chava felt relieved that her friends didn't think she was immature or that her mother was crazy. Maybe they were right. Maybe her mother should speak to someone who had done it before.

"I have a plan," said Gitty. "Devora, how about asking your mother to call Chava's mother and by the way mention the camping trip and say what a wonderful idea it is. And then they could talk about it. Meanwhile, Chava, let me take the sleeping bag to my house so that your mother doesn't see it before she talks to Devora's mother. How does that sound?"

"Sounds great!" said Chava. "Thanks, Gitty!"

"I'm sure my mother wouldn't mind calling," said Devora. "I'll ask her right now."

"I don't think it would be a good time to call now," Chava said uncomfortably. She couldn't explain to the girls about today's fight. Then they would realize what her mother really thought of her. She would be too humiliated!

"That's okay," said Devora. "I'll ask my mother to call tomorrow then."

"Thanks," said Chava.

As Chava opened the front door, her heart was beating fast. She wasn't sure what she would say to her mother. But she didn't have to say anything. Her mother was sleeping on the couch, her face swollen and red from crying.

Chava felt awful. She realized how much pain she had caused her mother by screaming and running out of the house like that. Her mother must have been worried sick about her leaving the house without telling her where she was going. Okay, so maybe her mother had been illogical and her fears totally irrational. But to her mother they were real fears which caused her real anguish, she realized as she looked at her sleeping mother.

She ran to her room, fell on her bed, and cried. She cried over the pain she had caused her mother. She cried over her own struggle to grow up and become independent, despite her mother not trusting her. She cried over her inability to deal with her mother's fears without hurting her and without feeling like a helpless baby. She cried over her inability to console her mother over the loss of her father and to help her mother get over her depression and live a normal, healthy life. She cried for all people suffering everywhere.

Somehow the tears made Chava feel better. Gradually, she stopped crying. She wiped her eyes and quieted down. She would apologize and tell her mother how much she appreciated her love and everything she did for her. She understood that her mother was worried not because Chava needed protection but because her mother had a need to overprotect. She was afraid to let go and admit that her daughter was growing up and didn't need her as much anymore. From now on, Chava resolved to be more sensitive to her mother's needs and to show her that she still needed her.

At eleven that night Chava heard her mother sighing and

getting up from the couch. She ran to the living room. "Ma, I'm really sorry," she said with tears in her eyes, hugging her mother.

"Chava," was all her mother said, hugging her in return.

They stayed up until two in the morning, talking about what was troubling each of them. Chava's mother told her about her worries at work, where she recently got a new manager. Chava talked about her dreams for the summer. The only subject they did not talk about was the school trip. Chava secretly hoped that her mother would change her mind and allow her to go, but she told herself that their relationship was worth more than a camping trip.

They went to sleep exhausted, but feeling more connected as mother and daughter than they had in a long time.

The next day, after dinner, the phone rang. Chava picked it up. It was Devora's mother. Chava handed the phone to her mother, telling herself not to put too much hope in the conversation. She went to her room to do her homework.

Chava heard her mother say, "Yes, my daughter mentioned a camping trip. I thought it was a crazy idea. What's wrong with just going hiking for a few hours, like every year? Why do they need to go camping for three days?" Chava's mother sounded angry.

After a pause, she said, "Teaches independence? But they're not old enough to become independent all of a sudden. Besides, isn't it dangerous? Aren't there wild animals in the forest? And what about poisonous berries?" Chava's mother asked in a worried voice.

After some time, Chava's mother spoke, her voice more composed. "So you think I should let Chava go? Maybe you're right. Devora's going to be right there and she's an expert camper. I guess she could make sure that my Chava doesn't go to any dangerous places or eat anything poisonous. What about the teachers? Do they have experience camping?"

Just as Chava was getting excited at the prospect of her mother allowing her to go, she heard her mother say, "I should probably call Mrs. Cohen and find out."

"Oh, no!" thought Chava. "I can't believe my mother is really going to call her."

Meanwhile, her mother was saying, "Thank you so much for calling, Feigy. I'll think about it."

After a couple of moments Chava heard her mother dial a number. "Hello, may I speak to Mrs. Cohen please?" her mother asked.

Chava hoped her mother wouldn't say anything embarrassing. To her surprise, her mother sounded quite sensible. She asked who was going camping with the girls. She asked who had experience camping.

After about ten minutes, Chava's mother came into her daughter's room. "So, Chava, you still want to go on that camping trip?"

Chava looked up from her textbook. "Yes. Can I go?" asked Chava cautiously.

"Okay, you can go," said her mother, sighing.

"Yeah! Thank you so much, Ma!" Chava jumped from her chair and hugged her mother.

Her mother smiled. "I'm glad you're excited about it. By the way, Mrs. Cohen asked me to sign a permission form. Do you have it?"

"Yes, I have it," replied Chava excitedly, getting the form out of her backpack. She would have a real signature! She was so glad not to have to lie and cheat.

Chava watched her mother take a pen. With shaking hands, her mother put down her signature. "Have fun camping!" she said with a smile as she left the room.

Chava stared at the paper in front of her. The shaky letters of the signature sent pangs of guilt straight into her heart. Her mother was finally being reasonable. But she was still nervous and fearful for her daughter's safety. Was it worth it to go camping and cause her mother all this anxiety?

Chava walked into the kitchen. Her mother was washing dishes. Her hands weren't shaking anymore, Chava noticed.

"Ma, are you sure you don't mind if I go camping?" Chava asked quietly.

Chava's mother looked up and smiled. "Yes, I'm sure, darling. You should really go with your friends and have fun."

"Thank you, Ma," said Chava. For some reason she felt like crying, but she held back her tears.

"Don't forget to call me!" her mother said. "I'll go crazy if I don't hear from you for three days!"

"Okay, Ma. Don't worry. I'm sure I'll find a phone. I'll tell you how much fun I'm having!"

"I'd love to hear it!" Chava's mother said. She looked genuinely happy.

As soon as Chava got off the bus at the camping site, she looked around to see if there was a pay phone. She didn't see any phones. She thought about asking someone. But how would she explain why she needed the phone? She couldn't say that she was going to call her mother. They had just arrived. She had just seen her mother a couple of hours ago. Everybody would think that she was babied if she had to call home so soon.

The girls were setting up their tent when suddenly they heard Mrs. Cohen's voice. "Chava, I've been looking for you. Your mother's on the phone." She handed Chava her cell phone.

Chava blushed. She looked around to see if any other girls had heard Mrs. Cohen. Fortunately, everybody seemed to be busy with their tents. Nobody was looking at her.

Chava took the phone. "Ma? Why are you calling? How did you get this number?" she asked in a whisper.

"Chava, I can barely hear you," she heard her mother say at the other end. "I just wanted to check if you got there safely. I called Rabbi Cohen and he gave me Mrs. Cohen's cell phone number."

"Everything is okay," she said, trying not to show her annoyance.

"I'm glad to hear that," her mother said. "Okay, have fun! Bye!"

"Bye, Ma," Chava said.

She gave the phone back to Mrs. Cohen, who was tactfully standing a few feet away.

"Chava, I know your mother was worried about this trip," said Mrs. Cohen gently. "If you ever need to call her, feel free to use my cell phone, okay?"

"Okay, thank you so much, Mrs. Cohen!" Chava said, glad to hear that Mrs. Cohen didn't think that her mother was neurotic.

Chava returned to her friends.

"So your mother is still worried about the trip?" Devora asked sympathetically.

"Of course she's worried! This is the first time you're going camping!" said Gitty.

"I guess you're right," said Chava.

"Yeah, any mother would be worried," said Devora. "It's okay, don't take it personally."

"Thanks," said Chava, relieved that her friends weren't criticizing her mother and laughing at her. The girls were right.

There was nothing terrible about her mother calling up on Mrs. Cohen's cell phone. Maybe other mothers wouldn't call on Mrs. Cohen's cell phone, but maybe they really were too busy with their other children and didn't have time to sit and worry. Or maybe they hadn't thought of asking Rabbi Cohen for the cell phone number. Anyway, it didn't matter what other mothers did. Her mother had a need to call, so she called. It wasn't embarrassing. It was a real need. And that was okay.

That night the girls returned to the camp late after hiking. It was getting dark. Chava, Gitty, and Devora sat quietly at the entrance to their tent, looking at the sky. It was dark blue, almost black, with a yellow crescent moon and scattered bright yellow dots, which looked very different from the stars in the city.

"This is amazing!" Chava whispered, afraid to break the silence. "I feel so tiny here, compared to this huge, dark universe!"

Devora nodded. "It makes you realize how little you are before Hashem, doesn't it?"

"You know, I should call my mother," Chava heard herself saying all of a sudden. For a second she regretted her words. Now the girls would surely think that she was overprotected and that her mother was paranoid.

But Devora nodded understandingly. "You should. She's probably worried about you."

"She'll be so happy if you call," agreed Gitty.

Chava got up. There was nothing to be ashamed about. If her mother was unreasonable sometimes, that was okay. She was her mother. And she should try to make her happy.

She went to look for Mrs. Cohen.

16

Tamar was her best friend from childhood, but after Zeeva arrived on the scene in tenth grade, things were no longer the same.

Best Friends

BY RAFAELLA LEVINE

I had always taken our friendship for granted. Tamar and I were best friends because we had been best friends since first grade. We often laughed over the seemingly random instance which initially bonded us. We were six-year-olds sitting next to each other in the circle in Morah Sharon's class. She was teaching us about bar graphs, and she used eye colors as an example.

"I have hazel eyes," Tamar announced.

I jerked sideways to look at her. "Me too!" I shouted. We both burst into giggles.

We compared eye colors at recess in the bathroom mirror and discovered that mine were more green, while Tamar's had a tiny hint of blue in them.

"My eyes change colors depending on what color shirt I'm wearing," I bragged.

"That's cool," Tamar said, smiling. "My mother says my

eyes change when I'm happy or sad. What color are they now?"

I examined them carefully. "They're, ummm, more green-ish-blue. Not so brown."

"That means I'm happy," she said, smiling wider. She was very friendly.

We remained best friends ever since.

I never thought about what else we had in common, or whether there would have been a reason to spend so much time together if one of us, for example, had brown eyes instead. We were just friends, and happily, unthinkingly so, spent many afternoon and weekend hours enjoying each other's company—until tenth grade, when Zeeva joined our school.

It was the first day of tenth grade, and as class had begun, we all noticed the new girl who shyly found an empty seat at the side of the classroom. She introduced herself as Zeeva Blau to the crowd of friendly and curious classmates surrounding her desk. As the empty seat she had found happened to be directly in front of Tamar, my desk mate, I had the opportunity to observe her as class started. I can't say what it was that attracted me to her on that first day. Perhaps it was because she was somewhat reserved, or maybe it was the organized, serious way she took notes, or the mature way in which she responded to our teacher in class. At recess I introduced myself to her, and we found ourselves in avid discussion by the time the bell rang.

The seeds of conflict were not yet apparent at lunchtime, when I seated myself between Zeeva and Tamar and proceeded to introduce them, nor did I notice the awkwardness with which conversation flowed, as I tried to steer it smoothly between the three of us. Afternoon recess found Zeeva engaged by a couple of other girls while Tamar and I giggled together as we had always done. It was only when Tamar and I parted from Zeeva, after walking halfway home from school together, that I noticed how something had clicked between the new girl and me, and how somehow Tamar had been left out.

Tamar lived two blocks away from me, giving us a full ten minutes together in the clear late summer air.

"Yonit," she was saying to me, "you know what I want to do this year?"

"What?" I had stopped trying to guess the answers to her questions years ago. I could never be sure what to expect from her.

"You know the area on the side of our house that's grown over by weeds? It used to be a flower garden. Now we call it the jungle. I'm going to get rid of all the weeds, fertilize it, and make it into a vegetable garden. I decided I want to learn how to garden, but I mean, really learn. Like know how to grow organic vegetables and stuff like that."

I wasn't surprised. "You want to start an organic vegetable farm?" I was only half teasing.

"Maybe," she grinned. "Wanna help?"

"Sure, I guess," I said. Any of Tamar's projects were bound to be at least fun. We had attempted many such undertakings with varying degrees of success. I had always been happy to follow through on her ideas. Now, however, I listened to ourselves as we talked together and made plans for the organic garden on the side of Tamar's house ("And then we can make an herb garden between the trees in *your* yard!"), and a breeze of discontent began to whisper around me. Tamar didn't feel it, excited as she was about the books on agriculture she had taken out from the library, but when she offered to bring them over to my house to share with me, I temporarily declined, wondering how Zeeva was spending her evening.

The first few weeks of school passed. Fascinated by Zeeva,

and excited by the friendly intellectual stimulation, I noticed a growing boredom when I hung out with Tamar, shmoozing about issues that weren't that exciting to me. Nonetheless, I refused to hurt Tamar by letting her catch on to my new interests. I continued to spend time with her as usual, barring the time I gladly gave to my new companion. I ignored the tiny, growing resentment that would often plague me when I was with Tamar. I stood between my two friends, juggling my time with each of them, with the poor skill of one who has little experience juggling. I dropped balls at recess, forgetting (not trying?) to include Tamar when Zeeva offered a philosophical explanation of an experience she'd had, and I dropped a ball studying for a *Pirkei Avos* test with Zeeva, before Tamar even had a chance to ask me to go over the notes with her. I was losing the balls fast and was beginning to get exhausted by the whole juggling act.

One Sunday I was at Tamar's, nestling tomato seeds in the earth she had weeded and tilled, no longer denying to myself my resentment at being stuck with this boring project. She was chatting about what kind of vine to have growing up the fence. I opted for flowers—morning glories, maybe—just to contribute to the discussion, but Tamar wanted string beans.

"So do string beans then," I agreed, with a shrug in my voice.

Tamar's hands, patting down the soil above a seed, stopped slowly. "You're not so into this, are you?" she asked me, quietly.

"I think it's a great idea, Tamar. You know I think you're so creative," I said in a desperate attempt to catch the ball before it came crashing down. I couldn't admit to her that I kind of felt I was losing out on something by crouching there in the dirt with her. Nor could I tell her how much I was looking forward to getting home so I could wash the brown out of my nails and call Zeeva to discuss *Dune*, the science fiction novel we had both just finished reading. It was such an intriguing story, written with so many conflicting undercurrents, and I couldn't wait to hear Zeeva's take on it, and tell her my ideas. It just wasn't the kind of book I could discuss with Tamar. When I had told her the plot, she had smiled her friendly, carefree smile, and said, "Cool!" and that was the end of that.

Tamar wasn't fooled. "Yeah, but you don't really want to be doing this with me," she said. She wiped the dirt off her palms and stood up. "I'm sorry to have dragged you into this, Yonit. You really don't have to help me with this if you don't want to."

I stood up as well to meet her eyes. She was right that I wasn't so into it, but I definitely had nothing against her, and I didn't want to hurt her feelings. I tried again. "Tamar, I might not be so excited about organic farming, but I like spending time with you."

"Usually, but it doesn't seem like you're having much fun right now. Maybe if we did something else?" Her tone begged me to say it was just the activity, not her company which had disenchanted me. As we went inside to wash our hands and make ourselves some lunch, I noticed her eyes were almost brown. ("That's 'cuz I'm sad," I heard her fourth-grade voice explaining when our teacher criticized the science project she had worked on so diligently. "Brown is my sad eye color.") I felt so bad for having hurt her that making lunch together wasn't so much fun either, and I went home early, saying I didn't feel well and wasn't hungry.

I didn't call Zeeva the minute I got home as I had planned to do. I made myself some cheese toast and took it to my room with my diary. I had to straighten things out in my head and extract myself from the mess I was in. I quickly finished the toast and began to write.

Dear Diary,

I finally dropped all the balls I've been juggling for the past month and a half since school started. I think I even lost some. I really hurt Tamar by not being so into her garden. But the truth is I'm not into her garden, and I see now that all the things we always shared weren't really things I'm so into anyway.

But I thought I was into them then… What happened that I was so happy with Tamar for so many years, and suddenly I'm no longer satisfied to hang out with her? What has taken my sweet childhood friendship and turned it sour?

Getting to know Zeeva made me realize that Tamar and I really don't have very much in common, at least not anymore. I have finally found a like-minded friend in Zeeva, someone with whom I can discuss ideas, and not just plan fun projects. I wish Tamar weren't so sensitive. I like her, but what can I do if Zeeva fills a gap that Tamar cannot? I always knew Tamar and I were different—that she was more creative and fun-loving, and I was more philosophical and into school, but that was just the way it was between us. I just thought I was boring. But now that Zeeva enjoys so much of what I love, time with her is so refreshing. I feel like I don't need Tamar anymore, but that's just too mean. She is my best friend, isn't she? I mean, she always was… What does it mean to be best friends?

The phone rang. "Hi, it's Zeeva. How are you?"

"Good," I said, wondering why I wasn't so excited to hear from her. After all, I had been looking forward to her call. "What's doing?"

"Well, I just reread the last pages of *Dune*. It's planned out so well, and I got so involved in it. I can't believe it's over! *Baruch* Hashem, it's just the first of a trilogy, so we can start the other two, though often the first in a series is the best."

She paused. I wasn't sure how to respond. I threw in a belated "Uh-huh."

"What do you think about Jessica? I couldn't tell if the author wants you to like her, or not."

"What? Oh, Jessica." I tried to figure out what I thought about the character. Right then, I didn't really think anything about her. I tried to get into the mode of evaluating the characters, but I just kept seeing Tamar's sad, brown eyes and felt too guilty. "Zeeva, actually, I'm kind of, umm, busy right now. I'm trying to analyze—something else."

"Oh, really? Another book?" She was interested and enjoyed hearing my ideas on literature.

"No, actually, I mean, I'm just trying to think about stuff right now." In a foolish, subconscious attempt to make things better between Tamar and me, I added brusquely, "I don't really want to talk about the book anymore. At least not right now."

When I hung up the receiver, I knew I hadn't improved the situation with Tamar, and I had instead succeeded in making Zeeva a little upset with me as well. I felt annoyed at Tamar for being so sensitive and wanting to prevent me from developing and expressing myself through this new friendship. I felt trapped. But really, I slowly admitted, I was most annoyed at myself. It was really me who couldn't figure out how to be nice to my friends. Tamar and Zeeva hadn't done anything wrong. Poor, sweet Tamar! I really did like her. And, if I thought about it honestly, we actually had many things in common. I also had a fun-loving side, for example, and enjoyed creating projects. I knew that if I had let myself get into it, I would have found Tamar's garden a lot of fun.

At some point, cross-legged on my bed with my diary half-open in my lap, I began to laugh at myself. Here I was, with not just one good friend, but two, and instead of being grateful, I was mulling over problems that I had created myself. I knew I would still have to figure out how to get myself out of my dilemma. I had hurt at least one of my friends' feelings, as well as building up resentment within myself towards parts of her personality. For now, however, inspired by the ironic humor of my situation, I picked up my pen again and scribbled some verses about appreciating the good in our lives. *Baruch* Hashem, I had been able to see what a gift I had before it was too late. When I fixed up the rhymes a bit and moved some words around, I had a short poem that, in a roundabout way, expressed my gratitude for the friends Hashem had given me.

I knocked on Tamar's door Monday morning to walk with her to school. The weather had just begun to get frosty, and I hadn't dressed warmly enough.

"Wanna jog to school?" I asked cheerfully.

"Sure," Tamar agreed, less cheerfully.

As we headed down the block, I handed her a packet of green bean seeds. "I thought about it, Tamar, and I think you're right about the green beans, since it is a vegetable garden. And I read up a little on vines, and morning glories are pretty much weeds. They appear on their own. So you may end up with both."

"Really? That's so funny! They're such beautiful flowers, who would think they were weeds?" She accepted my peace offering and smiled softly. "Thanks."

"I wrote a poem yesterday. I'll show it to you in school."

"Cool," she said, just as she always had. Her reaction echoed in my head the rest of our jog to school.

After she had read the poem, Tamar's response was somewhat more developed. She didn't just say "cool." "This is great, Yonit!" Tamar responded. "You're such a poet. You always write good stuff. You should show it to Mrs. Amsaloff. She'll be impressed." She gave me the "thumb's up" sign.

I didn't show it to Mrs. Amsaloff, our English teacher, but I did show it to Zeeva.

"I see you were thinking about life yesterday," Zeeva smiled, impressed. "This poem really captures the folly of humankind. Hashem surrounds us with so much good. Too often, people don't realize that the source of their frustration is actually a great gift, and if they would only view it as such, their problems would disappear. You've succeeded in expressing important ideas in a humorous way. I didn't realize you wrote poetry, though now that I think of it, it suits you."

I took my poem to my desk with me, slowly laid it down, and stared at it blankly. *"Cool! You always write good stuff. You're such a poet..."* one voice played in my head. And then the other: *"This poem captures the folly of humankind. The source of their frustration...thinking about life...if they would only view it as such, it would disappear. I didn't realize you wrote poetry. It suits you."* And then again, *"This is great, Yonit! Cool...I didn't realize..."* I could hear them speaking in my mind. I didn't notice that *Chumash* class had started. One voice echoed with the camaraderie of childhood; the other spoke from an appreciation of deep thinking. As they blended together in my mind, I saw that I needed both of them. Zeeva had helped me discover something new about myself, and I was grateful for that. But I had a fun side as well and didn't want to study the intricacies of life all the time. I liked Tamar's simple admiration, and I could enjoy her spirited activities if I would only let myself.

I grinned at the *"Cool! This is great, Yonit!"* now fading in my head. I nodded in comprehension of Zeeva's breakdown of the human plight. I now would be able to enjoy Tamar when

I was with Tamar, and Zeeva when with Zeeva. I had nothing to hide from either. Surely Tamar wouldn't be hurt by my relationship with Zeeva if it left our old friendship intact. I caught my juggling balls in one relieved swoop and put them away, along with the term "best friends." Neither one of them would be my "best friend." I would just be a very good friend to each of them.

I took out my *Chumash*, smiling at the girl beside me taking notes in colored pencil sketches, and at the girl in front of her, meticulously organizing the material in outline form. They had such diverse approaches to life, and I was glad I was now ready to enjoy them both.

Open Your Eyes
By Yonit

Thunder clouds roll out
over the sky
Uch, another storm, we sigh
We don't think of flowers so dry
That the raindrops come to satisfy.
Hashem rains down
vast cloud-fulls of good
We complain we're getting wet
And put on a raincoat with a hood
Resenting the rain as a threat.
Opportunities to learn,
occasions to grow
We view them as troubles
we'd wish to forgo
With a classroom of friends
in which to revolve

We create inner politics
and problems to solve.
Sometimes, if we move
the hood off our eyes
We see roots that needed
the water so.
Raindrops aren't problems,
school will make us wise,
And lots of friends is more fun,
Don't you know?
Open your eyes and
you will see
The gifts Hashem gave
to you and me.

17

There was something terribly wrong with the gown that Sari was supposed to wear to her sister's *chasunah.*

The Gown

BY ROCHEL YAFFE

Sari stared at her reflection, watching the tears slide down her face. The large wall mirror showed brushes, combs, and bows scattered across the table, a discarded crinoline lying in a heap in the corner, and schoolbags strewn across the floor—all left in the rush of getting ready. She could hear Dina's voice from upstairs saying, "Ma, hurry, the photographer said to be there at four sharp," and her mother's hurried reply, "Don't worry, Dina. No one is ever on time. I'm just giving the boys their bath."

Sari knew she should be helping her mother with the younger children, but she could not move. She was staring at the girl in the mirror, crying in earnest now, the tears smearing the makeup Leah had applied. She saw a girl with a round face and thick, curly, brown hair, wearing a shiny pink satin gown.

The gown. It looked terrible. Worse than it did at the last fitting. Mrs. Rosenberg had promised she would tuck it in here and let it out there, and it would be perfect. Perfectly horrible. Like a perfect pink house. *I look enormous*, thought Sari, *like the fat lady in the circus*. A sob escaped her.

"Hey, what's the matter with you, Sari? Ma needs help with the little boys. The photographer is waiting," Leah scolded in her big-sister voice. "Sari, is something wrong? Don't you feel well?" she asked with sudden concern. "You look awful."

"It's my dress." Her voice caught. "Look at it!"

"It looks fine to me! Come on, Sari, you chose the material and the style yourself. It's what you wanted."

"But it's not what I wanted! I thought it would be gorgeous—like Esti's gown at her brother's wedding."

"Come on, Sari, Esti is a size four."

"Right. And I look like size twenty." Suddenly Sari crumpled to the floor. "I can't go. I'm not going in this dress," she sobbed.

"We're ready, we're ready," Levi and Yossi came tumbling down the steps. "Hey, what happened to Sari? Come quick, Ma, something happened to Sari," they yelled.

Sari heard her mother's hurried footsteps and her anxious voice. "What's the matter now? Sari, don't you feel well? Are you sick?"

Sari did not look up.

"Sari, get up," her mother ordered. "Let me look at you."

Sari raised her tear-soaked face. "Ma, I'm not going. I can't go. My dress is too awful. I look like the fat lady in the circus." She felt calmer, now that she had made her decision. "Don't worry about me. I'll straighten up and put a load in the washing machine and start preparing for the *sheva brachos*."

There was a moment of stunned silence.

"Sari." Her mother's voice was like a whip. "Don't you dare ruin this day for Dina. Wash your face, and come right now."

At that moment, Dina came down the steps in a whirl of white. "Ma, we've got to go. It's late. Listen, the taxi is here. It's beeping."

Mother stood, undecided. Finally, she said, "Dina, I feel terrible about this. But I can't go yet. Go ahead; go to the hall with Leah. Tatty is already there with Mendel. Leah, take the little boys as well. Tell the photographer to get started with the *kallah* pictures. Tell him an emergency came up. I'll be there in ten minutes."

"Sari, I'll never forgive you for this!" Dina whirled, scooped up her long skirts, and ran out. Leah and the boys followed.

Suddenly, it was very quiet in the dining room. Sari picked up the brushes and lined them up on the table. "Sari," her mother's voice was no longer angry, just tired. "I know you are disappointed. I know how you planned this dress, how you dreamed about it. Partly, we are all to blame. We get so caught up in the preparations, the clothing, the menu, the color scheme. We forget what a *chasunah* is all about."

Sari felt a rush of contrition. She was ruining the day for her whole family. All because of a stupid dress. "I know. I know, Ma. It's the most important day in Dina's life. And for you, too, Ma. The first *chasunah*." She gave a ragged sigh. "I'm being a big baby. I'll go and get ready." She smiled wanly. "I'll just make sure not to look in any mirrors."

At the hall, the band was already playing. Dina sat on a white chair adorned with tulle, surrounded by cousins and close friends. Girls were dancing in the center of the wide, brilliantly lit room. Esti, her favorite cousin, came running towards her. "There you are, Sari. I was looking for you. Your sister is stunning. She looks like an angel." She grabbed Sari's hands and twirled her around. She caught a glimpse of two girls in the mirror. They wore matching dresses. One was slim as a pencil, the other was neither fat nor thin. She looked fine. Sari gently disengaged her hands from Esti's. "I have to go to Dina."

Her sister was smiling and nodding at relatives and friends. Then she bent her head over her Tehillim. She looked beautiful, but a little sad. Her eyes seemed red-rimmed. Had she been crying as she recited Tehillim? Or because she had to go to the hall without her mother on her wedding day?

"Dina?" Sari said hesitantly.

Dina looked up. "Hi, Sari," she said a little coolly. "I'm glad you could make it!" Suddenly both sisters burst out laughing.

"I'm sorry, Dina," Sari choked out. "I'm sorry. I was an idiot."

Dina smiled. "It's okay. I forgive you. I was also fifteen once."

"Right, about a hundred years ago," grinned Sari, and gave her sister a tight hug.

Sari threw herself exuberantly into the dancing, determined to help the *kallah* rejoice. Her mother joined the circle, slipping her hands into Leah's and Sari's. She gave Sari's hand a squeeze.

Suddenly, the music changed to a deep and solemn melody. The mothers took their places next to the *kallah*. Sisters and relatives followed, framing Dina with a bouquet of colors. As if drawn by the music, a cluster of black-clad men moved down the hall. The *chassan* was coming slowly, advancing towards the *kallah*. Dina glanced up shyly. Her eyes met her *chassan's*, gravely. He placed the white cloth over her face. Sari heaved a great sigh. Her sister was really getting married.

18

The Stars That Shine

BY NECHAMA DINA SMITH

I stood there in front of a class of twelve girls, ages six through twelve. They were breathless with excitement. A new year, new teachers, and new friends from nearby towns. As terror filled my mind, my heart, and my lungs, I let the advice of a friend of mine pound in my ears: "Give the rules and enforce them." Another directive resounded in my head: "Do not smile!"

The principal stood near me and said the worst thing I could imagine.

"Girls, this is your teacher, Morah Malka. I hope you'll all behave and show her proper respect."

Even before she left the room I had to grasp the reigns of authority. I heard the oldest girl announce to the class, "Let's say *brachos* out loud."

Crisply—very crisply, I said, "Good morning, girls. There

is to be no talking. The two rules are to stay in your seat and raise your hand for permission to speak. If anyone misbehaves—" and here I drew a box on the board, "*chas v'shalom*, I write her name in this box. That is a warning. A check next to her name is five minutes off of recess, and two checks is a bigger consequence. A third check—I call the mother. Please begin *davening. Brachos* to *yourselves.*"

The room was quiet. The children *davened*. And then that oldest girl giggled. I imagined her to be a ringleader, and I wanted to put an end to it.

In the quiet of the room I clicked open the board marker and wrote her name: Devorah.

I took a walk between the rows like a general. Then I heard another noise from Devorah. At first I thought it was laughter. Then I saw tears. I wanted to go over and put my arm around her and tell her that this is just a show! But no, I was firm with myself and said not a word.

After *davening* I took the five oldest girls, Devorah, Sara, Chani, Ilana, and Shoshi, to their classroom and taught them. They had to stand up for me when I came into the room. I couldn't believe I was forcing them to respect me like this. I taught, gave them classwork, homework, and a general knowledge test. The girls obediently did their work, though with a few sighs.

During recess I passed by the younger class. Some girls were eating their snacks indoors. Devorah was writing on the board: "School Rules: 1) Talk in class. 2) Bring tons of nosh."

She saw me. "I'm teaching them the rules of the school," she explained. I raised my eyebrows and erased "School" and wrote "Camp." The children laughed, and I said, "Class is starting."

Well, that night I took a walk in the cool air. I cried and

cried. It was a side road and no one could see me in the dark. I was in a strange place, and I was shy with the other teachers with whom I was sharing an apartment. They had hung up beautiful posters and calendars on the walls of their classrooms. They knew what they were doing. My students barely looked at me, sullenly following Devorah's lead.

The next morning before class began, one of the *rabbeim* from the boys' side came over to me. "Hi, I'm Sara's father," he introduced himself.

Uh, oh.

"Well, Sara doesn't like you, but that's because no one can be like last year's teacher, Morah Yehudis. She was a real mentor to the girls."

I smiled a big smile corresponding to the big burst of tears inside of me. That's what I wanted to be, a mentor to my class, a perfect role model.

But from the whispers and looks between my students, I realized they thought I was mean.

That second morning I *davened* again with both classes. One little girl stood on her chair and stared out the window. I felt desperate. Would this be the beginning of a free-for-all? I wrote her name in the *"chas v'shalom"* box.

After *davening*, Ilana tugged my arm. "I must do my math problems over! I left them at home, and my mother said I have to do them now."

"Fine," I answered, "but hurry up."

I didn't see Ilana the rest of that morning. I think she found a computer game to play with.

I put a decorated envelope on the wall. "For the month of Elul," I told the class, "write notes about nice things your friends did and put them in here."

I took out a note later. It said, "Chani lent me a pencil."

I don't know what kind of notes I was expecting, but it wasn't that kind. I thought they were playing a trick to show me how babyish my idea was.

When Devorah said, "Won't you read the note?" I replied, "It's not worth reading."

Then I noticed a quiet, pained look on everyone's faces.

Oh, no, I thought, I'm crushing them. They're only sixth and seventh graders. Lending a pencil was a sixth-seventh grade level of a favor. What was I doing to these girls? They were sweet and fresh and willing to learn. How could I have control without stomping on them?

"I mean... I'll only read aloud the really special ones," I finished lamely.

On my walk after school, I begged Hashem, "Please help me reach the girls. Help me break the ice. Help me teach them Your Torah, and help them love it."

Well, the next day for the *Ivrit* lesson I told them that we'd only be speaking *Ivrit*. I told them the story of Rabbi Akiva's daughter and the snake. They barely understood a word, but with motions and drawings on the board, and the fact that they already knew the story, we got through it. Everyone was laughing and smiling. I felt light and happy.

A bunch of new girls came the next day. One told me her name and smiled shyly. Before I could help it, I smiled back.

"It seems Sara likes you better," Sara's father told me that afternoon. "She still says you don't compare to Morah Yehudis, but *she* was really something."

I was teaching *Chumash Shemos*. In the *Rashi* on the first *pasuk* he says the Jews are compared to stars. My nightly walk had me looking up at the clear dark sky with millions of beautiful, bright stars. Wow. I thought about how, like the stars, we are counted—to show the preciousness of each individual, each with his or her own talents and qualities.

And I thought about my students, each beautiful in her own way, each waiting to shine and blossom. To count them meant to reveal them, to bring out their strengths.

I hoped I could do my part.

19

During World War II, in the midst of famine and poverty in Tashkent, fifteen-year-old Rochel Shagalov receives a not-to-be-believed offer.

Almost a Princess
(A True Story)

BY STERNA CITRON

Rochel Shagalov held on tightly to her frayed scarf as the train lurched from side to side, getting closer to the mysterious place called Tashkent. It had been eight days since she, her mother, three brothers, and older sister had left their hometown of Melachovka, on the outskirts of Moscow, as they fled the advancing Nazis.

The cold desert wind seeped through the train floor, the cracks around the windows, and the edges of the doors, penetrating every limb in Rochel's body.

"Ma…" she was about to complain. Not that her mother Mariasha could help. It was just instinctive.

"What do you want from Mommy?" Rosa, her sister, muttered. "Can't you see how worried she is about Yisrael?"

"Huh?" Rochel turned around to look at her brothers. While Berel, the older brother, and Shlomo, the youngest in the family, seemed fine, Yisrael, age twelve, was leaning list-lessly against his mother.

"What's wrong with him?" she asked in a whisper.

"Mommy thinks he might be coming down with some skin disease," Rosa said in an undertone. "He might have caught it from any of the hundreds of refugees on the train. And it isn't the *makkah* of *kinim* either that we're talking about." The two girls sighed. It was disgusting, this lice infestation. They couldn't wait until they could have a bath and get rid of the pests. But this skin disease of Yisrael's wasn't repulsive like lice. It was scary.

The train chugged on while they watched the changing landscape from the window.

At the train station in Tashkent, the train emptied out. As expected, no one was waiting for them at the train station.

"Where are we going to live?" Rochel asked her sister, as they sat forlornly among their bundles.

Her sister shrugged. "I heard someone say that we refugees are not wanted here. They're hoping we'll continue to some town farther away called Hungry Steppes."

Rochel made a face. "I don't like the sound of that name."

The sisters observed their new surroundings curiously. Tashkent was the capital of Uzbekistan, a republic of the U.S.S.R. at that time, but the native Uzbeks spoke a different language, and their dress was very distinctive. The men wore loose white blouses and pajama-like pants tied with a string at the waist. The women wore long flowing dresses. Married women covered their faces with veils.

They heard their mother calling. "*Kinder*, look who's here. I can't believe it."

There was Reb Chaim Tashkenter (his real name was Chaim Horowitz), with his smiling, friendly, round face, just as Rochel remembered him from when he would visit them in Melachovka.

He explained to them the state of affairs. "The housing situation here is terrible! I myself live with my wife, who is sick, and my daughter in a teeny-tiny room. With great difficulty I managed to find you a place. Don't be shocked now… it's the stable next to my place, but don't worry. I emptied it of all the animals and cleaned it out. The good part is that there's lots of straw to sleep on. I'm sorry, but it's the best that I can do."

"Reb Chaim, you've saved our lives! Thank you!" Mariasha said, and meant it. Hundreds of other evacuees were still milling about the station, with no place to go. The Shagalovs were well off as they would have a roof over their heads and be sheltered from the cold and rain. Officially, they were not even supposed to be living in Tashkent at all, but they had no choice. They had to survive.

The Shagalovs made themselves as comfortable as they could. The problem was Yisrael; his condition was getting worse. His mother took him to the hospital. Apparently what Yisrael had was diagnosed as very contagious, and so he was immediately admitted. There was some good news, though. Because of Yisrael's hospitalization, the family was granted official permission to stay in Tashkent and, even better, given a house to live in.

Their new home, which consisted of two rooms, was built on stilts. It had no furniture. They would have to sleep on the floor and use boxes for chairs. Perhaps it was a good thing, after all, that their first place had been a stable. They had gotten used to living without such amenities as electricity and running water. It wasn't such a shock that their new place didn't have them. All baking was done outside over a small hole in the earth filled with coals. The biggest shock, though, came when they looked for the bathroom and found it outside, under the building—a semi-open outhouse.

Human nature is such that one can get accustomed to almost anything. Though it was a far cry from the civilized cities of Russia, the Shagalovs lost no time in acclimating themselves to the primitive new way of living. After a while, they were given good news. Yisrael was *baruch* Hashem recovering and was ready to go home.

Rochel was happy that her brother was back home again. But not all her family was there. Her oldest sister was married and lived elsewhere. As for her father—ever since he was arrested in 1937 by the KGB, *yemach shemom*, when Rochel was ten years old, no one had seen him. If only they knew where he was held prisoner! If only they knew that he was still alive! Her heart ached when she thought of him and what he must be going through. She missed him so much!

It was rare for their little hut to be occupied only by their family. Usually there would be other people staying there too. Every available inch of the floor space was taken up by anyone remotely acquainted with them. Her mother Mariasha had a good heart and could not bear the thought that a fellow Jew should be wandering about without shelter. So she invited them to stay with them as long as necessary.

Soon illness struck again. First Shlomo contracted typhus, a sometimes fatal disease, and then Mariasha herself was diagnosed with a dangerous case of pneumonia.

It became Rosa's job to stay home and take care of the sick. Rochel was responsible to go out every day to get food for the family.

Food was rationed in wartime. Each family was given a coupon. It entitled their family of six to exactly one loaf of bread a day. It took the better part of a day to accomplish this task. It wasn't an easy task either, which is why the job fell to Rochel, as she was the fighter in the family. When anything difficult had to be done, Rochel was usually chosen to do it. Every day she had to walk for half an hour on a narrow dirt path which led to a wider road, still unpaved, where she would catch her first bus. The second bus was where the problem started. Often it was so full that she could not get on and instead had to hang on for dear life to the outside of the bus. Sometimes there wasn't even room for her hand on the outside, so she'd have to walk the rest of the way, which took a couple of hours. When finally she arrived at the commercial bakery, hundreds of people, some of them irritable and impatient, and all of them very hungry, were already waiting in long lines.

During the first part of this tiresome, daily journey, while striding down the dirt path, Rochel would pass by a *tchaychana*, a tea house, where dozens of Uzbek men, mostly middle-aged, sat, drinking cups of tea and eating raisins out of small bowls. Apparently, the men each had several wives who worked while they met with their friends at the tea house. Many of the men turned to look inquisitively at her as she passed. Was it the fact that she was fair while the Uzbeks were naturally dark? Or that her clothes were tattered and they pitied her? She cringed at the unwanted attention every time she went by.

Day after day, Rochel made the long trip to the bakery where she bought the loaf of bread. And after all that, what kind of bread was it? Its crust was inevitably burnt while the inside was raw. Apparently the loaves weighed more that way, so the bakers got more money for them.

Out of necessity, Rochel developed a technique for acquiring bread. She had to be aggressive; if she wasn't, she could end up going home empty-handed, which happened to some people. She was short, but she made that into an asset. She would manage to squeeze between people and get to the clerk's window where she would raise two hands with money in each hand. Rochel was so short that her face was not seen above the window. The clerk would sometimes assume that the two hands belonged to two different people, and so Rochel would come home with a treasure—an extra loaf of bread. Not that even two loaves a day were enough to still the hunger pangs of the growing children and their mother. Nor was it like the good, old days when there would sometimes be an onion, a potato, or a piece of herring to go along with the bread.

Life seemed to have settled into a kind of routine—if struggling for existence can be called routine. But one day something happened that was quite out of the ordinary.

It happened as Rochel passed the *tchaychana* one day. All the Uzbeks stood up as one and bowed down deeply to her. "Pretty girl," one of them said with awe in his voice, "you will be Irtoi's wife."

Another Uzbek said to her, "Do you know that you are betrothed to the prince?"

Her heart beating with fright and confusion, she hurried on. Who in the world was Irtoi, and why were they saying that she would be his wife? At fifteen and in their dismal circumstances, marriage was not exactlyuppermost on her mind.

As for marriage to a non-Jew, that would never be an option.

Still, she was curious. What was it all about?

Three days later, a dignified young man, elegantly dressed, was waiting for her at the tea shop. Rochel guessed that he must be Irtoi.

"Hello," he said.

Rochel just went on.

The next day he was there again. "*Dyevutshka* (girl)," he

addressed her, "would you like some pita?"

Rochel had noticed a pita store opening up opposite the *tchaychana*. But she had been intimidated by the throngs of people and all the noise. It was a pity because the pita was made of better flour than the bread, and was thoroughly baked too. Like the bread, it was kosher, being made only of flour and water.

"I don't think so," Rochel replied.

"Don't worry about the lines," he said. "Come with me."

As Rochel followed him into the shop, the Uzbeks made way for him, bowing to him and Rochel as they passed. It was the strangest feeling, having people show her all this honor when she was just a teenager, dressed in rags.

Ignoring the masses of people waiting to buy pitas, Irtoi strode up the head of the queue and commanded the owner, "Fill this girl's bag full of pitas."

"Yes, Sir Irtoi," replied the owner. He took Rochel's bag and filled it up to the top with six or seven large pita breads— a treasure! Rochel paid the owner and hastily left the shop, dumbfounded at her good fortune. Because of the rationing, the pita owner was normally only permitted to give each family two or three pitas. And here she had more than twice that amount!

She opened the door to her home nervously. "Home so early?" Mariasha asked, surprised. She was *baruch* Hashem feeling a lot better. Her eye caught the overflowing bag of pitas. "Where's the manna from?"

"I don't know," answered Rochel, groping for an acceptable explanation. "It must have been Eliyahu Hanavi."

Her mother dropped the subject. "We'll eat some of the pitas and sell the rest on the black market," she decided. "They'll fetch a good price."

The next few days Rochel came home with a bag brimming over with fresh pita breads. For the first time in a long time the Shagalovs went to bed without the usual hunger pangs gnawing at them. Yisrael especially appreciated the extra food, having lost so much weight during his illness.

But Rochel was worried. The extra food was very welcome, but all this talk about being betrothed—how serious was it? As she and Rosa prepared to go to bed, she casually asked her older sister, "How old are the Uzbek girls when they get married?"

"You've seen them with their veils and their babies, haven't you? They're very young. They get married at twelve or thirteen. You'd be an old maid by their standards!"

"Yeah, and what about you?!" Rochel retorted.

"Hey, why the sudden interest?" Rosa asked.

"Just curious."

"Well, if you're curious, I'll tell you some more of their interesting customs. First an Uzbek marries one woman. Then, when she gets a little older, he takes another woman, a younger one, for his second wife. He can have up to three or four wives. The older wife, *nebbach*, goes to work, while he does nothing."

"I know," answered Rochel. "I see them at the tea house, gabbing with their friends all day."

"And I'll tell you something else," Rosa continued. "Once a girl is engaged, she may not talk to any man other than her betrothed. I heard about a Russian refugee, not Jewish, who got engaged to an Uzbek. When her fiancé heard that she spoke to another young man, you know what he did?"

"No, what?"

"He had the young man's ears cut off and sent to her."

Rochel's tongue went dry. She tried to say something but couldn't.

"Rochel? Are you there?"

"I'm tired," she managed to mumble. "I think I'll go to sleep," she said.

But she couldn't fall asleep. She was worried. This betrothal thing wasn't a joke. And even though there had been no proposal, it was quite possible that by accepting Irtoi's favors, she was giving her agreement to be his wife.

Her sleep was filled with strange dreams of opening up envelopes and finding chopped body parts in them.

The next morning Irtoi was waiting for her as usual. "Good morning, *dyevutshka*." He motioned for her to follow him.

"No, thank you," she said.

Irtoi's handsome face clouded over with disappointment. Rochel hurried away to catch the bus to go to the bread bakery. Her father had been *moser nefesh* for *Yiddishkeit*. He could easily have joined the Communist Party when he was asked and thereby avoid arrest, but he didn't. She would happily give up a full stomach rather than give up a life of Torah and *mitzvos*. She thought about her brothers who would no doubt be upset when they saw the old half-baked bread again. Well, that was life.

That night the Shagalovs heard a knock at the door. It was a stranger, an Uzbek, and he asked to speak to the mother.

The visitor said, "My master, Prince Irtoi, has fallen in love with your daughter. He is the richest man among us and will one day be the leader. If your daughter agrees to marry him, she will live in his palace and have magnificent clothes to wear and delicious food to eat."

Rochel's mother listened attentively as the matchmaker continued, "As a prince, Sir Irtoi is entitled to a total of seven wives. Your daughter will be the main wife, and the others will be her servants. In exchange for her hand, he will give you camels, sheep, donkeys, and generous living accommodations. You will have everything you want."

He paused, waiting for her response.

Mariasha replied noncommittally, "I need to think about it."

As soon as the stranger left, Mariasha became highly agitated. "What do you know about this?" she asked her daughter.

Rochel told her.

Her mother took a deep breath. "We have to leave Tashkent," she said. "It's too dangerous to stay here. This prince is obviously quite powerful and can take you forcibly if he wants to."

They hurriedly packed up their things and that same night moved to a town called Kuluk. Mariasha was confident that Irtoi could not find them there. The living conditions weren't great. Their new home could best be described as a shack, and the unpaved streets became swamps when it rained. Rochel expected her mother to be upset by the harsh conditions, but to Rochel's amazement, her mother was far from it. In fact, she was exultant. "We beat them, just like we beat the KGB!" she exclaimed. "As for food and sustenance, I know Hashem will take care of us as He has until now."

And that is the story of how Rochel Shagalov turned down an opportunity to be a princess. She and her family happily chose near-starvation and extreme poverty rather than a life of extravagance with bountiful food. And never did they regret their decision, not even for an instant, not even during the famine which grew even more terrible the following year in 1942.

In 1945, WWII ended. Not long after that, Mariasha and her family escaped Russia and made their way to the U.S., where the family was able to live full Jewish lives amidst abundance and plenty.

Years later, when the Communist government collapsed, the Shagalovs finally received word of what had happened to their righteous father, Yitzchak Elchanan Shagalov. He had been murdered in cold blood by his captors shortly after his arrest, martyred *al kiddush Hashem* for the sake of the Torah and *Yiddishkeit*. May the merit of the *mesiras nefesh* of those steadfast Jews stand us in good stead!

20

Ilana had finally arrived at the mountain summer getaway. Now Rachel Leah would not have to spend her vacation following her mother to all the adult events. Now she'd have fun. Or so she thought.

Dream Vacation

BY NECHAMA DINA SMITH

Rachel Leah's golden-brown curls blew in her face as a breeze sifted through the tree branches. The sun shone bright and beautiful in the clearest sky Rachel Leah ever remembered. Her shoe scraped the earth back and forth impatiently as she sat on a large smooth rock.

"Where is Ilana?" She abruptly stood up, alarming the lizard which had been sunbathing next to her. It scampered off, leaving Rachel Leah to wait alone. The lake with its canoe glistened and beckoned to her, and the hiking paths were cleared and ready for the tread of her sneakers. The scent of pine trees and sequoias filled her nostrils. The pressures of school and life seemed far away. All she needed was someone with whom to share her bliss. Then life would be perfect.

"Oh, Ilana, can't you show up already?" She looked behind her to make sure no one heard her talking out loud to herself.

At the sound of a car coming round the mountain dirt

road, Rachel Leah jumped. A Grand Jeep Cherokee minivan appeared around the bend, and Rachel Leah's heart leaped. The windows slid down and the Zahavi girls called out, "Rachel Leah!"

Rachel Leah waved with gusto. Ilana was finally here. Now she wouldn't have to spend her ten-day vacation following her mother to all the adult *shiurim*. Now she'd have fun.

She ran after the minivan up the hill until the cabin grounds. Rachel Leah caught up as Mrs. Zahavi parked. Ilana emerged, stretching. It was the same Ilana, with her glossy dark brown hair, deep, contemplative eyes, and shy smile.

"Ilana!" Rachel Leah could barely contain her joy. "I'm so excited! Can we go for a walk?"

Ilana giggled. "Gosh! Let me just help my family unpack and I'll meet you at your cabin."

Rachel Leah remembered to say "hi" to Gila and Rena, Ilana's younger sisters, before she skipped away.

"Rachel Leah?" Ilana called out softly, not long thereafter, as she approached her friend's cabin.

"Oh, hi, Ilana," Rachel Leah responded. "You're probably hungry. Let's go to the dining room and see if they have soup or something."

The girls grinned happily. They only saw each other once a year, at the Wild National Park Learning Getaway. A group of *frum* families from several cities organized it every year. For four years now, since Rachel Leah was ten, Ilana was the only other girl her age at the Getaway. There was so much to talk about, so much to catch up on. Ilana was the best listener. She was also an excellent sport. Interesting, she seemed different now. More mature. Her long hair lay neatly in place; her blouse, starched and ironed. Maybe high school did that to her. Rachel Leah was curious to hear if Ilana's experiences had been anything like hers.

"So how's school?" Ilana began as they both turned down the path towards the dining room.

"It's incredible. Nothing like elementary," Rachel Leah answered. She started talking about the lively G.O., the difficult tests, and the teachers that shmoozed a whole period long. At some point she wanted to disclose to her friend her difficulties with the girls in school whom she thought were snobby, but not now. As usual, Ilana listened attentively.

Rachel Leah stopped her chatter for a minute. She suddenly felt so lucky to have a good friend with her in the beautiful mountains, and one who was always game to join her in any escapade she chose.

"Wait here," she instructed, "and I'll go in and get you some soup." She patted a huge tree stump as wide as a kitchen table, so that her friend should be seated.

"Oh, by the way, is that what you wanted? Soup?"

"Sure," Ilana smiled. She sat on the stump, crossing her legs at the ankle.

"You're such a lady," Rachel Leah joked as she ran inside.

When Rachel Leah returned with the two bowls of soup, she was in for a surprise. A girl about her age with short black hair, glittery earrings, and a camera looped around her neck, stood just feet away from Ilana. They were talking.

So a new family had joined. Rachel Leah's dream vacation seemed to come to a screeching halt.

The girls were having an animated discussion. They didn't even look up until Rachel Leah was only two feet away.

"So I can't believe you actually know Tova," the new girl was exclaiming.

"Yeah, we were in the same bunk in Camp Chayelet for three years," Ilana answered.

"Who's Tova?" asked Rachel Leah. If Ilana wasn't going to make the introductions, Rachel Leah would just have to squeeze her way in.

The new girl just stared at Rachel Leah. *Now, that's kind of rude*, Rachel Leah thought. *Or was it rude of me to ask?*

Ilana came to the rescue. "Tova is her best friend," she explained. "Uh, what's your name again?"

So they didn't know each other.

"Debby."

"Well, hi. My name is Rachel Leah," Rachel Leah tried to be friendly, but strangely, her voice sounded sullen to her ears.

Debby just said "Oh," in a bored way. She turned back to Ilana and went right on talking about Tova.

"Here's your soup, Ilana," said Rachel Leah. Now her voice sounded gruff.

She handed Ilana the bowl and sat down next to her on the stump. She ran her fingers through her curls as she half listened to their conversation. She daydreamed about canoeing on the lake, her fingers dipping into the cool, still water.

"Um, Rachel? Is that your name?" she heard Debby ask. Rachel Leah turned.

"Do you mind taking a picture of us?" She handed her camera to Rachel Leah and climbed onto the stump. She stood behind Ilana, her hands on Ilana's shoulders. Rachel Leah felt her face burn red. How could they shame her by excluding her like that? Why didn't Ilana say something? *Well*, she reasoned, *I guess she can't. It's not her camera.*

Rachel Leah pressed the button and hoped the picture came out bad.

"That's for Tova, right?" Ilana asked, after a glance at Rachel Leah. Good old Ilana. Trying to make her feel better. But it wasn't working.

"Hey, let's go for a walk," Debby proposed. She did not meet Rachel Leah's eyes. *Does that mean I'm not invited?* Rachel Leah wondered.

She joined the walk anyway. Yet whenever she said something, Debby would stare at her without replying, and then continue with whatever she was saying. Ilana sometimes tried to smooth things over, but she was so involved in what Debby was discussing, it seemed to be a chore for her to include her old friend.

They walked along a narrow path. Two could barely fit side by side. Rachel Leah walked behind. *Naturally*, she thought. *Who wants me here, anyway?*

"Oh, I can't believe it!" Debby squealed. "Your father is a cardiologist, too?"

"My uncle's a homeopath," Rachel Leah interjected, loud enough to be heard. Debby stared at her again, this time with unmistakable disdain.

Then, without Rachel Leah's input, both girls crossed the pebbled brook to continue on the other side. Rachel Leah decided she'd had enough.

"I think I have to go," she said, struggling to keep her voice even. "I need to take care of something."

Ilana turned around. "You're going? Oh… We'll see you later, okay?" Debby just continued talking.

As Rachel Leah dragged her feet back to her cabin, she heard the girls' voices fading in the background: "So does your father have crazy hours, too, or does he make his own hours?"

She opened her family's cabin door. It was empty. Just three beds, a night table with a lamp, and a small fridge. She'd brought a few books with her, but the truth was she was in no mood for reading. Or eating. Or even crying. She just felt like a nobody.

There was nothing to do. So she went to the social hall where Rabbi Schluss was giving a *Chumash* class to the women. Her mother, delighted to see her daughter joining the *shiur*, asked her friend to move over and motioned to her daughter to sit next to her.

For the next hour she sat, her heart heavy, not even bothering to try to understand the class. During the break, her mother whispered, "Isn't this great?"

"Yeah, it is," she answered, her face and voice expressionless. "Excuse me, I need to take a walk."

Her mother squeezed her daughter's arm and said, "Go ahead."

Rachel Leah breathed the sweet mountain air as she walked down the hill. She'd head towards the playground where the little kids played. Perhaps she'd be momentarily distracted from her thoughts.

On her way she heard girls' voices. From a distance she could see Ilana and Debby. They seemed to be exercising. Or was it dancing? Curious, she came a little closer. Ilana spotted her and ran over.

"Oh, Rachel Leah, we wanted to ask you..." She was breathless. Debby stopped prancing. She smiled—for the first time.

"What?" Rachel Leah didn't even pretend to smile.

"We're planning a dance that we'll perform in front of all the women on Motza'ei Shabbos. Do you want to join?"

Rachel Leah's voice got colder. "No, thank you." Then she added, "I can't dance for the life of me."

She turned on her heels and marched away, fast, towards the playground.

By the time she reached the play area, her steps had slowed down. She felt as if she were bearing heavy weights.

It took all her strength to push open the heavy gate to the

playground. Several toddlers were bouncing around. She sat down wearily on a picnic bench, offering a wan smile to one of the mothers, who was pushing her baby to sleep in a stroller.

Two of the little boys were exultantly shouting non-discernible syllables, each repeating the other's pronunciations.

"Ga ga!" shouted the kid called Eli.

"Ga ga, doo dah!" responded his friend Shmuel.

They're having the time of their life, Rachel Leah thought.

Just then another small boy approached. He grinned at Shmuel and made some comment in their secret language. Within two minutes, Shmuel and the new kid were holding hands, jumping up and down. The two hopped away, leaving Eli behind, visibly dejected.

Then came the inevitable: Eli went up to the new kid and gave him a push.

Her heart went out to Eli. *Poor child*, she thought. *He's jealous, and he can't even express himself. I know only too well what he's feeling.*

After a few more punches from the unhappy Eli, the mothers of the boys stopped chatting and went to see what was going on.

Fascinated, Rachel Leah waited to see how the mothers would handle the problem. One of the mothers who seemed to be Shmuel's mother quickly assessed the situation and took action. She took her son's hand, the one that wasn't holding the new boy, and attached it to the hand of Eli.

"There you go, boys," she said brightly. "Why don't all three of you hold hands and play together!"

The three of them scampered off happily. Rachel Leah wanted to jump up and hug the mother who had solved the problem so simply and beautifully.

It was time to go. She stood up. But go where? Do what?

She started to head back to her cabin, her thoughts still preoccupied with the scene she had just witnessed. She had been meant to see this, hadn't she? There was something there for her to learn. Something…

And suddenly she got it. She understood. Those two little boys who had rejected Eli—they hadn't meant to hurt him. They were just so excited about getting to know each other that they had momentarily abandoned him.

Tears of thankfulness and relief rolled down her cheeks. No, she wouldn't go to her cabin. She retraced her steps and followed the path to where Ilana and Debby had been practicing their dance. The tears were still dripping down her face, and she felt drained from all her emotions, but she was light of heart and content with her decision.

"Ilana!" she called. "Debby!" They were sitting down on the grass, apparently exhausted from all their practice.

"Um, do you still want me in the dance?" She couldn't believe she'd said the words. She instantly felt elated, even before she heard their reply. She was… proud of herself. It didn't even matter so much what they would say. She had been *dan* her friends *l'kaf zechus*. And she had swallowed her pride.

Both girls immediately jumped up. "Yes!" Debby cried.

"We were just thinking it wouldn't work out with only the two of us," Ilana explained.

Boy, Rachel Leah thought to herself. *They still don't want me. They just need a third person.*

"What about Gila and Rena?" Rachel Leah asked, smiling mischievously.

Ilana laughed. "Rachel Leah…!"

"Well, you know I can't dance." Rachel Leah looked at Debby. She took a deep breath. "You'll have to teach me, okay?"

And that is how Rachel Leah ended up having the most

wonderful vacation she'd ever had. She learned to dance, which she never thought she would. She also learned the benefits of judging favorably, but even more importantly, of being humble and willing to ask to be a friend.

21

Shira liked to do everything with her friend. Sara, on the other hand, often enjoyed being alone.

We're Friends, Aren't We?

BY BRACHA GOYKADOSH

"Hey, Sara, what's up?" Shira asked as we stood side by side in front of our lockers.

"Nothing much," I answered, dumping my books and backpack. "How are you?"

"Great, *baruch* Hashem! I went shopping last night and got a really nice pair of shoes and a Shabbos outfit." Shira dropped the book she'd been holding onto the floor next to Rachel's locker.

"Why did you do that?" I asked, pointing to the book.

"It was next to my stuff when I came in this morning. It's probably Rachel's," Shira said with a huff. She placed it upright on the floor, leaning it against Rachel's locker. She bit the corner of her lip but returned to the topic of her shopping experience. "Anyway, I got the stuff at this new Orange County Mall. They were having some really great sales there.

My sisters also got tons of stuff, and you know how hard it is to find things for my sisters."

Shira wasn't kidding. I went shopping with them once. Let me assure you, once was enough for me. Shira's sisters analyze every outfit, pair of shoes, dress, shirt, and skirt. Every single item gets a detailed fifteen-minute discussion of why or why not it should be bought. Not what I consider a very enjoyable shopping experience. I came out with a raging headache! That convinced me never to go shopping with them again. Ever.

The bell rang, and Shira and I headed to the auditorium together for *davening*. On the way down, we met up with some mutual friends and chatted about the upcoming Chanukah *chagigah*. What a great way to start a day!

After *davening* I went to Halachah class, my first period of the day. As usual, Shira was sitting at the desk next to mine.

"Hello, Sara!" she said happily and gave a little wave.

"I feel honored to receive such a warm welcome," I said, placing my notebook and *sefer* on my desk. "I might add: my *second* welcome of the day."

"Good. I feel honored to be the one to make you feel honored to receive such a warm welcome." Shira opened her looseleaf.

"So, I feel honored that you feel honored—" I said, turning to a blank page in my notebook.

"Okay, okay, we get the point!" said Rachel, who sits behind us. Shira and I giggled.

Rabbi Heller, our halachah teacher, walked in, and the class began.

Shira kept leaning over to see my notes. "What was that?" she whispered, her hair spilling onto my loose-leaf. "I think I missed that sentence, and I can't decipher your messy handwriting."

"Shhhh!" I said gritting my teeth, "I'll show you my notes after class."

The next class was *historia*. I love the class. I just find Jewish history so fascinating. Shira, on the other hand, does not share my view. For some reason, she absolutely loathes the class.

Our teacher, Morah Rivkin, was sitting at her desk, writing in her roll book. "Girls," she said as we settled down. "I have your tests to return."

Our tests…! I was so excited, I shivered! I had studied very hard for that test, and, though it was murderous, I thought I had done well.

Morah Rivkin started handing out the tests. "Tehilla Kerem… Rachel Kahn… Sara Cohen…" That's me! I ran to get my test and Morah Rivkin handed it to me with a smile.

I peeked at my mark and proceeded nonchalantly to my desk.

"What did you get? What did you get?" Shira danced around me.

"A mark," I said, trying to be casual.

"Oh, but how did you do? Good, bad? Did you pass, did you fail?" Shira asked nervously.

Just then, Morah Rivkin called Shira up to get her test.

Are you wondering why I didn't tell Shira my mark? Well, the thing is, I'm a very private person. Some things I just like to keep to myself; I don't think my mark needs to be publicized to the whole world. Shira can live a very happy and contented life without knowing that I got a hundred on the test. Anyway, I just didn't feel like telling her.

In less than a minute, Shira was back to nudging me. "So, nu, tell me! What did you get? I got a sixty-four. Of all the nerve! She could've just given me one more point and then I would have passed. So what did you get?"

Shira was acting like my younger sister. When Esty (Pesty is more like it) wants to know something, she will not leave me alone.

"I told you before. A mark." I put my test in the folder with the others.

"Well," Shira huffed. "If you don't want to tell me, just say so!"

"I don't want to tell you," I said very clearly.

Shira crumpled her test into a ball and threw it into her desk. I stared at the paper for a moment. I wished she would stop throwing things everywhere.

"Okay, your mark is your business. No one is going to force you to tell me anything." Shira is a master of reverse psychology.

"You're absolutely right," I agreed. Her little subterfuge was not going to work on me.

Morah Rivkin chose that exact moment to start class, which I considered a blessing. I didn't want the conversation going any further.

At recess, the seniors were having a muffin sale. Yummy! I couldn't wait to get my hand on a cranberry crumb one.

"What are you doing, Sara?" Shira asked as I fished through my bag.

"Oh, I'm trying to find my dollar. I really want to buy a muffin. Ah, here it is!" I said, happily locating the green piece of cotton. (Fun fact: money is not paper; it's cotton!) "See you in a few."

Whether Shira chose to ignore my last comment or didn't hear me, she followed me down the staircase to the auditorium, kvetching about the injustice done to her by Morah Rivkin.

"I can't believe that teacher!" Shira moaned, leaning against the staircase. "Like, what is wrong with her?! Can't she just give me a passing grade!? Does one point really make such a difference to her?!"

I wished I could just tell her to leave me alone, or at least to stop following me around! But, it wasn't like she was some pesky little sister I can firmly tell to get away when she starts to annoy me. Shira is one of my closest friends, and she's very sensitive!

The thing is, I never know when she is going to take me seriously or make a joke out of what I say. Like sometimes even when I indirectly insult her, she'll laugh, but sometimes when I have no intention of offending her, she'll get hurt.

I got my muffin. It was delicious. On the way back up to the second floor I met my cousin, Chana, and I started chatting with her. Shira hovered in the background. What was she doing here? Her loyalty and sense of attachment flattered me, but couldn't she see I wasn't in the mood to have her tag along and be my shadow?

During lunch I planned to study for the French test. I study best by myself. Shira, however, had other plans for us. She wanted me to come with her to visit Chanie Ross. Chanie lived in the vicinity of the school and was home, sick with the flu. I had no intention of forgoing my study period, even for a good friend like Chanie. French is not my strong point, and I really needed that review. Besides, we could visit Chanie after school.

Shira offered to stay and study with me for twenty minutes and then we'd visit Chanie together in the other twenty, but I'm the kind of person who values my privacy. I love to study by myself; it helps me think and relax. I guess you could call me introverted. It's not that I'm shy or quiet. It's just that I enjoy being alone sometimes. I'm not really alone. I'm with Me, Myself, and I—a great bunch, if I do say so. Not all the time though, just sometimes.

Shira just couldn't seem to understand that! Besides, she didn't really even need to study for this test! First of all, she's like a polyglot; she's great with languages. And second of all, her father was born and bred in France, and her mother grew up in Montreal, where they speak French. So Shira knows French better than Madame Klein, our French teacher.

I suggested she visit Chanie without me, and I would stay in school and study French verbs and prepositions. Shira seemed insulted by this solution. I guess I would probably be too.

"What do you mean, 'No, that's not a good idea,' Sara? You've practically been insulting me to my face the entire day. Aren't we friends? Or maybe that's just what I think," Shira said angrily. Her face was red. She was starting to make me tense. I could feel my temples throbbing.

"Just because we're friends, and we are, doesn't mean we have to spend every second of the day together. I really need to study for this test, and I am not in the mood at the moment for a social call," I said as I started to open up my French book to the test material.

"Fine. You know what? Be that way! See if I care!" Shira marched away from me resentfully. I scowled and stared at my French workbook. *Qu'est-ce qu'il se passé? Qu'est-ce qu'il faut faire? Elle m'enerve! Je ne l'aime pas! Je pense qu'elle et moi sont tres bonnes amies!*

I decided that as soon as she came back we would have a nice long chat about the meaning of friendship and overstepping boundaries. But unluckily I did not get that chance because as soon as Shira came back, I realized she was still angry.

"Oh, so now you want to talk, Sara? Well, you know we don't have to spend every second together. You could've talked before. Besides, don't you have a French test to study for? *Que pensez-vous? Le fou!*" Shira said sarcastically while rolling her eyes. French is a very beautiful language to be angry in, and Shira sounded fabulous yelling at me.

"Come on, Shira!" I pleaded. I was ready to pull the hair out of my head.

But I guess there is a reason why Bnei Yisrael are called stubborn; she refused to answer me.

She wouldn't even look at me, let alone talk to me in class. It felt as if I was sitting next to an ice statue. It was not fun at all. Shira just sat there with her French book in front of her, as if to mock me. But then the thought struck me. Had I been too harsh with her?

During recess I tried once more to talk to her.

"We're friends, right?" I asked Shira. She was sitting at her desk, eating an apple and studying for the French test. (Why was a bilingual genius like her studying anyway?)

She nodded.

"Okay, let me be blunt with you: sometimes I just like to be alone. I enjoy your company, but sometimes I want to be by myself," I said slowly. Hopefully, she wouldn't explode.

"So why didn't you just say so? You can't expect me to be a mind reader! It's like this morning, how was I supposed to know you didn't want to tell me what you got on the test until you said so?" Shira said, throwing out the core of the apple she had been munching on.

"I don't know. I just assumed you were prodding me in order to find out what I got. And then you kept complaining about your test; that was just a little annoying. And you were, like, following me everywhere I went." I threw out my orange peels.

"I thought that maybe you also got a bad mark on your test and didn't want to say because you were embarrassed. I didn't know I was annoying you!" Shira looked genuinely surprised.

Oops! That was a little dumb of me. I shouldn't have been so secretive. It wasn't like my test was some top-secret FBI file!

"I'm sorry," I said with a smile. "So... everything's settled now? I can be blunt with you, and you won't get offended?"

"Well, not too blunt. Everything does have a limit, and I'm sorry you felt as if I was following you around the whole day. Maybe you didn't notice, but I also bought a muffin from the sale. I didn't mean to purposely come with you."

"Oh..." I blushed. I guess I hadn't been so nice. "So... friends?"

"Only on one condition," Shira said seriously.

I was nervous! What would she ask me?

"Mmm... what?" I said, trying to hide the anxiety from my voice.

A hint of a smile crept across her face. "What *did* you get on that *historia* test anyway?"

22

As I slip my baby boy into his crib, pull the hat over his little ear and tuck the warm blanket all around his body, my memory goes back to a very different sort of home, one I visited when I was in high school...

The Volunteer

BY NECHAMA DINA SMITH

They greeted me at the door, all smiling. Esther, the mother, rosy-cheeked and bright-eyed, was holding a baby boy in one arm. From behind her skirt a little girl peeked out at me. Three older children stood by, watching curiously.

Nice beginning, I thought. I hoped I could be of help.

"It's so nice of you to come." Esther was looking intently at me.

"What's your name? What's your name?" the girls asked.

"I'm Shoshana. What's... everyone's name?"

In order, they were Chavi, Reuvi, Sara Leah, Naomi, and Chaim. The oldest brother Baruch was still in yeshivah.

Naomi must have been about three. She had her thumb in her mouth and did not stop staring at me.

I came into the dining room. Here I saw the poverty: a plain folding table—the ones used in shuls for *kiddushim*. Old metal folding chairs. No curtains, just blankets hanging from the windows. No carpets or rugs, only wooden, unpolished, stained and crumby floors. A sunken torn couch. And a kitchen with half the tiles missing.

"Are you in high school or seminary?" Chavi asked.

"Are you married?" Sara Leah asked.

"I'm in high school," I answered. "And no, I'm not married. What grade are you in, Chavi?"

"Third. Reuvi's in first, Sara Leah's in nursery, Naomi and Chaim are in 'no-school!'"

I nodded. "So what can I do?"

"This is really wonderful of you to volunteer," Esther told me. "Are you sure you have time? Well, maybe you can clean up this room."

She brought me a broom. I began to sweep. Esther went to the kitchen. Candy wrappers, plastic bags, crumbs, food spills, odds and ends, all were rolled into one pile while I engaged my helpers in putting away toys and books. Naomi just followed me around with her thumb in her mouth. She seemed to enjoy watching me.

Wow. It's easy to help families in need, I thought.

I progressed to the living room. Chavi, the oldest girl, was called to the kitchen. I continued cleaning. Suddenly, I heard a shriek that sent my broom and dustpan clattering to the floor. "Why did you do that?" I heard. It was a high, shrill scream. "Why did you do that? Answer me! Answer me, do you hear?"

My heart was beating fast as I struggled to breathe slowly, calmly. I looked at the children. They paused briefly, but then continued pressing me with questions.

"What did she do?" I asked.

Reuvi shrugged. "She probably bought the wrong kind of oil. She never listens."

The wrong kind of oil. The broom moved monotonously

back and forth through the room, back and forth.

Chavi was crying. "I didn't do it on purpose. I didn't do it on purpose."

My hands were cold. "Sara Leah, Naomi, Reuvi, you did a beautiful job cleaning up. Look how nice the room looks."

I gave them each a light pinch on the cheek or a touch on their head. From that moment on all I wanted to do was surround them with love.

Esther came out of the kitchen. Her face was flushed. "Wow, thank you so much, Shoshana. It's amazing how much you finished!"

I didn't want to smile back, but I did. "My pleasure. When can I come back?"

We agreed that I would come back Erev Shabbos.

On Friday afternoon I was assigned to help with the children's baths and showers. The children accompanied me to their rooms. The carpet was filthy and smelly. Clothing was everywhere; on the floor, on the backs of chairs, under the beds, around the hamper, in the bathroom. They told me that almost every week they would have a bath.

I washed Naomi's hair and then proceeded to brush it. She cried out. Yes, I knew it hurt. Her hair was one tangled mess. I handed her my watch. "Here, Naomi," I told her, "you can play with my watch while I brush your hair." Naomi smiled.

As I brushed, she held tightly to my watch and forced herself not to cry. I brushed as softly as I could, but I had to take out those knots. And when Naomi peered into the mirror, she looked stunning. She remained gazing at herself for a few minutes. She didn't, or rather couldn't, say a word. But her smile was more than enough thanks.

We picked out Shabbos clothes for everyone. I felt so good

about myself. The children seemed happy! And I was making their home more pleasant.

But then I came downstairs. I saw the older brother. "That's Baruch. He's ten," Chavi told me. Baruch was sitting on the couch.

"Why aren't you helping me?" barked Esther. *Oh, no*, I thought. *Not again*. And I tried to talk to Esther through my mind: *Please don't scream at him.*

"Let go of that book and HELP!" she yelled. She rushed over to him like a madwoman.

Baruch lifted his leg and defensively put up his arms in front of his face.

And then, in the highest pitch I had ever heard, his mother screeched. "What? You're kicking your mother? You're kicking your mother?"

And then she kicked him. Over and over she kicked him.

All I wanted to do was call the police. Just call the police and get rid of this horrible woman.

My baby whimpers in his sleep. "Sh…" I whisper and run my fingers over his forehead to smooth the little wrinkles. I bend down to kiss his soft cheek and breathe in his sweet baby smell.

I'm remembering those adorable children. How they loved it when I came! And how I enjoyed coming to them!

I didn't call the police. Of course not. As much as Esther was hurting them, she was their mother. She did love them. She did give them food. And they had each other, those children. They had a father too, though I never met him as he came home very late every night. I would have no part in helping them be torn from their parents and shuttled into different homes, perhaps not even Jewish homes, maybe even homes which mistreated their foster children.

But Esther needed help, and I didn't know how to give it.

I came every week for months. I worked hard and hoped I made life a little easier for the children.

But one Friday, Esther asked me to change the beds. The old sheets were crumpled on each bed. I collected them and put them in the laundry room. I decided to treat the kids to nicely made beds and began to spread out the clean sheets, tuck them in, spread out a top sheet, and over that the blankets so they wouldn't have to breathe in the blankets directly.

In middle of making the second bed, I heard Esther call up: "Shoshana?"

"Yes?" I called back.

"Are you finished?"

"Not yet!"

After a few minutes I heard that fearful scream. This time it was directed…at me.

"Shoshana? Shoshana! What's taking so long? Come out this minute! Do you hear? Shoshana! This is crazy!"

I couldn't believe it. I put the rest of the sheets down and calmly walked out of the bedroom.

"What were you doing?" shrilled Esther. "What took you so long?"

"I was making the beds."

"But I just throw on the new sheets! That's all I do! It takes two seconds! Just throw them on!"

"Well," I answered, "I wanted to do them nicely."

She kept on screaming. My voice quivered as I said, "I have to go." I glanced at whichever children were there, gave them a shaky smile, and left.

I didn't come back. I couldn't. I pitied those poor little children who got yelled at every day. It had happened to me once, and I couldn't handle it. I ached for them and felt guilty that I didn't return.

Esther needed help, I knew. She needed therapy, parenting lessons, something.

My angel wakes up. It's dark, and he's scared. He cries out. Quickly I lift him up. He buries his head in my shoulder and keeps crying. His arms flail and his legs kick. I walk back and forth singing him a song. He is soothed.

Two years passed and I was already in seminary. I remembered Esther and the children and visited them. Esther was happy to see me, and the older children smiled shyly. Naomi looked at me curiously.

"Remember me?" I asked her. "You used to hold my jewelry while I brushed your hair!"

Naomi brightened. "Oh, yes!"

"Can I help with something?" I asked Esther. Now I didn't speak like a timid student but as an equal.

Esther spoke to me quietly in the kitchen. "Sara Leah has trouble reading. Her teacher says she just needs to build confidence. Maybe you can help her read."

So I sat with Sara Leah on a mattress on the floor, with Chaim, now three, jumping all around us. I asked Sara Leah to read, but she kept changing the subject. I let her. Then I tried to get her to read one more line. She fiddled with a water bottle.

Esther saw what was happening. "Sara Leah! You're supposed to be reading. Not fooling around," and she grabbed the bottle out of Sara Leah's hand and mouth. She walked away and Sara Leah started crying. The inside of her lip was bleeding.

"Come, let's wash it," I told her.

Esther said, "What's going on? You're bleeding. Let me see." She pulled at her daughter's lip. Sara Leah screamed.

With forced self-control, I spoke calmly: "You pulled the

bottle out of her mouth, so she has a little cut. Let's just wash it out."

"I know what to do. I was a doctor's assistant," Esther stated, and again she pulled at Sara Leah's lip. Then she let her go.

Esther told me how I wasn't teaching her right and that's why she wasn't behaving.

"But if the teacher says she needs confidence to do well," I countered, "you have to build her up instead of putting her down."

Oh, was that the wrong thing to say! I could tell it didn't register. There was an awkward feeling between us. I left saying I'd be back to help.

I called a teacher of mine and related the entire story to her.

"You have to build Esther up and not put her down," she advised me, using the very same line I'd used about Sara Leah. "Compliment her, praise her, and find her good points. Dwell on those good points and encourage her to continue with them. If you criticize her, her low self-esteem will simply worsen, and that will not make her a better parent!"

So I tried. I told her, "It's amazing how you handle six kids! My family only has three, and my mother has it hard."

"You think it's amazing? No, you're joking. You're making fun of me."

"I'm not," I said. But we both got distracted by the kids.

She still screamed, and I still tried to find nice things to say. Once I told her, "Oh, that potato dish smells delicious."

"Oh, really? Here, taste it," she said.

The dish looked strange, but I forced myself to taste it. It wasn't bad at all.

She gave her daughters haircuts and I praised her work. They actually were cut pretty well.

I would take the children on walks every Erev Shabbos.

They adored me. I almost felt like I was coming so I could feel good about myself.

Esther still screamed. Sometimes I'd ask her to tell me about herself. She related how she was planning to be a doctor one day and how her brother did indeed become a doctor. I could tell she appreciated my interest, but at times she still was a nervous wreck. I did believe, though, that she began to scream just a little less.

Soon I moved away. I flew off to a teaching job. Before I left, I recruited a high-school girl to volunteer for the family, and I informed her of my plan. I hoped and prayed it would work. The last time I was at their house, they all gave me hugs. It was touching. I told the kids, with a smile, to behave themselves, and I told Esther what wonderful children she raised.

I hold my little son tight and caress his thin, downy hair. I hope Esther and her family are okay. I wonder if the high-school girl was successful in the building-up plan. I hope Esther got counseling. I pray the children grow up normal, healthy, and happy.

I rock my baby gently, back and forth, back and forth.

Note to our readers: the above is a fiction story, dealing with a serious issue. Should you ever encounter a situation of grave abuse, we suggest that you contact a *rav*, parent, or teacher.

23

The New Girl

BY NECHAMA DINA SMITH

Oh, no! It was almost 8:15, and I needed to leave by 8:10 to make it to school before Rabbi Stein held out his watch and raised his eyebrows in disapproval.

I slammed the door, heaving my backpack over one shoulder. Which shoulder had I worn it on last? I couldn't remember, but I didn't want to look lopsided. No one carried their backpack on both shoulders. That was unheard of.

There was no time for the elevator, so I ran down the hall toward the stairs, sidestepping loads of boxes in front of an empty apartment. Oh, finally someone was moving in! I hoped they were nice people. I wondered if the leaks ever got fixed and if the old, torn carpet had been replaced. A scrunched-up ball of tape got stuck on my shoe, and I nearly fell down the steps.

Believe it or not, Rabbi Stein was busy in his office. I reached the *davening* hall unnoticed. "*Baruch* Hashem," I panted under my breath, sliding into the seat between Rai-zy and Faigy. "Thanks for saving it for me!" I murmured to them. They had started *davening*, but Faigy pointed to her earrings. Dainty gold studs. I gave her a thumbs-up and be-gan to *daven*.

In the middle of our first learning period, there was a knock on our tenth-grade classroom door, and in came Rabbi Stein followed by a tall girl with a wide grin and disheveled, light-brown hair.

The principal introduced the new student as Rena. Everyone stared at her. I felt bad. I would not have liked to be up there.

"Hi," she said in a loud, awkward voice.

Oh, no, I thought, *that's the wrong thing to say*. No one says "hi" when being introduced to a class. You just give a quick smile and sit down. But the new girl finally did sit down, and I forgot about her.

At noon, Faigy, Raizy, and I headed toward the lunchroom. The three of us were best friends since first grade, and we al-ways had lots to talk about. We always stuck together, espe-cially now in high school with such big classes. Faigy bit into a whole-wheat sandwich with sprouts. "My latest diet," she chewed and explained. I'm not fat, and Faigy is skinnier than me, but I could never bring myself to diet. Chocolate brown-ies are too tempting.

I took out my tuna sandwich, and just as I took my first bite, I remembered. "The new girl," I sputtered, trying to swal-low first. My friends looked at me. "The new girl," I said again. "She must be all by herself."

Raizy peeked up from a science textbook she was skim-ming for a quiz. "We should introduce her to a clique." She popped a tangerine wedge into her mouth.

"Well," said Faigy, "she could eat with us."

I disagreed. "How about we finish eating, and then, when we pass her on our way back to class, we'll smile and say, 'If you need anything, come to us!'"

"But she just might be all alone, like you said, Chani," Faigy pointed out.

"No, wait," I insisted. "If we'd be the first to befriend her, she'd want to be part of our group." I kept chewing. "Can we just finish eating?"

Raizy stood up, closing her book. "Maybe only two of us should go."

Boy, we were making such a big deal of this. And I had started it! "I'm sure lots of girls are already busy talking to her," I said.

My friends smiled at me. "Yeah, right," Raizy said. They gathered their stuff and headed towards the door.

Something stuck in my throat and it wasn't food. Not only might a nerdy girl join our little group, but I could be left out of it.

"Hey, wait, I'll come too," I said, moving to catch up.

The new girl wasn't in the lunchroom. When we reached our class, there was Rena, all alone. She didn't seem to be worried, though. She was reading a book on self-esteem. A book on self-esteem right there in public! And she was eating something from a sardine tin that filled the room with its oily scent.

We introduced ourselves. Rena smiled broadly. "I'm so glad you came over to me. I didn't know where everyone disappeared to!"

"Did you just move to town?" I asked.

"Yes, last night!" Rena replied.

"If you need anything, we're here to help," Faigy offered, as other students started filing in.

"Chani here is the best in the class in *Chumash*," Raizy

patted me on the back, "so she'll be glad to help you catch up."
I was ready to pinch her, but the bell rang.

After school, I hurried home. I wanted to finish all my
homework and then soak in a hot bubble bath and just think
about life.

As I turned a corner, I saw Rena about half a block behind
me. She waved and jogged to catch up.

"Where do you live?" I asked her.

"18 Rochester Place."

I swallowed hard.

"Do you live near there?" she asked.

"Actually," I answered slowly, clearing my throat. "I live
there, too. Apartment 3F."

Rena clapped her hands. Literally clapped her hands with
delight! "That's wonderful," she exclaimed, and though I didn't
know why, I had to smile.

We had a pleasant walk. She was as fluent in Israeli politics
as my father was. We made up to walk to school together.

But as we started down the stairs the next morning, I
couldn't do it. She was wearing her knapsack on two shoulders! It was just too embarrassing to be seen walking with her.

"Oh, I'm so sorry, Rena," I stammered. "I think I'm going
to be late today. I remembered an assignment that I have to
finish."

"Oh." Rena looked disappointed. "I was hoping to have a
nice talk with you."

I squirmed inside. "Don't wait for me. Rabbi Stein is serious about coming on time. We'll walk back together, okay?"

And so I waited in my home until I thought she arrived at
school, and then I ran the whole way there. Somehow, I made
it on time.

Throughout the day Rena seemed hesitant in the Hebrew

subjects. She'd wear a puzzled look on her face and write notes half the time, and the other half she'd concentrate and look bewildered. In the general subjects, though, she was a whiz.

Biology class was especially intense. Our teacher had information that could easily fill ten periods a week, but she had only three classes a week with us. So she rattled off pages of notes as we frantically scribbled. Once in a while someone in the front row whispered, "Can you slow down a tiny bit?"

Rena didn't seem to get it. When the teacher taught about dominant and recessive genes, she asked questions. "My father has a dent in his ear and my mother doesn't, and I have one. Does that mean my mother has a recessive gene for a dent in the ear?"

I wished I had mental telepathy to tell her we don't ask those sorts of revealing questions.

Then Rena wanted to clarify the lecture on X and Y chromosomes, so she asked if she could sum it up to make sure she understood it.

"She's so different," I whispered to Raizy. "She's smart, but she's different."

"Well," Raizy whispered back, "we can all thank her for giving us a few extra minutes to catch up on our notes!"

Rena was so independent, I thought. Was that what it was?

I walked home with her, swallowing my pride for the first three blocks where everyone could see us together, and Rena with her backpack on both shoulders. After that I was fine.

We agreed to learn *Chumash* in her apartment, though it was messy, she warned me. I didn't offer my place. My younger sister was having friends over, and I wouldn't want them to think this was my best friend!

After dinner I knocked at her door. Her father ushered me in. He was really tall, and he wore a gray suit and a straw hat.

He looked nothing like my father, who wore the typical white shirt, black pants, and black hat.

"So you're the famous Chani!" he exclaimed, as the whole family—Rena, her mother, and about five girls and four boys—greeted me. I was honored by all the attention, though it was a little overwhelming.

Rena and I went to one bedroom and started learning. I taught one lesson several times over to her, and by the fifth time she grasped it really well.

"You're a great teacher," she complimented me. I felt proud.

Her sisters kept coming in, begging me to play a new board game they had just bought. Rena and I promised them that when we finished studying, we'd play.

When we finally left the room, I beheld the sweetest sight. Rena's father was bent over a guitar, strumming and quietly singing a song. Her mother was feeding a baby on a rocking chair, and the other children were dancing to the music.

Rena, who looked at the scene calmly, was not the least bit self-conscious. She told me to have a seat. Then she reached up to a bookshelf and, to my surprise, took out a harmonica. I sat and marveled at the harmonica, the guitar, the singing, and the dancing. I'd never seen a family musical exhibition. Wow.

It was very nice, but I felt funny about telling anyone of my experience at Rena's house.

One day at recess, Rena showed a bunch of girls some photos she had of her old school. Her class had performed a play, and their costumes were impressive. "We were a class of only seven," she told us. "Every girl had her own specialty."

"What was yours?" someone asked.

Rena looked shy for a minute. "I was the lead in the play. I'm a good actress. You want to hear?"

Now I was nervous. I didn't want her to embarrass herself

in front of so many people! I quickly tried to distract her. "Oh, Rena," I said, "the production heads will probably love you! You should meet with them. The school will finally have a good play!"

"Oh, can you please perform for us now?" asked a sincere girl who sits near me. I winced.

Rena took a deep breath. A different look came over her, as if she were becoming whoever it was she would be imitating.

"Wait!" I said, desperate. "Don't forget Mrs. Tennenberg is giving us a huge quiz in five minutes."

There was a scurry of papers as information was passed and shouted in the five minutes until the bell rang, and we were all ready for the quiz. Rena looked at me. What was she thinking? I almost cried. I didn't want to hurt her. Inside I was a wreck. Was I helping Rena or harming her? Or was I trying to save my reputation somehow?

On Tuesday, Rena celebrated her birthday. She invited Raizy, Faigy, me, and Leah, another classmate who had gotten friendly with Rena, to her home.

The apartment was decorated with handmade streamers and balloons stuck with tape to the walls. Rena's brothers and sisters were running around with their markers and glue. Rena's father was manning the barbeque, wearing a big apron that said something like "Great Dad." The little children showed us all their decorations, toys, bedrooms, and schoolwork.

After the dinner, which we ate with gusto because we had to wait for forty-five minutes for it to be ready, Rena, two sisters, and a little brother put on a lively play for us. All the guests clapped. It was excellent!

We left in good spirits, each to our own home, but soon Faigy and Raizy phoned me. "You didn't tell us she has such an interesting family," they said.

"I'm glad you got to see them for yourselves!" I said.

They went on and on about what a great girl Rena was.

Something was bothering me, but I didn't know what it was. "Can we go to the pizza store tomorrow, just the three of us?" I asked.

As Raizy doled out the pizza slices the next day, she asked me, "What's up? You look frazzled or something."

"I'm confused."

"What's wrong?"

I didn't know what to say.

Faigy said, "Don't be upset, Chani, but Raizy and I discussed things, and we think we can help you."

"Eat," said Raizy.

I took a tiny bite of my pizza.

"We all like Rena, correct?" Faigy asked.

"I guess…yes," I answered.

"But what bothers you is that you like everyone to be the same, and you think that everyone should be like you and that everyone wants the whole world to be the same."

"I just don't want to stand out in the wrong way," I said.

"Maybe we should all just change our perspective, and enjoy Rena's differences and appreciate her without being embarrassed." Faigy eyed me seriously but lightly.

I blushed. "I guess I'm an open book."

"Basically, you are a super person. That's why we love you. You're sensitive and smart," said Raizy.

"Just like us," said Faigy, laughing. "And super friends are open to super people."

Well, Rena ended up becoming very close to all three of us. And I really thank Hashem for bringing her into my life and especially for enabling me to appreciate her uniqueness and learn from her.

24

The Lonely Summer

BY NOMI DAYAN

If my friend reads this, she'll kill me.

Okay, not kill. That's strong language. She'll probably just call and say in that stern little voice of hers, "Nomi, what's up with that thing you wrote?" (She's a very private person.) And I'll say something like, "Oh, ha ha, did you like it?" And she'll just let there be a thoughtful silence on the line.

I met Leah in, let's see, tenth grade. All right, if you want to be official, make it the very end of ninth grade. There was this really big school function where all four grades of high school (400 girls, mind you) went up to a camp in the Catskills for a Shabbos.

Well, you know how "cliquey" ninth grade can be, and I had my own bunch of friends. On Motza'ei Shabbos, everyone was sitting around this big bonfire getting really emotional, especially those twelfth graders, vacillating between the joy of graduating and the gloom of not being with high school friends forever. (I remember thinking, *What is* wrong *with those twelfth graders?*) I wandered around into a bunk full of a hodgepodge of girls whom I only semi-knew, but sat down with anyway. And we had nice, civilized conversations. One of the girls lugged out this huge suitcase (I said suitcase) of candy. Junk. "Take, guys," she said, peeling open a Laffy Taffy. I sat there awestruck, my mouth open like a codfish.

"You mean somebody else actually brings a trunk full of food for a three-day trip, just like me?" I asked.

Fast forward to the beginning of tenth grade. The principal made this snuggly-wuggly speech about how this was the year to get to know *everyone* in the grade, and how we shouldn't just hang on to the same set of friends. Subsequently, there was this mad rush to the classroom to get the "best" seat next to your same old set of friends. Seats were grabbed and "saved" left and right. I decided not to make a big deal about it and kept scanning the room for an open seat. Finally I saw a nice empty place right next to the girl I had met at that camp in the Catskills with the suitcase full of candy.

Oh, it was a dangerous move—to sit next to someone I didn't know! (Don't make fun. You think the same thing!) But I summoned up the courage, walked up, and asked if the seat was taken. It wasn't.

That was the beginning. It only seemed natural that Leah and I would get to know each other better since we were sitting right next to each other. At first it was awkward. In first grade, you made friends through sharing sparkly stickers and wearing the coolest headband to class. And you might even ask the person outright, "Do you want to be my friend?" And if they say "yes," that's it. But what do you do in high school? No stickers to stick on the end of your nose this time. You don't ask someone if they want to be your friend. (Heavens, no!) It kind of just… happens.

Well, it happened. At first, it was kind of complex—are we friends or what? We started spending lunchtime together. Keep in mind, our own separate sets of friends were very different. But she and I felt the same. Different and the same at the same time. I think the big break was when she found out that I *wrote*, and I found out that *she* wrote, and, two nutcases that we were, we just had to be friends now. I mean, we were both writers! (And good ones, too, if I may add.)

We were alike in many ways. Nutcases, as I just said. Different too, which kept things interesting. We wore our hair differently. We had different opinions on lots of things. But hey, that's what friendship is about, liking each other despite differences.

We boasted about never having a fight until, well, until we had a fight. Oh, was it stupid, as many fights tend to be! We were editors of the school journal together. We had lots of time off from class to work on the journal. And—all right, I'll tell you the truth—here's what happened. There was a big history exam coming up. We had time off from class, as I said, and so I, like the responsible, studious person that I was, decided to spend it preparing for the test, which was that day. I would do the journal work after school when I got home.

My friend sat down to work on the journal. She didn't say anything about my studying. I knew she didn't like that I was studying for the test and was annoyed that I wasn't working with her on the school journal; it was unethical, maybe. She typed away. After some time, I ran downstairs to the office to grab something. Leah, seeing I was going downstairs, asked me to get something from the office. I ran downstairs.

This part gets fuzzy. I forgot to bring the paper she had asked me to bring. Leah said, "Go back down and get it please."

I said, "Sorry, I have ten minutes left to study, and you're done working, so you get the paper. It's not a big deal."

She got mad.

I still defend myself. I do see her point—she typed stuff up, she worked, I didn't. But she was done with the work, so why was she making such a big fuss? *Go get it yourself; you're not doing anything now*, I thought. I was desperate. I had to prepare for the test.

That's how the fight started. After that, she wasn't talking to me, and I wasn't talking to her. We were both stubborn. When I want to be stubborn, I can be so stubborn it hurts. (I wore a sweatshirt for four years of high school because I didn't want to tuck in my shirt because A, I felt fat and B, I thought plain, thin, white uniform shirts were see-through. So I wore the school sweatshirt every single day, winter and summer.) I liked to tell Leah that she was just as stubborn as I was, but she would never hear of it.

We didn't talk for months. Soon summer flew in.

All of a sudden, my day was so—oh, it was so empty. There was nothing to do. Everything I looked at reminded me of my old friend. I thought about her constantly. After a while I thought about her so much and felt the loss so deeply that I began to scorn her, scorn her for the whole stupid fight and the whole stupid thing. I hated myself for getting into it. So when I started to think about her, I switched channels and thought about something else. There was no point in thinking about her as a friend because that would never be anymore. Obviously, it was all just a mistake. The whole friendship was a mistake. What a fool I was to have thought it was real! The little private jokes we had together now filled me with anger when I was reminded of them.

Who knew how empty a day could be? How silly it all felt!

How much I missed her!

And then my family became suspicious. They wanted to know why I wasn't on the phone anymore. I avoided telling them. I hated making big deals of things. But they figured it out somehow.

"Oh, Nomi," my older sister said, "just call her up and apologize."

But I didn't.

My mother was worried about my sitting outside all by myself. The thing was, I was beginning to get used to my loneliness. I forgot how much fun it was to laugh with your best friend in the world, to have ice cream together on a humid summer day, to call her up at the craziest hour to make her laugh, to talk about anything and everything in the world. I forgot what it was like to share my world with someone, and partake in the sharing of hers. I didn't really forget—I made myself forget. I just didn't think about it. There was nothing to think about. It was awful.

Then one day a letter arrived in the mail, addressed to me. I glanced at the return address and saw—it was from her! My heart froze. She had written to me. What would she say? I immediately ripped open the envelope and read the contents of it. It was her official "I'm sorry" letter. I was astonished to read that Leah felt that our fight was my fault, but she wanted to apologize anyway. She was putting up the white flag. She wanted to talk. She was sorry.

I stuffed the letter back into the envelope. I didn't want to write her back. I was angry. Just because she decides it's time to write means I have to answer right away? I went to my room and wrote down all my thoughts on paper. I kept that paper for a long time in my room, never giving it to her and never reading it myself again, just knowing it was there. One day when I was cleaning my room, I threw it out. *There*, I thought. *I have separated myself from anger, from bad feelings, from fight, and I am throwing it out. It's gone.*

Eleventh grade was approaching. Remember the journal we did together? It still wasn't finished. It was "on hold" all summer. She and I weren't speaking, remember? The teacher in charge of the journal called me up at the end of the summer and said that we would have to get together to work on it and finish it up so it could be distributed to the school. For part of the phone conversation I pretended everything was all right between us but then bluntly told her that Leah and I weren't speaking.

The teacher was very surprised. Nomi and her friend weren't speaking? Knowing how close we had been, she gave me this little speech about friendship and insisted that I call Leah and get the whole thing straightened out and over with. I told her I would, not sure if it was true. At first, I thought, *What business is it of hers?* But it was her business. She had a right to try to break up this silent fight.

So I called. We spoke politely. Civilly. We spoke about the journal—only. She sounded… the same as I remembered. I almost expected her to change. But there was a mutual coldness we radiated toward each other, an aloofness. We talked about the layout of the journal until we were… done. We would have to meet. I couldn't come on this day because of this. She couldn't do it that day because of that. All right then, how 'bout this day? All right with you? Fine. Have a good night.

"Do you have anything else to say?" Leah said.

"No."

Tension. What was she getting at?

"You don't have anything else to say?"

I shrugged and stared out of my bedroom window, at the

brick wall. "No."

"You didn't get my letter?"

Sure I got her letter.

"Why didn't you write me back?"

So I told her I didn't feel like writing back. Who said I had to write back right away? I was angry.

Leah said something like, "*You're* angry!"

She was always the one to say she was sorry for arguments. She hated that. No one ever made her say it; it just happened like that. She would always complain, "Why am I always the one to say I'm sorry?" I realized how much it had taken for her to write that letter, especially after so long. She had spent time and made the effort to sit down and think and write about the loss she felt, and I hadn't even shown her the common courtesy of answering her letter. Now that I thought about it, it was insulting. Really. I regretted it.

We talked for hours that night. And that was it. The shaky but glad beginning of the patching-up process made me want to jump for joy. I realized how much I had missed my good friend, who was so devoted to everyone she loved. I missed how I was truly myself with her, how she overlooked my short-comings and cherished my accomplishments, how she knew all about me but loved me just the same. She was so reliable. She was always there. I was the luckiest person in the world.

Click. I stared at the phone. I couldn't believe we just did that! Talked!

School began. There was Leah—I hadn't seen her in months. Months! With her deep eyes, she looked even more beautiful than I remembered.

We are the best friends I know (and I'm not trying to gloss up the story!). We rarely talk about what happened because it is a sensitive (yet healed) wound. (We call it "the fight.") But when we do talk about it, it's so we can understand what happened and know each other better and be able to handle such things in the future (because I can tell we have a long, long future together!). I see what happened as a bout of miscommunication. I used to think we were so close that we were immune to petty fights, but it wasn't true. They affect everybody, and you have to work through them and not lose contact with each other. So learn from me and don't be stubborn. I was too "tough" to call and admit that maybe I wasn't right. Don't let the same thing happen to you. Don't let a petty argument swell up into a full-blown fight, don't be afraid to discuss the matter, and don't think the other person doesn't want to start talking again. Of course she does! She's going through the same thing you are.

My friend now points out to me that it was the journal that put us back together again, but I point out that it was the journal that broke us apart. In actuality, though, the journal had nothing to do with it. I should have behaved better. Whatever the case, neither of us regrets doing the journal. It came out a masterpiece.

25

I can do this, I told myself. I would walk over the George Washington Bridge. No doubt I'd be late for school, but what an adventure! "Where were you?" my classmates and teacher would ask. And I'd say, "Oh, excuse me, I was just walking over the George Washington Bridge."

Stranded

BY NOMI DAYAN

My mother is always terrified of my getting lost. To tell the truth, her fears are well grounded. I have little, if any, sense of direction. It took me a long time to master the challenging tangle of the NYC train system. Take it from me; it is not easy to navigate your way through that big city, between trying to figure out what in the world the signs say, dodging rebel cars, and falling into the rush of stampeding pedestrians. My older sister Nina can't understand why I have such a hard time figuring it out. She finds her way around easily, as if Manhattan were the back of her hand.

Well, recently, I gained a little more confidence in myself. My father was kind enough to offer me a ride to my seminary, located at the tip of Manhattan in Washington Heights. It was a nice break from being flattened and squished on the train during the dreary morning rush hour. We drove down the West Side Highway, which was a bit clogged with the infamous morning traffic. You could feel the impatience of other cars as they waited at the red lights. The view of the Hudson River, however, was lovely to see.

As the street numbers of Manhattan started to climb, the misty outline of the George Washington Bridge came into view. It is my mother's favorite bridge. I must admit it is beautiful and serene with its high cable necklace suspended over the Hudson River. I myself am a bit partial to the Verrazano Bridge, which has a tall, proud regality in its stature. But now the George Washington Bridge is high on my list, and you shall see why.

Soon the bridge came into clear view. Our plan was that my father would drop me off right before the bridge, and he'd go on to New Jersey for some business (another one of those car auctions!) while I would walk a couple of blocks to my seminary. The plan sounded good. Notice, I said "sounded."

Let me sidetrack for a moment. It's hard for me to be dropped off by a parent to go to school. It gives me a bad feeling. Here I am, having such a good time with my father, and boom, I have to go sit in some classroom all alone. As if that could be half as nice! I always get filled with nervousness, accompanied by a swishy-swashy feeling in the stomach. I know I *have* to go, but do I have to *like* going? That feeling has been with me since first grade. But now, back to the morning traffic.

My father said, "Get ready." I stuffed my loose papers into my knapsack. Our eyes darted back and forth on the road ahead, searching for a good spot to drop me off. But we could not see any. Hmm. Would we have to take an exit?

There was one more exit coming up before the bridge. My father swiftly switched lanes. Almost immediately the traffic began to slow down as if something got caught in a drain and all the water was piling up. The exit was so congested and clogged with cars that we saw there was no chance of getting out there. My father switched back to the lane he was in before. We'd just have to find another place for me to hop off. Right?

Before we knew it, we were on a ramp, which went up and up and up. "Abba," I said, looking down from the window, "what if we go over to New Jersey?" He was quiet.

At that moment, I realized we were on the bridge.

My father pulled over to the side. A few feet ahead was an inhospitable sign: No Stopping on Bridge. Behind us, cars honked intolerantly but discovered they could get around us easily. We opened our doors and nimbly stepped out.

The salty spray of the ocean mist hit me in the face. Wind combed through my hair and flapped at my skirt. It smelled like Niagara Falls! This was the first time I'd been on a suspension bridge standing outside of a car. It was a very exciting moment!

We peered down. We were so high—almost uneasily so. Could I walk off the bridge? There was a deserted staircase that was blocked off. Where was the walkway for pedestrians? Looking past the blurred lanes of whizzing cars were people walking—on the other side of the bridge. How inconvenient! Unless I could fly over, there was no way I could get to the other side.

Somewhat defeated, we climbed back into the car. I faced the fact: I was going to New Jersey. I immediately said, "Abba, I have no problem whatsoever with walking back. We'll just drive to the other side, and then I'll cross over and walk back." Of course, once we got over the bridge, we could just turn the car around and come back. But my father was already late for work. And I didn't want him to get caught in the rush hour traffic. Besides, he'd have to pay the toll.

I knew I could walk back over; it would be beautiful. Long, but beautiful. So we pulled out and drove over. I knew I'd be seeing the same cables and poles a few minutes later as I walked back. I tried not to think about the time when my mother walked over the Brooklyn Bridge with my younger sister Sara. When they were halfway over the bridge, they were *chalashing* with thirst. It was a much longer walk than they expected. That was the Brooklyn Bridge, which is half the size of this one.

Finally, we were over. You'd think hopping out was easy. Well, we couldn't find a sidewalk. We kept driving. I reassured my father that I'd be okay and we'd be in contact via our cell phones. Finally, we spotted a little walkway that bridged over the highway we were on. I'd walk over to the other side. Perfect. My father pulled over and let me off.

I watched his car drive away, waving. *I can do this,* I told myself. *Yes, I can. I am going to walk over the George Washington Bridge.* No doubt I'd be late for school, but what an adventure. "Where were you?" my classmates and teacher would ask. And I'd say, "Oh, excuse me, I was just walking over the George Washington Bridge." What a way to start an ordinary day!

I climbed up the stairs and stood over the highway leading to the bridge. It looked beautiful, yet unreachable. While I was up there, I saw all the streets leading to the bridge. Cars poured in from every direction possible, from overpasses and underpasses and thruways. There was no way for me to get to the other side with all the cars speeding by. For one slow, sick second I thought, *I am stranded in New Jersey.* But I blinked away the panic. *No, I can do this. There must be a way. I could look for a policeman, couldn't I? I could walk to the tollbooths and tell the people manning the booths my problem, and they'll show me how to walk over. Maybe they'll even drive me over.*

I saw a woman approaching where I stood. I stopped her and asked if she knew how to get to the pedestrians' walkway on the bridge. She said, "Oh, my goodness, I have no idea. How will you cross with all those cars? And there are no traffic lights!"

Well, I resolved, there must be a way. I would find it myself. It will be exciting. I imagined myself telling my mother when I got home how I crossed the George Washington Bridge. But how that would be I still did not know.

I climbed down another set of stairs. Then, I saw it! A bus, with people boarding it! Bus means going somewhere. Bus means New York! The last passenger boarded. The doors started to close. I ran up and hopped on. "New York?" I asked.

"Yes," the driver responded. New York! I could not believe my ears!

"How much?" I asked.

"A dollar." A dollar? Was that all? I fished around in my purse. Two twenties.

"Is a twenty all right?" I asked. He agreed to give me change, which most drivers never do. Victory! And there was even a seat for me! Was this a dream?

I sat down with renewed energy. I was going over the bridge! Back to New York! I usually avoid buses. I praised myself as the wheels started to roll. I looked out at the view. I could see the skyscrapers poking up at the blue stretch of sky, the waves below us lapping the rocks of the New Jersey shore.

I suddenly felt a pang of regret. I had really wanted to walk over, no matter how long it would take. Just then my phone rang. It was Abba. "Abba, guess where I am," I said. "I'm on a bus. I saw a bus and I just hopped on it, and now I'm almost over." He was really surprised, almost as surprised as I was. Then it occurred to me—where exactly does the bus stop? I asked the person next to me, who told me that everyone is let off where the bridge ends. Connections could be made to other buses or the subway. *Perfect*, I thought. It could not be better. All I really needed was to get over the bridge.

"Do you always go around hopping on buses?" my father asked. I told him briefly what had happened.

We were let off. I stepped off triumphantly. I turned around for a last look at that glorious bridge.

Well, I got to school on time that day. I actually got there early. (Can you believe it, even with all that *mishegas*!) Everyone was slowly coming in. For them, their morning was just like the morning before. But I kept quiet in my silent pride. Wasn't I just in New Jersey? Hadn't I just accomplished a feat?

I turned behind me to the window to see if I could see the bridge. Buildings were blocking it, but I knew it was in that direction. (But, honestly, I wouldn't trust myself about that now…)

I think of my adventure from time to time, especially when we drive near the bridge. I'm proud because, direction-challenged though I am, I found my way back. Sometimes people laugh at my story, as if to say, *what's the big deal*? But for me it was a big deal because I learned something from it. Whenever I see a dead end, I know I can find a way around it. When I'm faced with obstacles, I remember the bridge. You can always get through difficulties somehow, I tell myself. Just think it through and explore the possibilities. Think clearly and deal with what you have, and you'll find your way to the other side.

26

I worked just as hard as Tova all summer. We sweated the same, we were exhausted the same.

Last Day of Camp

BY NECHAMA DINA SMITH

The sun was bright that morning, as usual. The yellow rays soaked my face through the blinds and I rolled over to get away from the light...

My back ached. I had bent over the copy machine at Kinko's last night with Ahuva, cutting, pasting, copying, stapling, checking, and coloring in. We had planned, written, typed, edited, drawn, whited out, and perfected the end-of-camp goodbye newsletter for Bunk 7-Up. What a bunk. What a summer.

Well, I had to get up, didn't I? I wouldn't miss today for anything. I only missed one day of camp and that was when I had the flu. But today—though I could barely move—I had to be there. Today was payday. I was sure that all my loyal five-year-olds had told their parents how much they loved me and I'd get big tips. It wasn't like I was greedy, I assured myself; I just wanted to know that all my hard work was appreciated.

The stereo turned on to "*Ana Hashem*." I pulled myself up and washed *negel vasser*, splashing the extra water on my face to wake myself up.

"Morah Devorah!" Sara'le, her blond hair perfectly braided and tied with light pink ribbons, ran up to me in the line-up court. "Look at my new pocketbook!"

"Hi, Sara'le!" I grinned. As usual, she was there waiting for me. "You are so good! You always come early!" I told her. As for me, I wished I was still in bed.

"Well, do you like it?"

"Oh," I said. "Yeah, it's pretty! Where's Morah Ahuva?"

"I don't know." Sara'le danced away.

I went into the counselors' room.

"Hey, Devorah!" There was Ahuva, smiling, her pen poised to make notes on her schedule.

It was refreshing to see her. So tall, so beautiful, so relaxed. And most importantly, happy to see me.

"Can you believe it's the last day of camp? It's such an exciting day, isn't it?"

"Yeah, but what are we going to do with the girls until the carnival?" I asked. I plopped into a chair next to her and leaned over to look at her schedule.

"Okay," Ahuva began, "after line-up, I'll *daven* with them while you get everything ready—the sandbox toys, the costumes for the choir, the snacks, and your story—if you haven't prepared it already." Our eyes met and we laughed. She knew me so well! "Then you'll tell them the story, we'll do bathrooms, play in the sandbox, and practice our song."

"That's great!" An easy morning. And then after that, the carnival, and then—I closed my eyes... Then I'd sleep and sleep.

The morning passed by too quickly. I was going to miss

them, these sometimes impossible, but usually lovable campers. I made up a story about a bunk's last day of camp. The
children loved it, of course. "Was there a girl named Faigy?"
asked Faigy.

"Oh, yes," I told her. "And she had red curly hair, just like
you."

"And when camp was over and all the children went home,"
I ended the story, "in everyone's heart was a little piece of their
morah, which they'd always keep. And in the *morah's* heart
there was a place reserved for every camper. That way they
would never forget each other and always be friends!"

The girls all clapped.

During sandbox time, there was one fight instead of the
usual three or four. I watched the girls while Ahuva took Dini
to wash out the sand from her eyes and hair. Then Ahuva
watched everyone while I took a couple of girls to the bathroom because they "didn't have to go before."

We practiced our song for the performance. The off-tune
kids were still off tune, but they were sweet and they really
tried hard. We couldn't hurt their feelings, so we let them be
without trying to correct them.

Then it was time for the…

"CARNIVAL!" I exclaimed, and we all ran to the gaily
decorated courtyard. Helium balloons were bopping up and
down from the factory fans which blew on all sides. Brightly
colored tablecloths covered the tables. The games and prizes
were set up and ready. Some of the mothers had arrived.

Mrs. Greenberg, the director, approached us. She had been
shlepping odds and ends all over the campgrounds. "Can one
of you take care of the ticket booth? Aliza couldn't come today.
Thanks!" And she bustled away.

"Oh, Ahuva," I implored. "Can I do the tickets and you

take the kids?" I wouldn't mind taking it a little easier just today.

"I'll take the kids for the first hour, and then we'll switch," Ahuva told me.

Splitting the work as usual. *Fine*, I thought. Just because I was lazy didn't mean I should have it easier.

After two hours of tickets, hot dogs, chaos, games and good-natured yelling, Mrs. Greenberg took the mike. "Mothers, please take a seat. Counselors and junior counselors, please take your bunks!"

It was almost the end of camp!

"Please give your complete attention to each bunk's special performance in honor of the last day," the director said.

Ahuva and I quickly dressed the girls in the bright purple costumes which we had found in the camp garage. Soon our campers were on stage. Though we motioned to them to keep their hands at their sides, Rivki and Chava shyly curled their hair as they sang. It only added to their charm. Our bunk— the youngest bunk—got the loudest cheers. I must admit we had done a good job!

I watched Bunks Pepsi and Coca Cola perform followed by Bunk Sprite, which acted out a comedy. My mind, however, was on the tips which I was about to receive.

"And now," I heard Mrs. Greenberg announce, "I'll announce camper and counselor awards. Morah Kayla will distribute the awards."

I sat back to listen. Ahuva and I had nominated all the girls in our bunk for an award. Otherwise there would be tears.

And then Mrs. Greenberg said, "And the Counselor-and-Junior-Counselor-Team-Effort Award goes to…Ahuva and Devorah!"

What a nice surprise! Yes, we had worked hard together.

Ahuva was pretty easy to get along with, which made it fun. I liked the certificate. It was written in pink and purple letters. I knew the perfect spot for it in my room—just above my desk.

"Thank you all for coming and we'll see you *im yirtze* Hashem next summer. Have a great year!" Mrs. Greenberg finished.

Another, bigger round of applause, and the director stepped down as the mothers began to round up their children.

"Wait," Mrs. Greenberg called to all the staff. "I have something for you." She reached into a big Macy's bag and took out small white jewelry boxes. She handed one to each junior counselor. I opened mine to find a blue beaded bracelet interspersed with gold beads. I put it on and looked questioningly at Ahuva. Wasn't she getting one too?

From another bag, Mrs. Greenberg took out a bunch of envelopes. She handed one to each counselor. Ahuva said "thank you" and opened hers. A check! I came closer to see, but Ahuva quickly folded it and slipped it into her pocket.

I walked away, the blood pounding in my head. Ahuva got paid and I didn't. I couldn't believe it. This wasn't fair!

I rushed to the bathroom and in the privacy of one of the stalls cupped my head in my palms and banged my head into them over and over like a kid with a temper tantrum. Hot tears coursed down my cheeks.

"I am so angry," I whispered to myself through clenched teeth. I worked just as hard as Ahuva all summer. We split the work equally. Together we taught the children, *davened* with them, told them stories, and made up the schedules. We sweated the same, we were exhausted the same. I wasn't Ahuva's helper. We were partners.

I pinched myself. Bad girl! Why do you care so much about money?

But it wasn't the money I cared about. If I ever needed

anything, my parents always gave it to me. The money wasn't the issue.

It was the fact that there was no difference in the work that Ahuva and I did. It was the fact that I thought we were the same. I expected we would both just get tips. It never occurred to me that she would get paid and I wouldn't. How dumb of me! Of course! She was seventeen years old and the counselor, and I was the junior counselor and only sixteen, which was why she had gotten paid and I hadn't.

Then why in the world had I worked so hard? How stupid of me to have worn myself out for a bracelet!

I looked in the mirror. My face was set, hard, and red. I didn't care. I had every right to cry. I returned to camp grounds. The grounds were emptying as one by one the children and their parents said goodbye and left.

Ahuva spotted me. She waved something at me. I turned away. I hoped she was not asking me to clean up because I was definitely not going to!

"Hey, Devorah," Ahuva called. "Are you okay?"

I didn't want to say anything lest she see how angry I was. I nodded, making sure not to meet her eyes.

"Here are some tips you got from the mothers."

I grabbed them and shoved them into my pocket.

"Don't you want to see them?" Ahuva was surprised.

"Actually, not!" I muttered and quickly walked away.

Sara'le and Chaya ran over to me. "Bye, Morah Devorah!" They took turns dangling from my neck and hugging me.

I couldn't help laughing at their open display of affection. "Bye, girls! I'll miss you!" I really would, too.

When all the parents and campers left, I sat on a stool and looked at my tips. $10, $15, $20, another $10. And thank-you notes. At least the parents appreciated me! And then I thought of Ahuva. She probably got even bigger tips! It was so unfair!

Ahuva walked over and sat down next to me.

"Okay. So tell me what's wrong."

She was so understanding. I sobbed, partly in gratitude that she knew I was mad.

"Ahuva, I worked just as hard as you! I didn't know you would get paid and I wouldn't!"

Silence.

"I wouldn't have come here if they weren't paying me," Ahuva finally answered. "I need some spending money in seminary. My parents can barely pay the tuition!"

"Oh." I stopped crying. I had never known that about her.

"Well," I gazed down at my lap and caught sight of my tips. I couldn't even enjoy them, now that I suspected that we weren't treated equally with the tips either. Once more the tears welled up. "I feel like an idiot for working myself to the bone."

"Let me explain," Ahuva said. "You worked hard, that's true. But I had the responsibility. I had to deal with the phone calls from the parents. I had to go with Chaya to the hospital when she fell down and needed stitches. I had to meet with the director when there were problems. I had to worry about inspection day. And when we went on trips, the kids were my responsibility. Do you understand?"

I just looked at her. I hadn't really thought about that. Neither was I sure if that was enough of a reason for her to get a paycheck while I received a bracelet.

"One day you'll understand." Her voice was firm. No apologies.

"In the meantime," she said, standing up, "let me treat you to some ice cream. I had the best summer with you!"

I followed reluctantly. I wasn't totally happy, but ice cream was ice cream. And maybe one day I *would* understand!

27

Production tryouts had already started. Gitty just had to get a solo this year. If not... She looked at her hands and noticed they were clenched.

Listen to the Music

BY YOCHEVED LEAH PERKAL

"And now it's time for our eleventh-grade Chanukah choir!" the *chagigah* director announced.

Cheers broke out. Shoshana twirled her ponytail around her fingers as she watched Gitty and nine other girls in her class line up on stage. From her seat not too far back, she could see Gitty eyeing her. Gitty held up three fingers. Shoshana smiled back as broadly as she could. Of course, she hadn't forgotten that Gitty had the third solo.

The house lights went out, and only the spotlights on the stage beamed down. The choir began with an original rendition of "*Ma'oz Tzur*." Her lips clamped, Shoshana watched Gitty closely. It always took Gitty a minute or two to shake off her stage fright.

The choir paused, and a tall girl glided to the center of the stage. Shoulders erect, she slid right into her solo without a trace of nervousness. Oh, no, Vivi was never anxious. In the dim room, her face glowed from between the layers of her sleek, blond hair.

The song ended. Vivi stood poised in place as applause rang out. Shoshana couldn't help clapping too. Vivi definitely had a gift.

Another song, another solo, and then it was Gitty's turn. She stepped softly forward. "*Al Hanissim...*" Her voice was sweet as always. Shoshana let out her breath slowly as her fingers drummed in rhythm. "...miracles, yes, miracles today..." The spotlight was shining on Gitty, just as it had shone on Vivi, but somehow Gitty's face seemed to melt away and there was only the music. That's how it always was when Gitty sang.

Out of the corner of her eye, Shoshana sensed a slight movement near the front of the stage. Of course. Chaya Leah, one of the choir heads for the upcoming big production, was on the lookout for candidates.

Gitty's voice faded away as her solo ended, and she slipped immediately back into place among the other girls. But Shoshana barely saw her. She was focused on Chaya Leah. Was it too dark, or could she really make out the look of approval on Chaya Leah's face?

When the house lights went back on, Shoshana rushed toward the stage. Gitty came slowly down the stairs. She didn't say anything, but her hazel eyes were questioning.

"You were great, just great!" Shoshana breathed. "And guess who was looking at you? Chaya Leah! And she had this definite look of approval on her face."

Gitty still didn't utter a word, but her eyes gleamed.

"Let's get some refreshments." Shoshana led her friend to the buffet tables set up at one end of the large auditorium. "Those donuts look yum. You want custard or jelly?"

Gitty eyed the mound of donuts. "You know how much oil

is in them? With my skin, I don't think I can afford a whole one. Take whatever you like, and I'll break off a corner. You don't have to worry about such things."

"Maybe my skin can afford the oil, but I'm not so sure about my waist," Shoshana countered. "You, *lange lokshen*, don't have to worry about such things."

Gitty smiled. "As long as we all have something to worry about." She paused. "So you think Chaya Leah really liked my solo?"

"Of course! I know I wasn't imagining it. She's probably planning a solo for you this year."

Gitty shrugged her shoulders. "Maybe. If there's any left after Vivi gets hers."

Shoshana contained the sigh that threatened to escape her lips. Production tryouts had already started. Gitty just had to get a solo this year. If not... She looked down at her hands and noticed they were clenched. *Yes, and if not, then what?* A taunting little voice piped inside her head. *What exactly are you going to do about it? You couldn't do much about it last year either.*

Shoshana shook her head to clear it. Not now. Tonight was supposed to be fun—and fun only. "I think I'll take some latkes instead. I know they're oily, but at least there's no sugar."

"And don't forget those delicious-looking salads," Gitty said, picking up a small plastic plate. "At least we can eat those without feeling guilty."

The two girls filled their plates and headed to where the rest of their classmates were sitting.

When the *chagigah* ended, Shoshana got a ride home with Gitty's father. She let herself into her darkened house and tiptoed up the stairs to the room she shared with her older sister, Tzirel. Her sister was at the desk, hunched over a thick notebook. Shoshana's tiredness evaporated in an instant. "Is that for the production?"

Tzirel yawned. "Yes, it is, and no, you cannot look at it—not yet anyway. I have to get Mrs. Langer's okay first, and then everything will be official."

"Oh, come on. By then everyone will know. Can't you tell me something that no one knows yet? Don't I get anything out of having my sister as production director?"

"Depends whom you ask. Well, I can tell you one thing that's not a secret, but I don't think anyone really knows yet. Esther Segal is resigning her position as choir head, and we're looking for a replacement to work with Chaya Leah. Esther recommended her cousin, a girl in your class, Vivi Feldman."

Shoshana sank onto her bed. Vivi to be choir head? Poor Gitty. Always standing in Vivi's shadow. At least that's how Gitty viewed it. Vivi probably wasn't even aware of how Gitty felt. But why did Vivi have to flaunt her talent so much? Even if she was better... Shoshana shook her head. No. How could she even let herself think that? Gitty and Vivi both had beautiful voices, but for some reason, Vivi always came out ahead. Like being the first to be chosen for a solo. And last year, she had been in three choirs while Gitty had only been in two.

Tzirel shut her notebook and switched off the desk lamp. "So what do you say? Why are you so quiet all of the sudden?"

"I was just thinking about what you said. It's very... very... surprising, that's all."

"Isn't Vivi as talented as they make her out?"

"Oh, she is. She sings beautifully. It's just that..."

"That?"

"I'm not sure how good she would be at heading something. She's a bit flighty and disorganized..." Shoshana's voice trailed away. Was that her talking? Had she really said that?

Well, Vivi definitely was not strong in organization, and anyway…

Tzirel gave her sister a long look. "This sounds like it's turning into *lashon hara*. On the other hand, I need to know if she's dependable. A choir head doesn't only have to sing well; she needs to have initiative, authority, and reliability."

"I know, I know," Shoshana murmured. "Look, don't take my word for it. She's not my closest friend, so I can't really say I know everything about her. Maybe ask someone else."

Tzirel rose. "I'm going to brush my teeth, but I'm glad you told me this. It's very important. Of course, I'm not accepting it from you. I'll just check it out a bit before we make our final decision."

Shoshana dropped her head onto her pillow and ferreted underneath it for her faithful diary. As always, when she was caught up by the storm of her emotions, her pen flew across the page.

I can't believe what I just did! I'm a bad girl. To put it as plainly as possible, I don't want Vivi to get the job. She'll be on top of the world, and what about Gitty? Poor, poor Gitty. It's hard enough that Vivi outshines her. Okay, I'll admit it to you—never to Gitty though. Vivi is *better than her. There, I actually said it. But why does Vivi have to make it so obvious that she knows she's great, as if the whole world is listening to her? Now she'll really have what to flaunt, and I can't* stand *it.*

The production will be ruined for Gitty, whether she gets a solo or not. I'm dreading the day she finds out. But maybe, she won't have to… because maybe Vivi won't get the job. Am I doing something wrong? I have to be loyal to Gitty. What are friends for anyway? It's not fair that she should always be lagging behind. It makes her so miserable… and me, too. Hashem, please smooth it out somehow!

Shoshana tucked her pen inside her precious little book and dazedly got herself ready for bed. Determined not to think, she closed her eyes and dropped off into sleep.

It all came back to her, though, as soon as she opened her eyes the next morning. What had she done? How could she have besmirched Vivi like that?

As soon as the words of *Modeh Ani* were off her tongue, she called out to her sister in an urgent tone. "Tzirel? Tzirel, are you up yet?"

There was a long yawn. "Well, if I wasn't, I sure am now."

"Sorry, but listen. Forget about what I said yesterday."

"What you said yesterday about what?"

"You know, about Vivi and if she's good for the job or not."

"Oh, right. Vivi. I told you I wasn't going to take your word for it. It was never finalized anyway. I'll just do some checking to make sure she's the person we're looking for."

But you don't understand, Shoshana wanted to shout as she rolled out of bed. *I can't stand the thought of Vivi's being head, even now.* But Shoshana didn't say anything. How could she tell Tzirel and have her know what a horrible sister she had?

Shoshana picked up her hairbrush and examined her face in the mirror. Did she really look like a horrible person? But someone had to stand up for Gitty! Vivi was very popular and had many friends. Would it be so terrible if she didn't get the job? She closed her eyes and tried to picture Gitty as choir head. Gitty and Chaya Leah leading practice, teaching the motions, and standing at the bottom of the stage on production night.

Shoshana opened her eyes and shook her head. She couldn't see it. She simply couldn't envision Gitty shouting out directions, stopping the girls mid-note to correct them, demonstrating how to sing. Gitty was just too unassuming to be a choir head. Shoshana gave her hair one last pat. Oh, well…

The week passed. Tzirel didn't volunteer any more infor-mation, and Shoshana didn't ask. She would just wait along with everyone else until the lists came out.

She didn't have to wait long. They were posted Monday afternoon, just as the girls streamed out of their classes after dismissal. Shoshana took a deep breath and looked at the lists, shutting out all the shouting and exclamations around her.

There they were, the two choir heads: Chaya Leah Brown and Vivi Feldman.

She was suddenly happy that she had gotten to hear about it beforehand. What a shock she would have had seeing Vivi's name up there without warning! She looked at the choir lists. There were four choirs, and Gitty was going to be in all of them. At least that much. If Gitty would just get one solo this year, maybe she would be happy enough to overlook the fact that Vivi had gotten ahead of her again.

"So how do you like your part?" she heard Gitty's familiar voice behind her.

"Huh?"

"You know, part. As in p-a-r-t."

"Part? Oh, right, part." Shoshana couldn't believe she had forgotten. Her eyes turned to the pink drama list. Shoshana Pinter—Joseph as a young boy.

"It's a great part," Gitty was saying. "You get to be Joseph when they tell him he's a Jew and everything. It's perfect for you. I can just see you up there…"

Shoshana couldn't help smiling. It was a good part. Then she heard Vivi's voice behind her, crashing into her pleasant thoughts. Instinctively, she reached for Gitty's arm. "Come, it's late. Let's get going."

Obligingly, Gitty followed Shoshana down the hall and

out of the building. "I was offered soundtrack, by the way," Gitty said.

"You were? That's great!"

"Well, someone had to get Vivi's leftovers." Gitty's usually pleasant voice was tinged with a faint trace of bitterness.

"It's a nice job," Shoshana persisted. "Do you think you'll manage to do it and be in all four choirs too?"

"If Vivi can head choir, don't you think I should be able to do what's left for me? Anyway, who says I'm doing it?"

Shoshana felt a sudden spurt of impatience. Why did Gitty's happiness have to depend on Vivi? If not for Vivi's heading choir, Gitty would have been thrilled with soundtrack. But she didn't say anything. She didn't want to sound preachy. To Shoshana's relief, Gitty changed the subject.

The next morning, Shoshana ran breathlessly up the school steps and down the empty corridor. She hated being late. Maybe, just maybe, Miss Stern wouldn't be in class yet. But there was no such miracle. As she turned around to head to the office for a late note, she bumped into another latecomer. Vivi Feldman. Both girls looked up at the same moment. Shoshana was about to make some joke about both of them being in the soup, but she almost choked on her words as she took in the expression in Vivi's eyes. It was unfriendly, even hostile.

Shoshana felt as if she had been thrown backward. She couldn't remember anyone ever looking at her like that. "What's the matter?" she burst out.

"What's the matter?" By now, Vivi's eyes were practically flashing fire. "You get your sister to take me off the job and almost succeed, too, and then you ask me what's the matter?"

Shoshana stared. How had Vivi found out?

"You think that just because your sister is production director you can arrange things the way you like? Well, it didn't help me any that my cousin Esther recommended me. Your sister Tzirel suddenly came back to her asking her all these questions about me and if I could really handle the job. Apparently she heard that I'm not always reliable, etcetera, etcetera. Esther knows you're in my class and figured you must have stuck your nose in. After thinking about it all night, I decided she was right. It could have only been you. Don't deny it!"

Shoshana felt a bit relieved. So Vivi didn't know for sure. She was only guessing. The seconds ticked by as she tried desperately to think of something to say that would get her off the hook without betraying Gitty. But the words spun around in her brain, tantalizingly out of reach. By the time her head cleared, she knew she had been quiet for too long. She had given herself away.

"I see you're not denying it," Vivi said, her voice cold. "What do you have against me, anyway?"

"It was a whole misunderstanding," Shoshana heard herself say. "I even told my sister that you're great and that you'll do a good job. If I told her anything, it had nothing to do with you."

She knew she was being vague, but it wouldn't be fair to Gitty if she told Vivi the real problem. Because the problem wasn't Vivi's, she suddenly realized. She saw that now. Suddenly, Vivi seemed so human. Why had she and Gitty thought she flaunted herself? It was just Vivi's natural confidence which stood in sharp contrast to Gitty's inferiority feelings.

"I don't have anything against you," Shoshana continued. Well, that was true; by now she didn't.

Was she imagining it or did Vivi's eyes look softer? But Vivi still wasn't saying anything. The silence was killing her.

"Please believe me..." That was as far as Shoshana got. She couldn't say anything else. Clutching her loose-leaf binder tightly, she rushed blindly toward the bathroom for a tissue.

She could hear Vivi coming after her. "I'm sorry for attacking you. I believe you. I believe you. The truth is that I couldn't imagine why you would do such a thing." She handed Shoshana a tissue. "Let's just forget the whole thing. I'm really sorry. I never wanted you to start crying."

Shoshana looked up and couldn't help smiling. "Believe me, I didn't want to either."

Vivi smiled back. "Think we still need a late note?"

The ringing bell was her answer.

Vivi went right into class but Shoshana hung back. She had to get her mind in order before she spoke to Gitty. Because she had to talk to her—if she really wanted to be the good friend she had always believed herself to be. But how to begin? Shoshana was still thinking about it as she and Gitty left the school building together that afternoon, and then as they stopped for a red light on the corner, Gitty said, "I heard all about you and Vivi this morning."

"You did?" Shoshana squelched a wave of irritation. Couldn't anything she said remain private?

"Someone overheard part of your conversation and decided to tell me because if I'm your friend, I have to know." Gitty smiled wryly. "I put two and two together and figured out the rest. I'm really sorry I got you into it. I know it's all because of me. But I never dreamed you would take it so far."

Gitty sounded genuinely contrite, but for once Shoshana didn't feel forgiving. "Did you decide about soundtrack yet?"

"Soundtrack? What does soundtrack have to do with this?"

"Are you taking it?" Shoshana persisted.

"I don't know yet."

"I don't understand you. It's a great opportunity. And you know you'll love it."

Gitty shrugged.

"You know, this is crazy!" Shoshana burst out. "I think I care about it more than you do! When are you going to decide already?"

Gitty still didn't say anything. Shoshana felt herself exploding inside. She turned away before she said something she would regret. She realized they were just outside the neighborhood pharmacy. "I-I have to go in here," she stammered.

"Will it take long?" Gitty asked. "I don't mind coming with you, but you know my mother doesn't like it when I'm late."

"You don't have to wait for me." Shoshana was so glad for the reprieve, she found it difficult looking Gitty in the eye.

"Speak to you later then," Gitty said and continued down the street.

Shoshana pushed open the swinging doors and instinctively headed for her favorite spot, the gift corner. The soft lighting and muted colors of the inviting display assuaged her outraged feelings somewhat. She picked up a small ceramic telephone. It would look great in her miniature collection. Maybe she would come back for it another time.

Her eyes swept over the next shelf. Here was something new: music boxes. So pretty and elegant. Just the right gift for Gitty, whose birthday was coming up next month.

Shoshana couldn't help smiling at herself. Here she was thinking about buying her friend a present when she had just been so furious with her that she'd grabbed the first opportunity to get away. Why the anger anyway? So what if Gitty was acting stupidly about soundtrack! It was her life, after all.

A poster on the wall stared at her. "There's no one like a friend who cares." That was true. But maybe a friend could care too much.

Shoshana glanced at the music boxes again. Each one was

engraved with a quote. She glanced over them quickly, then reached out and lifted one up. "Don't forget to listen to your own music," it read in graceful white letters. It couldn't have been more perfect. Gitty would love the sophisticated present, and maybe one day she would realize that even if she never got to head a choir, she would always have her own music.

Shoshana took out her wallet and stepped into line at the checkout counter. It had been a long day. She hadn't had a moment until now to think about the role she would be playing in the production. Joseph! What a great part! She wondered if she would have to deepen her voice. Hmmm, maybe. She couldn't wait to see her lines.

28

Helping Orah made me feel good—at first anyway. But then things got complicated.

Orah

BY NECHAMA DINA SMITH

Orah had big, beautiful brown eyes, framed by unkempt knotty hair. "I'm special, you know." Her voice was earnest. "I can't learn in a regular school. There are very weird, bad people in my school. They do crazy things all the time. But I don't. Because I'm Jewish."

We were sitting in the lobby of my building on a Monday evening, our first lesson together. Her aunt, Mrs. BenChaim, my French teacher, had introduced her niece to me and asked that I teach her.

Somehow our first lesson led us to the subject of *yetzer tov* and *yetzer hara*. "Orah," I attempted to explain, "Look at the *yetzer tov* and *yetzer hara* this way. The *yetzer tov* is the little voice inside you that encourages you to do the right thing. The *yetzer hara* is the voice that tells you to do the wrong thing. It's like the animal inside you."

"Oh, yes, I get it," Orah cried. "It's like that little fuzzy animal inside you that wags its tail and begs you to follow."

I nodded doubtfully. How important was it exactly how much she understood?

As we finished our lesson, I saw a sports car drive up. Her mother had come to pick her up. She was well dressed, middle-aged, and bathed in enough perfume to supply a roomful of ladies. She gave me the Sephardic kiss on both cheeks, and we arranged for next week's learning.

Later that night, as I sat with my friends finishing up a *Pirkei Avos* project, I was energized. It was an inner happiness that I experienced, as if I had made a difference to someone.

During our next lesson, we discussed kosher food. "My dad makes shrimp," Orah informed me. "I tell him it's bad, but he's not Jewish. He doesn't know. But my mom and I are, and now I'm really Jewish 'cuz I know you. Can I hug you, Yehudis?"

I quickly calculated and decided that yes, for a mitzvah I would bend my natural inclination and let her hug me. Her clumsy arms awkwardly embraced me. My mind raced for a comment I could make to get me out of this hug, and my mouth came up with a suggestion I would deeply regret.

"You know, Orah, you should really come to shul on Shabbos and have the Shabbos meal with my family."

That was the end of my relaxing *Shabbosos*.

I'd forgotten that every Shabbos either my neighborhood friends came over or I went to Faigy's house. I'd forgotten that sometimes I was so tired from working hard all week that I couldn't make it to shul until *Mussaf*. And I'd forgotten that once in a while I needed to spend Shabbos afternoon just reading a book.

Orah's parents walked her over to shul. It was a long way and the sun burned brightly. Her mother asked if she could drive over later to pick her up.

"Well," I said, "if you don't mind, pick her up after Shabbos. I don't want to make Orah get in the car on Shabbos."

Orah loved the *davening*. She could barely read even the English translation, but she listened to the speech, ate the kiddush crackers, and smiled when I introduced her to my friends. Mrs. BenChaim didn't go to this shul, but one of her daughters did. She and Orah didn't talk much. I wondered if Orah's cousin was embarrassed by her.

After our meal, I hung out with Orah in the living room. I reviewed some *Chumash* for a test while she looked at pictures in my album. We spoke occasionally and munched on raisins and cashew nuts.

My friends Leah and Ahuvah came over, but after an hour they said they had to leave, which didn't surprise me, as they're the action-loving type. They didn't invite Orah and me to come with them, which was okay because I didn't quite know how to include Orah.

The minute we made Havdalah, Orah went home, and I was left to myself.

But when the next Shabbos came by, and the next and the next, and each time she'd hint for an invitation for the next week, which of course I extended to her, I began to feel stifled. A tiny fear lurked inside me that I'd be stuck entertaining Orah every Shabbos afternoon for the rest of my life.

I needed a break.

I phoned Mrs. BenChaim. I took a deep breath. "Um, I wanted to tell you thank you for setting up the learning with your niece. I think she wants to be more involved with *Yiddishkeit*. Isn't that great?"

I paused. I wondered how her relationship fared with her sister's daughter.

"I've been inviting her over every Shabbos. I thought may-be...um...do you also want, maybe, to invite her for a Shab-bos?"

"Oh, yes, of course. I understand," Mrs. BenChaim re-plied. "I will call her up."

I hoped it would go well. I didn't hear from Orah for the next few days, and I made plans to sleep over at Faigy's.

Late Friday afternoon, as Faigy and I sat braiding each other's hair in Faigy's room, the cock-a-doodle-doo of my cell phone gave me a jolt. I gingerly let go of Faigy's braid and peered at the phone. It was Orah calling. My heart gave a little jump.

Her voice was low. It took me a minute to realize she was crying.

"You betrayed me. You were my best friend, the only friend I ever had."

I gasped and covered my mouth.

Faigy swiveled around and looked at me questioningly. "I'm her best friend!" I mouthed in horror. The pressure and the guilt were overwhelming.

"And now," Orah continued steadily, the most normal-sounding I'd ever heard, "you told my aunt you didn't want me to come. You'd rather be with your other friends."

My heart was pounding. It was true; I wanted to be with my other friends. But I didn't say that to Mrs. BenChaim. Senseless woman. Was she too lazy to invite Orah? Did she have to get me into trouble instead? Or perhaps Mrs. Ben-Chaim never said those things to her. Perhaps that was Orah's interpretation of what her aunt had said.

"I am very, very hurt. I was crying all day and I can't stop."

Faigy poked me. She had to know what was going on. I whispered to her quickly as Orah cried.

"Good riddance!" Faigy shouted in a whisper. "Tell her you're sorry, but you have a life."

I nodded to my friend, but I couldn't bring myself to say anything to Orah.

"Orah?" I finally said. My voice sounded cool and crisp to my ears, like a snobby teacher. "I didn't tell your aunt that I didn't like you coming. I just thought you'd like to eat at her house this Shabbos since I was going away to my friend's house. Please don't be so sad." And in a conclusive tone, I added, "Try to be happy this Shabbos," and I hung up.

On the surface, that Shabbos went perfectly. I did all the things I loved to do and didn't do anything I didn't want to do. I didn't have to help much either; it was not my house. We slept late; no one was waiting for us at shul. We talked the whole Shabbos long without trying to accommodate a stranger who wouldn't understand us. And we took a walk and visited some sophisticated relative of Faigy's whom we'd never have visited had Orah been with us.

But I went home heartbroken. The whole Shabbos, a little nagging uncomfortable feeling had grown and grown, until it catapulted into a huge depression.

Motza'ei Shabbos I tossed and turned in bed. Thoughts streamed at me from all directions. What was life all about? Was it about being comfortable? Was it selfish of me to want to have an enjoyable Shabbos? What did Hashem want of me? Could it be that He wanted me—and here I sat straight up in bed at the thought—to go beyond myself to help another person? But then, if so, could I *never* just relax and enjoy myself?

Surely Hashem knows that I can't always be helping others. I needed breaks. I needed to function like a normal person. I needed to spend some time with friends like myself, friends who understood me. I consoled myself with that thought.

268 : ONIONS ALWAYS MAKE ME CRY

Maybe now I was ready to resume sharing my *Shabbosos*—some of them anyway—with Orah—if she'd ever forgive me. I knew that by making her happy I'd make my deeper, inner self happy, too.

I snapped on the lamp and leaned over to my daily planner.

In great big letters, I wrote in Sunday's slot, in between studying for history and going shopping with my sister, "Call Orah. Resolve! And invite her!"

I just hoped she'd forgive me for what she considered a betrayal. I hoped it wasn't going to be all or nothing with her. I hoped she'd understand that I was human and that I didn't belong only to her.

But at least from my end I was ready to give up my comfort and make her feel wanted. But every once in a while, I would take a break and not feel guilty about it.

Yes, that was it. Finally I fell asleep, at peace with my decision.

29

Sometimes being around different people makes you feel most like yourself.

Long Skirts and Lizards

BY NOMI DAYAN

"Can I ask you a question?" she said.

"Sure," I answered, looking up.

"Your skirt," she said, "why's it so long?"

Before going to the Chirichuahua Mountains in Arizona to participate in animal and plant research, I thought that my long skirts would hamper me from hiking, rock climbing, and meandering around sharp cacti in the desert. And with my long sleeves I would surely roast in the scorching heat. But I was wrong. I turned out to be the one best dressed for mountain rambling. My long skirts protected me from the bristles, spikes, thorns, and needles of mesquite, cacti, and prickly shrubbery. The people who wore shorts had a much harder time. And thanks to my long sleeves and buttoned top button I did not suffer one sunburn; the material shielded me from the harsh rays of the sun and from the biting bugs as well.

I also thought I wouldn't know as much as the researchers and scientists. Me, a yeshivah girl from Brooklyn—how could I compete with them? On the plane ride there I hastily memorized the scientific name of every possible reptile living in the southwestern region of the United States. How silly I was to worry! Everything was just fine—in fact, better than fine. When a snake would cross our path during fieldwork, I would instantly call out its name. I hadn't realized this was meant to be a learning experience, and you weren't supposed to come knowing everything. You're just supposed to *leave* knowing more than you did when you came. Fortunately, I did leave having learned a whole lot, to my delight! (As for my family, however, that is another matter. They are not quite as delighted about my trip and learning experience. They think I talk about it *too* much.)

I was the only religious Jew at the research station. There were several other Jews there who were not religious. I had been apprehensive about not knowing as much as the other researchers, but I had been even more nervous about my being religious. I would not be wearing hiking shorts or eating from the same dishes as everyone else. I would not be joining in research from sunset on Friday until Saturday night. Yet, as I came to see, being Jewish did not in any way take away from learning or doing well in my studies. It actually enhanced my experience tremendously.

Interestingly enough, when we were not talking about western diamondback rattlesnakes, whiptail lizards, or screech owls, we were talking about Judaism. The people loved to ask me about it and talk about it. I got used to being thrown all kinds of questions: What exactly is kosher? Why do Jewish men have those little fringe things dangling beside their pockets? What's that little book I see you holding in the morning?

What is the Sabbath, and why do you keep it? What's that little candle I see through your window on Friday nights? Why can't you touch lights on Saturday? You mean you never, *ever* wear pants? Why do you always say "thank you?" How come you're always smiling? Why are you so nice to people? Is it hard to be Jewish? How is it that the Jewish people survived so *long*?

When I answered their questions, they never said or conveyed by their look, "Well, that's kind of weird," or "How ancient and outdated that is!" In fact, someone even commented, "You know why you guys are still here? Because you don't take the easy way out."

I was the only one in this group of scientists, biologists, botanists, ornithologists, and herpetologists who did not believe in evolution. When the others looked at a mountain, they saw millions of years of evolution. When I looked at a mountain, I saw Hashem's fingerprint. I was careful never to get into debates in this area, and most respected me for what they called my "decision."

Some of the Jews there became more interested in the heritage they had either left behind or had never had a chance to know, and some even lit Shabbos candles with me. They saw me as someone who does not leave Judaism behind because it's "too hard" to keep or because it "conflicts" with what one learns in school. They also saw how excited I got about seeing a spadefoot toad and how careful I was about checking the little labels on the foods that I ate. They noticed how I woke up early to have enough time to *daven*. They saw how much I loved talking about Passover and how much I loved discussing pythons. (For me, science and religion are not separate entities. All aspects of the world point to Hashem.)

Being far from home in a foreign environment, I became

more aware that I needed to make time to keep up my relationship with Hashem. Sometimes being around different people makes you feel most like yourself. I felt the significance and holiness of *mitzvos* much more than I did at home. At home I sometimes take saying morning *brachos* for granted, or preparing for Shabbos, or wearing a skirt that covers the knees. At the research station in the Chirichuahua Mountains I could not wait to say the morning *brachah* of *shelo asani goy*—thank You for making me Jewish! When Friday came, only Shabbos was on my mind—four hours left until Shabbos, three hours left… Did I have my matches ready? Were all the wrinkles out of my outfit? And when Shabbos came, I felt the Shabbos *kallah* enter my room. At home, it can sometimes be a mere weekly routine, but in the wilds of Arizona I was very conscious that I was now stopping work and all my activities for this one day, which I would share with Hashem. From Shabbos I gathered inner peace, quiet, and harmony for the coming week.

Out in the middle of the Arizona mountains, I got to feel closer to Hashem through the many different aspects of nature too. When I smelled the bark of Apache pine tree for the first time, let me tell you, if there is a hint of the fragrance of Gan Eden in this world, it is emanating from that tree! The others smelled it and thought, isn't it great—evolution! But what I thought was—isn't it great—what *brachah* can I say! (P.S. There *is* a *brachah* to say for trees that give off a pleasing smell—check in your siddur!) And when I caught the first glimpse of the Chirichuahua Mountains, I was filled with happiness about being able to say the special *brachah* upon seeing mountains. When I said Havdalah for myself, I really understood the meaning of *hamavdil bein kodesh l'chol*.

Learning about wildlife, from bees to hummingbirds, fills

me with wonder at Hashem's greatness. The woodpecker that woke me up in the morning (he was my alarm clock) has built in shock-absorbers in his skull so he can drill into tree bark, looking for insects. The little brown bats that flutter around at dusk can each catch 1,200 insects in just one hour! I noted the determination of the Harvester ant colony near my cabin; no one is supervising the ants, yet no ant is ever lazy. Each does her work (the workers are female) to the best of her ability—a model for us to do *retzon* Hashem with *zrizus* and enthusiasm. (I couldn't help but think—why can't I be like this little ant that just does what she's supposed to do?) I listened to the robin that sat on my roof every afternoon singing his little heart out, producing the most beautiful songs imaginable. I was amazed at the colors I found on lizards; is there an artist who can paint the world and everything in it better than Hashem? (And they talk about evolution!)

When you go out into the world, remember that we, as Am Yisrael, are an example for all the other nations of the world to see and learn from. That's why we must always be on our best behavior. People are watching us all the time (I learned from my experience at the research station), even if it doesn't look like it. When you smile at someone or say "thank you" or "good morning," it has an effect. If you hold the door for the person behind you, it sticks in their heads. If you throw your gum wrapper in the street, that also makes an impression on them. Be a model for everyone to learn from, and make Hashem and Am Yisrael proud.

Lastly, try to pick up the hints of Hashem's master plan that He leaves for you to find. Look for Him in the slopes of valleys, the crests of mountains, the delicate balance of creatures, the way the light hits the water, the way the wind teases your hair, the face of your friend, who is made *b'tzelem Elokim*.

And most importantly, leave time for Hashem. Then you will come to loving Hashem and feeling His never-ending love for you.

30

No one, not even her good friend Chaya Leah, could understand the suffering Sheindel endured during P.E. Here she was, an honors student, the one who helped others with their homework, and she couldn't keep up with a few simple exercises which all the other girls found a cinch to do. It was bizarre. It was humiliating.

Holler If
You Need Me

BY STERNA CITRON

Her long, blond hair swinging, her stomach muscles taut, the P.E. teacher bent over her CD player and pressed the button.

"Ready, set, here we go!" Janet Drew's Nike-sneakered foot came down in time to the quick beat of the music. The second exercise class of the year had begun.

Ugh! How Sheindel Bergman hated P.E.! It wasn't the physical activity that she minded. She actually liked that. It was the parts where you needed coordination, for which reason she also hated dancing. On top of that, she had this feeling that she and the teacher weren't going to get along. Maybe it was the over-confident way Ms. Drew swung her mane of dyed blond hair, or maybe it was the overly viva-cious way she smiled, white teeth against dark tan. From past experience, Sheindel knew those gut feelings were usu-ally not wrong.

"Everybody ready?" Ms. Drew called out. "March in place!"

Everyone dutifully marched in place, twenty girls in rows of four, in their baggy sweatshirts and their long pants un-derneath their skirts. Sheindel marched, too, in the last row, in the farthest corner, as far away as possible from the in-quisitive eyes of Ms. Drew.

"Inhale, step in, step touch, arms circle. Let's go!"

Oh, no. The teacher wasn't even demonstrating. Ms. Drew expected everyone to know exactly what to do. What, was everyone supposed to be born knowing? Sheindel watched Chaya Leah in front of her. Her good friend had no problem getting it. Lucky her. Sheindel tried her best to copy her. It wasn't too hard—yet.

"Exhale," Ms. Drew commanded. "Reverse your arms. Inhale. Reverse again."

This wasn't so bad. If it only stayed like this...

"Give me four punches." Uh-oh, things were picking up speed quickly. "Hit it, hit it, pull together. Three, hit it, hit it, pull together." Ms. Drew was finally demonstrating, but she moved too fast for Sheindel to figure out the sequence of movements.

Meanwhile the rest of the class, nineteen girls, punched out once, twice, pulled back and clapped simultaneously, all with perfect rhythm, while she, the twentieth girl, stood fro-zen.

Finally she gathered her courage and punched out, but by then everyone was up to the clapping part.

"Give me four. Give me three. Hit it, hit it, pull togeth-er," the teacher called out gaily.

It was going much too fast. Sheindel had no idea what to do. She was sure she looked like a total idiot in front of her classmates.

"Two, hit it, hit it. One, hit it, hit it." Oh, good, the end was in sight.

But it wasn't.

"Turn to the right and give me four!" Ms. Drew ordered. They were going to do this in all four directions! This couldn't be happening!

Sheindel turned to the right. She tried again, determined that this time she would get it. She punched with the left hand. She punched with the right hand. But now what? Where was she supposed to pull back *to*? And what were her feet supposed to be doing? It was all so confusing.

"Turn to the back."

Suddenly, everyone was facing her. She hastily turned around and faced the back wall. She was in the front row now, where everyone could see her from the back. No doubt all eyes were upon her, watching as she made all the wrong steps and clapped at all the wrong times. Every second was pure agony.

"Turn to the wall."

What a relief! At least people weren't looking at her any-more. From the row in front of her, Chaya Leah caught her eye and shot her a look of sympathy. Sheindel appreciated having a friend who understood her. But could Chaya Leah really grasp what she was going through? After all, Chaya Leah was an excellent dancer. She couldn't possibly imagine what it felt like to have two left feet.

"She's not bad," Chaya Leah mouthed encouragingly,

keeping up with the one-two, one-two of the teacher.

"Whatever..." Sheindel whispered back disconsolately.

"Hey, it's only gym," Chaya Leah murmured.

It was easy enough for Chaya Leah to say. How could she possibly understand the suffering Sheindel was enduring? Here she was, an honors class student, a star pupil, the one who helped others with their homework, and she couldn't keep up with a few simple exercises which everyone else found a cinch to do. It was too bizarre. And here Chaya Leah was encouraging her—Chaya Leah, who wasn't even such a great student. Good at sports, yes, but basically a B- student.

"Okay! Get ready for the karate kick! Think of someone you hate, and really give it to them."

Everyone laughed. Except for Sheindel. She didn't see anything funny about it.

"Turn out your kick!" the teacher shouted.

The teacher turned, flexed her foot, and shot out her heel backwards with perfect precision, grinning all the while.

"Turn it over!"

Sheindel made a half turn and kicked with all her might. So far so good.

"Now turn out your kick!" Sheindel turned out her foot and kicked again. It wasn't bad, this karate kicking. She actually felt like she was releasing some of her anger and frustration.

"Take it backwards!"

Backwards, backwards... Sheindel got it.

At least there was one exercise she could do. But just when she finally mastered it and congratulated herself for it, Ms. Drew moved on to a new exercise. Why did it have to be like that? Couldn't she stay with the same exercise for more than two minutes?

Sheindel glanced at her watch apprehensively. They were only ten minutes into P.E. There were thirty-five of pure torture left!

• • •

When the P.E. class was at long last over, Sheindel was the first one out the door. Chaya Leah, her face red and shining, followed her into the locker room where they changed back into their school uniforms.

Amid the opening and banging of lockers, Sheindel could hear her classmates commenting excitedly, "Isn't she great?" and "I really like her class!"

Out of loyalty to her friend, Chaya Leah had the good sense not to rave about the class. It made Sheindel all the more conscious that this problem was hers, and nobody else's.

Next to her, Leiba was sitting on the bench, tying her shoes. "Wasn't she funny?" she asked Sheindel.

"Umm, not exactly," Sheindel answered morosely.

Leiba turned to the person on the other side of the bench and asked her the same question. The two of them agreed that the teacher was not only funny but a fantastic teacher too.

What was with these girls, Sheindel wondered. Couldn't they see through Ms. Drew? Yes, she knew her stuff. And she knew how to make the girls work hard and didn't let them get away with goofing off like some of their previous gym teachers had done. But to call her fantastic? Well, if you think a sergeant barking orders to her troops is fantastic, then Ms. Drew was too.

Seeing how unhappy her friend looked, Chaya Leah tried to console her. "We don't have any more P.E. until after vacation."

"I know, but after the Yamim Tovim there's the whole rest of the year," she answered glumly.

"It's not so bad. You'll get better. You'll learn," said Chaya Leah encouragingly.

"Sure I'll learn," Sheindel answered sarcastically. "Don't you understand? It's not like learning an algebra problem, which you'll get if you work at it long enough. It's more like banging a nail into the wall with your fingers. If you don't have the right tools, if you're not coordinated, you'll never get it."

Chaya Leah didn't go for her *mashal*. "If you want, I'll help you," she offered.

"Thanks, but it's okay," answered Sheindel dryly. Since when was Sheindel the one to need help?

She slammed her locker door shut. She wasn't going to dwell on P.E. anymore. She was going to enjoy her Yom Tov vacation.

Yom Tov vacation was wonderful, but hectic. Even if Sheindel had wanted to, there wasn't much time to think about P.E. There was always something to do between the cooking, serving, clearing up, and dish-washing. She didn't mind the work, and the guests were interesting, especially her uncle Rabbi Yaakov Berger and his wife Rivkie. Trust Feter Yankel to talk about real issues. He never bothered with small talk.

As her father and brother lingered in the sukkah after the Shabbos day meal, the sun filtering slowly through the dappled leaves above them, her uncle said, "One thing I noticed about students today. They learn all these wonderful, lofty Torah principles in school, but when it comes to life, they don't put them into practice."

What was Feter Yankel talking about? Sheindel didn't say anything as she made a pile of the dessert dishes, but she listened carefully as her father responded.

"Really?" Mr. Berger said. "I'm surprised you say that. What about all the *chessed* committees that the girls have? The girls in Sheindel's high school do some marvelous things for the community."

"I'm not talking about that," her uncle answered. "I'm talking about the girls' *middos*. From *Chumash* and *Rashi* alone you can learn which *middos* are good and which ones to avoid. But the girls just study to get high grades on their tests, and they don't apply the lessons they learn. I see girls who are arrogant, who think the world of themselves."

"Arrogant?" her father said. "That's bad. Don't they know what the Maharal says about arrogance—that it is the root of all *aveiros*?"

Was her uncle right? Were the girls in her school lacking good *middos*? And were they really arrogant?

Thoughtfully, she scooped up the dishes and carried them out of the sukkah. Now that she thought of it, there were some girls who were conceited. They thought so much of themselves that they wouldn't talk to anyone they felt was beneath them.

• • •

Too soon, it was the last day of vacation. Sheindel spent most of her last free evening on the phone with Leiba preparing for the next day's *Navi* quiz. Together they went over the *perek* about Eliyahu Hanavi going up to Shamayim with the *peirush* of the Alshich Hakadosh.

"Thanks so much, Sheindel," Leiba said when they finished. "I have a feeling I'm going to do really well tomorrow, thanks to you."

Sheindel hung up the phone in a happy mood. It gave her a feeling of satisfaction to help someone.

Life was good. If only she didn't have P.E., life would be perfect!

The next day, there they were, all lined up in rows, like her little brother's toy soldiers. And there was Sergeant Drew, shouting orders.

"I'm not going to have any compassion on you today," the teacher announced.

Thrills.

Sheindel was determined to keep up. She'd concentrate really hard. If you try hard, you have to succeed, right? But no matter how hard she tried, she was always a beat behind everyone else.

And then came a new horror. It was a new movement called "kick-ball-chain." There was a little kick followed by a skip, and then some other quick step that she couldn't catch. As for the name—kick-ball-chain—she had no idea what it had to do with the step. The only thing she could think of was the iron ball and chain worn by convicts around their ankles to prevent them from escaping. It didn't do much for her spirits to think of that.

She tried to shrink into the back wall so the teacher wouldn't see her, which was hard as she was taller than most of the girls in the class, including Chaya Leah.

The teacher announced in a significant tone of voice, "This is an easy exercise. I hope we're *all* keeping up."

As there was only one person not keeping up, it was only too evident who that girl was.

"Let's see," the teacher stopped and gazed at her seating chart while the voice of Shwekey rose from the CD player. "Sh-shein-del. Did I pronounce it right?" She stared straight at Sheindel.

"Yes," the girls sang out as they kicked and skipped in perfect unison.

"Sheindel, just follow the girl in front of you, and you'll be fine."

She could barely answer, her throat was so tight. "Thank you, I'll do that," she answered finally, her voice sounding strangely raspy. What did she think she had been doing all along?

As she strove in vain to master the new step, Sheindel thought about those prisoners with the balls and chains. How miserable they must have been! She really felt for them. They probably had a taskmaster like Ms. Drew. Funny how misery had a way of making you more empathetic.

"Holler if you need me," Ms. Drew called out loudly.

Yeah, sure. Like Sheindel would really do that.

She stumbled along until the end of the class, by which time she had come to a decision. No way was she going to suffer all year long.

"Loosen up," Chaya Leah advised her when she saw her friend's grim face as they left P.E. "Don't take it so seriously. It's not like it's *Chumash* or anything."

She didn't tell Chaya Leah what she had resolved to do. She was going to get out of taking gym.

• • •

Knock, knock. Her heart raced as she waited for the principal to answer the door. She whispered a little prayer to Hashem that her mission be successful.

"Yes, how can I help you?"

Sheindel had expected to see the usual stern face of the principal, but instead Mrs. Rubin was smiling. Maybe she had caught her in a good mood. Maybe, just maybe, she'd be open to Sheindel's request.

Sheindel sat down on the edge of the chair. Gripping her notebooks tightly, she wondered where she should start from.

Something positive first, she thought. "I like all my classes. They're really good. All except one."

Mrs. Rubin looked startled. "And which class is that?"

"It's P.E. I just can't do it." She swallowed the sob that lurked below her throat. "So I'd like to take another class during that time. I can help out in the office," she offered, inspired by desperation, "or I can tutor someone. I'll do anything as long as I don't have to go back there."

"And what about the class don't you like?" Mrs. Rubin asked curiously, leaning forward in her swivel chair.

She gulped. How to say it? Well, she would say it like it was. "I can't keep up with everybody else no matter how hard I try. And it really bothers me. Not to mention it's extremely embarrassing."

"I can understand that," Mrs. Rubin replied thoughtfully. "You are used to excelling, and here you are in a situation in which you're not excelling. It must be very hard for you."

"Oh, thank you for understanding!" Wow! It suddenly struck her that principals weren't as bad as she had thought. They were quite *human*, in fact.

Mrs. Rubin sat quietly, chin in hand, her eyes fixed on the distant trees out of the window. Suddenly, she turned and focused her gaze on Sheindel. She had obviously come to a decision. "Although I feel for you, I think you should stick it out. And I'm not saying this only because the school has rules, and if I make an exception for you, I have to make it for others, too. I'm saying it because I think you'll gain from it."

"How can I possibly gain from it?" Sheindel asked, her heart sinking.

"You'll see that you don't have to excel in everything. Sometimes it's good enough just to try your best," Mrs. Rubin said in a final tone of voice.

Mrs. Rubin got up and ushered Sheindel to the door. The meeting was over.

Sheindel wiped away the tears of frustration that stung her eyes. Defeat was bad enough; nobody else had to see it. She had opened herself up to this woman, this stranger, and admitted something very personal, something she hadn't really ever put into words before—how important it was for her to do well and how awful it was to feel incompetent. And what had she gotten out of it? Zero.

"Why, Hashem, why?" she asked. Twice a week for the rest of the year she'd have to feel like a total fool.

She rejoined the class in time for Minchah. She *davened* with more *kavanah* than usual. No doubt other people had worse *tzaros*, but being humiliated in P.E. wasn't exactly a picnic. Surely Hashem had to have pity on her. She didn't mind asking Hashem for help. It was a lot easier than asking people. She really hated admitting her neediness to people.

The thought occurred to her: was that being arrogant, the fact that she didn't like asking for help from people? No, she wasn't one of those arrogant girls Feter Yankel had talked about. After all, she liked helping her classmates. It was just that she disliked asking others for help.

• • •

The next P.E. class took place two days later, too soon for Sheindel's liking. She changed into her gym uniform and didn't even attempt to hide her discontent.

"What kind of teacher is it who can't teach in a way that students understand?" she grumbled to Chaya Leah as they took their places. "Why can't she teach us the steps slowly so everyone gets the idea?"

Chaya Leah wisely refrained from pointing out that for everyone else it was slow enough.

"Okay, class. Today we're going to learn the cha-cha," Ms. Drew cheerily called out.

As if life wasn't hard enough.

But the other girls were all eager to learn. "We never heard of the cha-cha! What is it?" the girls wanted to know.

"It's a dance from the fifties. Your grandmothers probably know it. Here's how it goes. Forward with the right foot. One. Two. Cha cha cha."

The directions seemed straightforward enough. Two steps forward followed by a shuffle. She tried the first part and got it. Yay!

"Now back with the left foot. One. Two. Cha cha cha."

Back with the left foot! Why didn't the choreographer make it back with the same foot? Why did he have to make it complicated?

She tried switching over to the left foot. *Now where am I*, she asked herself, coming to a standstill, while the music blared on.

"Can I show you?" offered Chaya Leah. "It's really not hard." Without losing the beat she reached out towards Sheindel's hand.

Sheindel's hand automatically stiffened. She wanted so much to say, "No, thank you. I'm fine."

"Come on," her friend called out encouragingly, hand still outstretched.

Sheindel still didn't respond.

A little bell rang in the back of her mind. Could this be what her uncle meant about being arrogant? Was it pride that was preventing her from accepting Chaya Leah's help? No, that would not be a good thing, especially in view of the fact that Chaya Leah was trying to help her not look like a complete idiot. Besides, Chaya Leah was offering, and she'd be hurt if she refused.

Slowly, Sheindel stretched out her hand.

"Forward with the right foot," murmured Chaya Leah. "Okay, good! Now back with the left foot."

It wasn't easy taking instructions from Chaya Leah, to put it mildly. It was actually one of the hardest things Sheindel had done in a very long time. Thinking about that, she hesitated and missed a step.

"Don't worry, just keep moving in time to the music," Chaya Leah reassured her.

The next time Sheindel did it. Back with the left foot. "I think I got it," she murmured excitedly.

"You're doing great!" Chaya Leah exclaimed.

"I hear talking," Ms. Drew called imperiously from the front of the room.

"I'm showing Sheindel the steps," Chaya Leah explained.

"Okay, but as soon as you get it, go back to your place."

Sheindel stepped back to her place, careful not to lose the sequence. Right foot forward. Left foot back. Incredibly, unbelievably, she was doing it.

But even more exciting was that she had overcome her nature. She had let herself be helped and had survived the experience. Maybe next time she'd even ask Chaya Leah to help her with that kick-ball-chain thing.

Who knew? Maybe one day she'd even like P.E.

31

Friends Apart

BY NECHAMA DINA SMITH

Shaina was my best friend since first grade. People used to say we looked alike. We would sleep over at each other's houses, each stay ending in a play fight which would inevitably lead to a real fight, which would dissolve the next day when we'd be best friends again. Shaina was incredibly fun, and life was never boring around her. She was beautiful, graceful, talented, and brilliant. But unlike me, who was very studious and conscientious and wouldn't settle for any grade less than a 95%, Shaina's grades would fluctuate. One year she didn't get along with the teacher, so she hardly showed up. She'd say she was sick. That year her grades were practically failing.

As we grew up, our personalities continued to develop. From a quiet girl, Shaina became outgoing, funny, and with-it. I sort of continued down the quiet path, delving deeply into my studies and my books and having philosophical discussions, mostly with Shabbos guests. We still enjoyed sleeping over at each other's houses for Shabbos or weeknights and even outgrew our regular childhood fights.

When Shaina and I turned fourteen, we joined a thriving high school in the community. Ninth grade had many girls, and there was a branch—a smaller class made up of scholastic girls who wanted academic challenge—as if our regular studies weren't difficult enough.

A week before school started, my father approached me. "Leah'le," he said, "you know *kein ayin hara* you're a very bright girl, and one day you'll *im yirtzeh* Hashem marry a *talmid chacham…*"

What was my father getting at? I wondered. He mainly talks to me about serious things.

"You know, I saw Rabbi Gordon at last night's *chasunah.* He expressed surprise that you didn't choose the higher level of ninth grade."

Oh, that was it. "Ta," I sighed, "you know Shaina can't make it into that class."

My father nodded. "I just thought I'd tell you."

I knew why my father didn't argue with me. Although he was always proud of my learning accomplishments and would help me when I didn't understand my work, he was also very pleased with my friendship with Shaina. So he left his comment without further pressure.

The first day of school, Shaina and I were glued together. We each wore our clean, starched white shirts and new gray uniform skirts, our hair in neat ponytails and our new shoes (at least mine) hurting from the stiff leather.

We sat near each other at the school assembly. While the principal spoke, we listened as we looked at the masses of girls, all sitting perfectly still. We were looking for girls we thought looked nice and also for girls we should avoid, although I couldn't tell too much from just glancing around.

"Leah," Shaina whispered urgently, "we have to find seats next to each other in class!"

I smiled. Of course, I wanted to sit next to her. I was so glad she felt the same way.

But when we reached our classroom, I heard some girls groan softly and others giggle nervously. On each desk was a piece of paper on which was printed in large letters the name of a student. Our seats were assigned! To my dismay, Shaina's name was placed two rows away from mine! But at least, I realized hopefully, we were in the same row horizontally so we could still make eye contact with each other. I gave her a disappointed little wave and sat down.

Everyone around me settled down, and our *mechanechet*, Mrs. Green, spoke. "Welcome to a brand new school for you, to a four-year stay in which I hope you will learn a lot, grow a lot, and share a lot." She spoke warmly and confidently. "Please take out a piece of paper, and write down what special talents you have and whether you'd like to be on school committees, such as the *chessed* or library committee. This is just to get a rough idea, and later I'll present you with suggestions of group ideas."

I wrote that I loved reading and that I could help with anything to do with a library. I could also tutor, and I could write poems. I put the poem part in parenthesis because I wasn't sure if that was important or not. I glanced at Shaina, scribbling away. She was probably writing about her calligraphy and art skills.

When our papers were collected, Mrs. Green gave us an introduction to *Chumash*. I took notes neatly, keeping the margins clear. During questions I highlighted the important words. I wondered if Shaina was taking notes. Usually she'd only jot down one or two things and draw pictures on the side, although she did listen and remember better than I did—that is, what she cared to remember. But I was sitting too far from her to keep tabs.

I knew I couldn't ask for my seat to be switched. That would be the ultimate childish request! I was feeling upset, and to my surprise, my anger turned toward Shaina as I saw her smile to the girl in front of her when she handed Shaina back the pen she had dropped.

At recess I whispered to Shaina, "I need the bathroom! Can you come help me find it?"

"I know where it is," Shaina flashed me a smile. "Just make a right at the end of the hall."

"Okay," I said weakly and headed out with my shoulders slumped. Didn't Shaina understand that I couldn't be left alone in this huge strange school? But then I spotted Chavi from my old class, and we chatted while we searched for the bathroom. Okay, so I made it there fine.

I hurried back. To my chagrin, Shaina was standing with three girls around her. They were all laughing. I eased in, attempting to look comfortable. "Hi," I tried to announce, but only Shaina heard me. The three girls acted as if they didn't hear me. I decided right then and there I didn't like those girls and I didn't want to be their friend.

As the day wore on, my heart grew heavier and heavier. The discovery that Shaina was blossoming in the new environment hit me like a ton of bricks. She thrived with all the attention her charm brought. She joked around, she smiled, and she was friendly to everyone in sight.

And I sullenly looked on and cried to myself. My best friend had disappeared. She hardly glanced my way. True, when I'd approach her, she'd give me her wide, happy grin.

But…I guess, I thought glumly, *I'm just like one in fifty girls. I'll never be popular like her. She's already forgotten about me.*

The girl sitting behind me introduced herself to me. Her name was Bracha. She brought out her eighth-grade yearbook and showed me the pictures. She was sweet. She was nothing like Shaina, of course, but I was glad to have someone nice for a neighbor.

The whole first week of school was torture. One day Mrs. Green announced, "Here's a tentative arrangement for who will be in which committee: monthly bulletin board—Tzipora Feld, Shaina Shapiro, Chana Gold; *chessed* heads for ninth grade—Nechama Klein, Goldy Schwartz, and Yocheved Cohen; library—Leah Friedman and Bracha Weiss…"

That was all I needed to know. I was happy to work in the library. I'd busy myself in books until I'd forget my troubles.

I stayed in my seat during recess, as was becoming usual, while Bracha and I made some library plans. Out of the corner of my eye, I spotted Shaina and her bulletin teammates talking excitedly. I was so jealous. And when Shaina whispered to me that they'd be sleeping over at her house to work on the new bulletin, I blinked my eyes and forced a frozen smile.

"Isn't Bais Rochel great?" she exclaimed.

I nodded. "Oh, yes." And before she could ask me to join her for lunch, I slipped away.

That night after school, I made a decision.

"Ta," I said, "maybe you're right. I should be challenged more. Is it too late to join the advanced class?"

My mother jumped in. "But what about Shaina? I think social life is important for a young girl."

I wanted to cry to my mother and say that Shaina wasn't my friend anymore. But it was too painful to discuss. My father was already on the phone with the principal.

"Ma," I said, "don't worry—it's really still the same class."

But I knew it wasn't really the same class. And my mother's "oh" seemed to know it, too.

The next morning, without a word to Shaina, I joined the higher class. The girls there were very smart and actually comfortable to be with. I did, however, suddenly feel not quite as smart as I used to. But I felt proud to be able to partake in free-style discussions comparing *mefarshim*. The work would be harder, but I was one rare student who loved doing homework. My heart ached when I thought of Shaina, but then I couldn't wait for recess to tell her how excited I was about my move.

When I got the chance, I started racing down the hall towards Shaina's class, then noticed that my new classmates all moved sedately and serenely. They were not jumpy like the crowd that encircled Shaina. So I walked as quickly as I could while still looking calm until I found Shaina.

"Shaina! I moved classes!" I told her.

"You did?" Her voice was low, quiet. Oh, no, I couldn't believe it. She was shocked! Before my eyes she turned to her new friends and continued the conversation with them, completely ignoring me. This time I wasn't upset. I understood that she was most probably hurt. I'd give her time. Soon we'd be friends again.

I found Bracha and told her about my change. "Oh, really?" She looked disappointed. "I thought you were sick and didn't come to school today."

"Look at the library cards I made," I said, showing her. At least I could count on Bracha to be a friend!

I returned to my new class. Our *Ivrit* teacher spoke in *Ivrit* and would not accept even one English word from us. I loved it. This was the way to learn! We were a small group of ten girls and raising our hands was not an issue as it was for the regular ninth grade.

Suddenly, I was not so mad at Shaina. I was glad that she was happy. I just didn't want her to be angry with me. I wanted her to remain my friend. I walked with two of my new classmates to the lunchroom. I saw Shaina and picked up my hand to wave "hi," but there was no eye contact. I was scared if I'd say something she'd ignore me, so I didn't.

I called her after school. No one answered. I left a message. "Hi, Shaina? Can you please call me back? It's Leah! Bye."

She didn't call back. This had never happened before. I called again. I started to leave another message when I realized she might be sitting there listening to it with all her friends! So I got back to my schoolwork.

The next day when I walked up to Shaina, she didn't walk away. She pretended she didn't see me. "Shaina," I said anyway, "I tried to call you last night."

She shrugged. "Oh, I didn't…" Her voice trailed off and she looked distracted. *Didn't care less?* I thought. We went our separate ways.

In a homework period, I cried when I read the newspaper about the events in Eretz Yisrael. Another bombing and six precious Jewish lives extinguished. It was so horrible! I wished I could do something! At least, I reasoned, I can do my part and make up with my friend. I sat down to write her a letter. I poured out my heart and reminded her of all our good times. I told her I didn't care if she didn't want to be my best friend— just that she shouldn't hate me. And if she needed help with a poem for the bulletin, perhaps I could help.

I handed my letter to Shaina at the end of the day. And in the morning I spoke to her in front of some girls. I figured she couldn't outright ignore me! "Did you read my letter?" I asked.

"Yeah," Shaina said, trying to sound breezy, but her voice quivered. "I had fun making it into a paper airplane!"

I stormed away. I couldn't believe it! I didn't try to speak to her after that.

One morning there was a school assembly. A guest rabbi was lecturing. I noticed Shaina wasn't around. Then I saw her enter the auditorium. She glanced around nervously at the packed audience. I felt so bad! And there was a seat next to me. I waved until for sure she'd see me and then pointed to the chair. She came and sat down next to me.

We both stared intently at the speaker. I didn't hear a word he said, though I tried to listen.

And at the end of the speech, during the girls' applause, she smiled wanly. "Thanks," she said.

"No problem," I answered.

"I'm sorry," she said.

I said, "I'm sorry too. I should have said something to you before I changed classes."

"It's really the perfect class for you, though," she admitted.

"But maybe I can sometimes join your committee to help with writing things so we don't forget each other completely!"

We both gave laughs of relief.

BIOS OF AUTHORS:

STERNA CITRON

Sterna Citron, author of several books including *Why the Baal Shem Tov Laughed; 52 Stories About our Great Chassidic Rabbis*, was publisher and editor of *Shoshanim, the Magazine for Jewish Teenage Girls*. She lives with her husband in Los Angeles and is currently working on a biography of her grandfather Rav Zalman Schneerson z"l and a children's book book entitled *The Miracles of Elisha*.

NOMI DAYAN

Nomi Dayan received her BA in English Creative Writing from Hunter College and MA from Bank Street College. She enjoys historical fiction and imaginative writing exploring world cultures and nature. She loves Carlebach music and is currently the Director of Education of the Cold Spring Harbor Whaling Museum. Nomi lives in Long Island, NY with her husband and daughter. The stories which appear in this anthology—*The Empty Chair, The Lonely Summer,* and *Long Skirts and Lizards*—were written by Nomi when she was a teenager.

BETH FIRESTONE

Beth Firestone is the author of *Candles in My Window*, recently revised and reprinted by Targum Press. She is a mother, grandmother, and high school English teacher. Her most recent work, a children's serial called "To the Edge of the Galaxy," was published in AMI magazine.

BRACHA GOYKADOSH

When Bracha Goykadosh read the first issue of *Shoshanim Magazine* in 2002, she was inspired to send in her own short stories for publication. Many of her earliest stories appeared in *Shoshanim Magazine*. Bracha was in her teens when she wrote the following stories which are included in this anthology: *The*

Big Move, Monday Morning Trouble, A Taste of Perfection, We're Friends, Aren't We? Since then, she has had two novels published, *Footprints in the Sand* (Jerusalem Publications, 2005) and *Shadows on the Moon* (Israel Book Shop, 2009), and a collection of short stories, *Go Bananas* (Israel Book Shop, 2011). She lives with her family in New York City.

YONINA HALL

Yonina Hall enjoys writing stories for teens, children, and adults. She grew up in Los Angeles and now makes her home in Yerushalayim.

RAFAELLA (FOX) LEVINE

Rafaella Levine is a Hebrew-English translator living in Yerushalayim with her husband and young children. Fiction writing is her passion, and she thanks *Shoshanim* for having provided a space for her stories.

YEHUDIS LITVAK

Yehudis Litvak lives in Los Angeles and is busy raising her family and home-schooling her children. In her spare time, she writes and maintains her website and blog. She is also actively involved in the local Russian Jewish community and helps out with outreach and educational events.

YOCHEVED LEAH PERKAL

Yocheved Leah Perkal is a writer, translator, and copywriter living in Yerushalayim with her husband and children. She writes regularly for children and teens and is presently published in *Hamodia* and *Binah Bunch*. She is also the co-author of the well-known *Mrs. Honig's Cakes* series.

NECHAMA DINA SMITH

Nechama Dina Smith delighted *Shoshanim* audiences with her

stories from the inception of the magazine through all of its issues. She was also associate editor of *Shoshanim*. She has co-edited this anthology. Nechama Dina lives with her husband and children in Surfside, Florida.

ROCHEL YAFFE

Rochel Yaffe is the author of *Rambam: The Story of Rabbi Moshe Ben Maimon* and *Lost and Found and Other Stories for Jewish Girls*.

For All Your Plumbing and Heating Needs
EZ Roth Plumbing
5747 Melrose Ave.
Los Angeles, CA 90038
323-469-5692